The Adventures of
Harry Stone

The Adventures of
Harry Stone

Larry Horowitz

Larry Horowitz

Library of Congress Control Number:		2019901601
ISBN:	Hardcover	978-1-7960-1511-9
	Softcover	978-1-7960-1510-2
	eBook	978-1-7960-1509-6

Print information available on the last page.

Rev. date: 05/23/2019

To order additional copies of this book, contact:
Xlibris
1-888-795-4274
www.Xlibris.com
Orders@Xlibris.com
792133

I would like to thank all of those who supported me in this effort, giving me encouragement, reading my story online, and urging me to publish it. Special thanks go to: Gordon, Charlie, Randall, Russell, John, Tim, Dean, Barry, Eve, Deb, Carol, Paul, James, and Dave.

Cast of Characters:

<u>The Crew of the *Galaxis*</u>
Harry – Hero of the story. Tall, husky, strong, smart, courageous, loyal.
Rachel – Harry's girlfriend. Pretty, smart, kind.
Sherman – Extremely intelligent, arrogant, social misfit, overweight, selfish.
Linda – Intelligent, good with animals, kind, sympathetic, scientific.
Sammy – Stuck at 17, can be vulgar, uncouth, street-wise intelligence.
Kluco – Very advanced (male) robot, pilot of the *Galaxis*, has the ability to learn from his environment and past experiences, logical, emotionless

<u>The Trinollians</u>
Minzi – Female, surgeon, scientist, sympathetic.
Tsedo – Male, assistant to Minzi, practical, analytical, acquires data and runs projections.
The Elders – Leaders of The Emerging Species project. In charge of Minzi, Tsedo, and other unnamed Trinollians also on the ES project.

<u>Friends</u>
Wendell – Harry's roommate at the Juvenile Detention Center.
Dr. Vance Bowman – Scientist at NASA. Sherman's boss.
Tica – Female Cyborg from a distant planet, intelligent, attracted to Kluco.
Dremmil – Glarb slave. Friend of "the crew".

Snurdles

Jibly – Loyal, brave, intelligent. Swaps minds with Linda.

Glarbs

Torka – Big, strong, ugly, ruthless, sadistic. Harry's trainer.

Gritzel – Leader of the Glarbs, tough, cunning, cruel.

Ditzen – Gritzel's right-hand assistant. Not that smart or very good at his job.

Corrigan – Guard at the airstrip where the *Galaxis* is kept.

The Farmer – Mad Scientist. Extremely intelligent, evil, sadistic, insane.

Rebel Glarbs

Dravitz – Owner of the house where rebel Glarbs headquarters is.

Chapter 1

Little Timmy grimaces as the bully sitting on top of him applies pressure to the back of his head, pushing his nose deeper into the grass.

"Say it," the bully demands.

"No—get off, Wally!" Timmy wails.

A crowd is gathering around the fight. Some of the kids take pleasure in Timmy's distress.

"Make him eat a bug!"

"Don't let him up until he says it."

"Make him cry, Big Wally!"

"Leave him alone, you big bully," Rachel shouts.

Many are not on Big Wally's side. Certainly not Rachel, who has bully problems of her own to deal with. And certainly not some of the other smaller boys, who have also had the misfortune to feel Big Wally's wrath, but are afraid to speak up fearing that they may be the next victim. Rachel's pleas, as well as Timmy's, are completely ignored. Big Wally presses down harder.

"Say it, Dorko!"

Timmy is fighting back the tears. His nose really hurts—he has had enough. He is on the brink of surrendering and saying that he is a little girl who likes to wear pink panties—the escape clause that Big Wally is waiting to hear. But he knows that if he utters these hated words, the other kids will never let him forget it. If he can just hold on a little longer maybe a teacher would come to his rescue?

Harry is on his way home and spots the crowd of kids in the distance. A fight, perhaps? Harry has plenty of homework and is already in trouble for getting a low grade in social studies. He really should go straight home. Let whatever kids are fighting kill each other, it's none of his business. He continues on his way.

Harry is determined to go home, crack open his books, and do some serious studying. He has to get his homework done before dinner each day, as he had promised his parents he would, if they didn't ground him for his D in social studies.

Just then, he thinks he hears Big Wally's name being cheered on. Now Harry is a lot smaller than Big Wally. Well, all the fifth graders are, for that matter, seeing as how Big Wally had been left back. He certainly doesn't need to be Big Wally's next victim.

Nevertheless, when one of Timmy's pleas reaches his ears, Harry turns around and heads over, not sure yet what he's going to do. But he sure knows that he hates Big Wally, and bullies in general.

When he reaches the crowd of kids and sees what's going on, he can contain himself no longer. Big Wally is sitting on little Timmy's back, shoving his face into the ground, and rubbing dirt in his ears.

"Say it or it's gonna get a lot worse," Big Wally taunts.

"Okay, okay, just get off and I'll say it," Timmy begs.

"No, Dorko, that's not how it works…"

"Get off him right now!" Harry bellows.

Everybody turns to look at him.

"Why, what are you going to do about it?" Big Wally shouts back.

Big Wally puts on his most menacing look and, while still sitting on Timmy's back, challenges him, "You want to be next, *Hairy*?"

It's the best insult that Big Wally can come up with on the spur of the moment. And it's also exactly what Harry doesn't want to hear. He doesn't want to fight Big Wally, he just wants him to leave Timmy alone.

A hush falls over the crowd—a new wrinkle has developed. They are astonished that someone is going to challenge Big Wally. Harry had drawn the line in the sand and Big Wally had stepped over it. Now Harry is obligated to follow through.

"You're just a big bully!" Harry shouts.

"That's my job," Wally replies.

That one gets a few chuckles.

Big Wally is feeling pretty good. He likes being the entertainer, the center of attention, especially while sitting on top of someone. He looks over at Harry and warns him, "You just shut up and stay right there and I'll get to you next!"

Big Wally turns his attention back towards Timmy. He is determined to break this puny weakling, and then he will teach Harry a lesson. He forces Timmy's head deeper into the ground. Timmy tries to scream out his protests, but they are muffled. Big Wally grabs Timmy's hair, pulls his head back, and then rams it into the dirt, drawing blood from Timmy's nose.

"Say it, or it gets worse!"

Timmy is crying now. He opens his mouth to say those dreaded words. But those words are never uttered.

Something about Timmy's distress and Wally's arrogance has touched Harry in a way that he can't ignore. Somebody has to teach this big bully a lesson.

Before the phrase can leave Timmy's lips, Big Wally is walloped with a vicious kick to the head. He falls off Timmy, and goes down to the ground, dazed and confused, holding his head. Harry had not opted to just pull Wally off. He had gone berserk and meant to hurt him as much as possible in a full, to-the-death fight, with that kick.

Harry is on top of him now, swinging away with everything he's got. The kids are screaming and cheering. Nobody has ever challenged Big Wally like this before.

Wally is bewildered, astonished, and getting pounded. He manages to get his big, burly arms up to block the punches. A new feeling is stirring inside him, that of fear and cowardice. He wants to get out and run away. But that isn't an option with this crazy kid sitting on top of him, trying to kill him.

Out of desperation Wally lashes back, and his long, thick arm catches Harry with a clean shot to the nose. It starts to bleed, and Harry is rocked back enough so that Wally can roll onto his stomach and get to his hands and knees while Harry is still recovering. Big Wally recognizes his chance to get away now. But something inside keeps Wally from fleeing.

After all, he's good at being a bully. He is thirteen and in sixth grade, having been left back once. And in this elementary school, sixth grade is the oldest class before going on to middle school. Wally is the biggest, strongest, meanest kid in the entire school, and up until just now, the toughest one as well. He doesn't want to lay that reputation to waste, and he's not used to losing fights. Harry is down with a bloody nose, and Wally seizes his chance.

Harry looks up just in time to dodge Wally's kick. Wally goes for another one and this time Harry catches it, holds on, and Wally falls on top of him. Now they are rolling around on the ground, each trying to get the advantage. The kids are going crazy. Almost all of them are now cheering Harry on.

"Come on, Harry!"

"Teach him a lesson."

"Kick him, Harry."

"Smash his head!"

Unfortunately for Harry, he is no match for Wally when it comes to grappling. He is out-weighed by too much.

Wally pins Harry down, crawls on top of his belly, straddling him, their situation is now reversed. He starts to rain down punches like a piston. He is going to show this kid who's the king of this school after all.

Harry, on his back with his arms in front of his face while Wally pounds him, is in dire circumstances. He needs to do something fast, he's desperate. Blocking his face from Wally's punches, his nose still bleeding, Harry sees Big Wally's ugly mug through his splayed fingers. It's clear that Wally has no intention of letting up. That big nose, that sneer, those big ears...and suddenly an idea comes to Harry.

Some would say it was a good idea, at least for getting out of his current predicament. But in the long run, it may have been better to just take Wally's beating, heal, and get on with life.

Because, although this idea was great for fighting, it would ultimately change the course of Harry's life.

Chapter 2

[11 years ago]

It first happened when she was just learning to walk, at around 11 months old. As a toddler, Rachel's world was half reality, half fantasy anyway. She didn't really understand the grey areas of visibility. Some things were very easy to see, other things let you see them only when they wanted to. She didn't judge or try to figure this out, just accepted it as another strange and wonderful fact of how this magnificent new world works.

She was in her high chair doing a relatively fine job of distributing the mushy food all over the table, chair, floor, her face, everywhere she thought it belonged.

"Rachel, you are a messy eater," her mother playfully scolds her.

"I'm messy eating," Rachel agrees, and giggles uncontrollably.

And it was right after that, as her mother leans over and starts to clean her, when she looks over her mother's shoulder and sees it dashing across the floor from one side of the room all the way to the other. It looks like a tiny little man, sometimes referred to as a brownie, or urisk.

Midway through his dash, the little man glances at Rachel, acknowledges her presence, and smiles and waves at her. And then he is gone. Out of the kitchen, into the living room, back to his hiding place, wherever that may be. Rachel giggles and points in his direction.

"There, you like that? Isn't that better?" her mom coos.

Rachel points towards the living room, "Mommy it go there."

"You want to get out, honey? There you go."

Her mother gently removes her from the high chair and places her on the floor. Immediately, Rachel waddles after her little friend, still a bit shaky on her new chubby, walking legs.

She then stumbles into the living room and looks around. But there is no funny little man to be found anywhere.

Rachel surveys the room carefully, and her eyes land on some toys scattered outside of her playpen. Especially that ball toy where you keep putting the balls on top and they roll down and around, making that delightful noise.

"Oh, that's fun, let's do that," she thinks. Temporarily forgetting her little friend, she toddles over, plops herself down, and begins putting the balls on the top hoop. They trickle down making that noise and she smiles and keeps it going. She is totally absorbed. Her mom is in the kitchen, hears her daughter playing happily, smiles, and returns to cleaning up.

While giggling and playing with her toy, Rachel notices something out of the corner of her eye—a wavering in the air, something is blurry. It moves behind her playpen and goes out of sight. She continues playing, when, there it is again—going in and out from behind her playpen. She pauses for a moment and all the balls come to rest in the bottom tray.

What is that near her playpen? The air is funny; crooked, unclear, just wrong somehow. Rachel crawls over to investigate and reaches out her hand to touch the funny air, but there is nothing there now. Everything is back to normal. Just then, a small rubber ball rolls across the carpet a few feet, completely on its own.

Rachel looks at it, giggles, and crawls over to get the ball. She reaches out and grabs the ball and is startled to see the little man standing behind it—and he has a little hat on his head.

He smiles and waves. He is so cute. Rachel giggles with glee. She reaches out to touch him, but he darts away. Rachel pushes herself up to a standing position, balancing carefully on her new baby legs, and the chase is on.

She toddles after him, laughing, and sees him go behind the playpen once more. As she approaches, he smiles and waves again. She plops herself down next to him, and suddenly, he isn't there as much as he was before. He seems to be only half there.

Rachel reaches out to grab him, but he darts right through the living room wall. That is really funny. Rachel stares at the solid wall he just went through and giggles. She loves this game and her new little friend.

And then, out from the wall, comes a tiny hand.

The hand is opened in a "shake me" position, looking for something, or someone, to grab.

Rachel reaches out and squeezes her chubby fingers around it. The tiny hand reacts instantly, and clutches her back in a surprisingly strong grip.

Chapter 3

Harry is in serious trouble, on his back, trying to cover his face as Big Wally rains down bombs. But when he peeks out and sees Wally's big mean face, with those big dumbo ears sticking out, an idea comes to him that may give him a chance to turn the tables.

As Big Wally is rearing back, getting ready to deliver another blow, in a split-second Harry lurches out with both hands, grabs those big ears, and jerks Wally's face forward and down hard, right into his own forehead. And although Harry had only seen head butts on professional wrestling, and never performed one of his own, this one was executed perfectly.

Wally hears a dreaded crack as his nose smashes against Harry's head. The pain is immediate, agonizing, and completely debilitating. He falls off Harry, onto the ground, holding his bleeding, broken nose. The kids go wild.

"Way to go, Harry!"

"That's showing him."

"He did it. He did it. Harry beat up Big Wally!"

It was an implied consensus that the fight was over and Harry was the hands down winner. After all, Wally was down and bleeding, not fighting any more. This was how playground fights were supposed to end.

But unbeknownst even to Harry at this time, is the dark and dangerous side that lurks deep within his psyche. God help those who have hurt Harry's friends and opened this up.

Harry gets to his feet, looking down at Big Wally whining, and kicks him hard in the stomach. A hush falls over the crowd. They were about to celebrate his victory, pat him on the back, even carry him off on their shoulders if they could. But now they step back in astonishment. Apparently, the fight is not over, not in Harry's mind anyway.

Again, Harry lands another kick—and again. Big Wally is rolled up in a ball, too disabled to fight back in any way.

Harry lifts his foot up high and brings it down as hard as he can, stomping on Wally's head. Wally's cries change tone. He is not just in pain now. He is terrified and unable to defend himself, at the mercy of this crazy kid who didn't know that the fight was over.

"So, you like to pick on smaller kids, do you?" Harry taunts.

He jumps up and comes down on his knees, right into Wally's gut. The other kids gasp.

"Okay, you...win..." Wally feebly manages to get the words out.
CRAACKK!

While Wally was holding his stomach from that knee drop, Harry punched him square in the face, punishing his already broken nose. Wally howls in pain and astonishment. He has never been in this position before and is starting to see how it feels to be the victim instead of the bully. It sucks.

Wally now begins to be afraid for his life, or at least serious injury. And so, he does something that he has never in his life done before—he begins to beg.

"Please, no more. Okay, you win," he sobs, his voice quivering with fear and genuine remorse.

But Harry doesn't hear him and continues to pummel him mercilessly, landing clean blows to Wally's head and face. The crowd of kids begin to realize that something is very wrong. While before it was extremely satisfying seeing Big Wally finally get his comeuppance, now it was scary. Wally is now lying still, not defending himself in any way, his arms at his sides.

"Harry, that's enough, he's not moving!"

"Harry, stop it, he's unconscious."

"Harry, stop, you're going to kill him!"

Harry doesn't hear them

Finally, Harry is knocked to the ground by some of the boys who decided to take action. This is supposed to be a playground fight, not a murder scene. As terrible as Big Wally is, nobody wants to see him die, especially while they're all watching and cheering, making all of them in a way, accomplices.

But Big Wally never manages to take another breath. Multiple blows to the temples and his head have caused his heart to take its very last beat.

The kids stand around staring at Wally's body, watching his face turn blue.

"You killed him, Harry!"

"I can't believe it, you really killed him, for real."

Some of the kids start to whine and cry, others flee. The ones that are left are in a state of shock, scared to death of what they have just seen.

"Harry, what have you done?" Rachel exclaims.

"Well, I..." he starts.

"My God, what have I done?" he thinks to himself.

"I mean, he was hurting Timmy. I couldn't take it anymore! I just couldn't. Someone had to do something!"

"But you didn't have to kill him! Look he's all blue."

"I didn't mean to," now Harry's voice is quivering.

"It just happened. I lost control."

"You can say that again," Roger says. "Wait, maybe..."

He pauses, then gets an idea, and wonders aloud, "But maybe he's not dead? Maybe we can get him alive again?"

"How?"

"He means CPR," Sarah, a girl in a light blue jacket, says.

"Do you know how to do it?" Rachel asks.

"No," Roger admits.

"I think I do," Harry says.

"Well, hurry up and try it then," Rachel exclaims.

And so, Harry leans over the boy that he just killed, and does the best he can to perform mouth-to-mouth resuscitation. Absolutely nothing happens.

"Blow harder!" someone suggests.

Harry does, but is not getting any results. He does not really know how to do mouth-to-mouth resuscitation. He fails to tilt Wally's head all the way back, and Wally's air passage is somewhat blocked, with blood and swelling. Not that it would make a difference.

Harry tries his best, but after five minutes gives up. Wally hasn't responded at all. He is dead.

Harry looks up at the other kids with tears in his eyes. He has never been more frightened.

"It's not working," he complains.

"It doesn't work if he's already dead," Sarah says.

Timmy is still there. He holds no remorse for Big Wally.

"So what if he's dead? He deserved to die!"

"No, he didn't Timmy. He was only 13," Rachel answers.

"He was a big bully and I hated him, too," Roger shouts.

"Well, he'll never bully anybody again," Rachel says.

"Guys, what are we gonna do?" Harry pleads. "I can't go to jail! I'm just a kid."

"You won't go to jail, you'll go to juvie," Mark pipes in.

"What's that?"

"Juvenile Delinquency Detention Center," Mark answers. "I know a kid who did two years there. It's kind of like a jail for kids. But with school work and stuff."

"C'mon guys—I didn't mean to kill him. We were just fighting. He was gonna hurt Timmy. I had to do something!"

"But why didn't you stop when he stopped moving?" Sarah asks.

"I didn't notice!" Harry wails.

"What was I thinking?" Harry thinks to himself. *"There's no way out of this. Unless..."*

And then Roger says what Harry was thinking, "We could hide the body."

Chapter 4

[11 years ago]

Baby Rachel had reached out and grabbed the tiny, barely visible, hand sticking out of the living room wall behind her playpen. And, it had grabbed her back.

She now feels a tingling sensation all over her little body. It's kind of funny, and she giggles. If her mother were to witness this event she would faint in disbelief. Rachel is becoming semi-transparent.

And when she fades enough, the tiny hand jerks her forcefully right through the wall.

Rachel is wide-eyed and full of wonder. What kind of great game is this? Boy, this world is sure full of strange and fantastic things. She feels no fear, only excitement and awe. She looks this way and that at her surroundings.

Here, on the other side of the living room wall, is a bunch of tiny little people, just like her funny friend here. They are all looking at her and smiling. She chuckles. They are so funny.

Behind them she sees...well, she's not sure of what she is seeing—colors mostly—swirls of orange, blue, yellow, green. If she looks hard enough, she can almost see the studs and insulation within the wall, but it's wavy and not fully there.

Her little friend has let go of her hand, and now a new little person approaches her. It is a female, and she is holding out a toy—a toy like she's never seen before.

It is kind of like a rattle, but contains rings of color circling around an oblong shaft. The rings of color just float in the air rotating around the shaft, kind of like the rings of Saturn circling around the planet. It hums and vibrates.

The tiny lady extends this device to Rachel, and she reaches out and takes it. She holds it in front of her, looking at the circles of light floating on the shaft. Then the circles start to move, going around and around. Rachel giggles at this.

The top circle, the yellow one, then comes off the shaft and grows much larger. It rings itself around Rachel's head, then travels down to her neck. As it spins around, it grows larger still, and then floats down a little more, encircling her belly.

Now the blue circle has left the shaft, grown larger, and rings itself around her neck. The red circle then leaves the shaft, and follows the blue one. Now Rachel has three rings of light encircling her body, spinning around and around, trading places with each other and going up and down, from her head to her feet.

Rachel can't contain her joy any longer and bursts out laughing. She has a coat of pretty circle lights, and she just loves it.

The rings of light are humming as they pass over all parts of Rachel's body. Finally, they finish (their examination?) and float off Rachel, grow smaller, finally returning to the shaft.

Now while this is going on, in another dimension of the room resides a peculiar object, somewhat translucent, but not entirely. It is some type of central data storage, or computer, of sorts. It also has a rather pleasant hum to it, and streams of data flash across the monitor recording Rachel's information. The little people look at each other and nod.

The female approaches Rachel, who's head over heels in love with her new toy. She is giggling, and about to see how it tastes, when the floating colors disappear. Her eyes grow wide, she furrows her eyebrows. Rachel liked those circles and wants them to come back.

The female stands in front of Rachel and extends her hand out towards her. She would like her instrument back now, please.

Nothing doing. Rachel has a good long time to go before she gets tired of this cool toy.

"Mine!" and she clutches the toy to her chest.

The female starts at her, then stops.

"Just take it from her," one of the others demands.

"If I do, then she's going to be distressed," Minzi, the female in the white lab jacket, replies.

"So what? She'll whine a little, and then get over it."

"We can't just put her back and leave her crying," Minzi insists.

"Why not?"

"Her mother will rush over and wonder what happened."

"So what?"

"Well, it's cruel to put her in such an unhappy state," Minzi replies.

"Nothing will happen, she'll get over it."

"But she'll think we're mean, and won't like us."

And this part matters to Minzi. She wants Rachel to like all of them. It becomes quiet for a just a couple of seconds, then...

"The mother may come in at any moment," one of them warns her.

"Just give her another toy and get the ratudil from her in exchange," someone suggests.

Minzi goes over to the barely visible computer, waves her hand over something, and picks out a colorful toy on the screen. Shortly thereafter, it materializes in her hands. She approaches Rachel again.

Rachel looks at her. Her eyes grow wide when she sees the red and yellow stuffed chimpanzee in Minzi's hand.

Minzi extends the toy to Rachel while holding out her other hand as well, to receive the ratudil back.

Rachel understands this gesture perfectly and she's not about to give up her wonderful toy. She clutches it tightly to her chest and says, "Mine."

"For God's sake, Minzi, just take it from her," Tsedo exclaims.

"Just let me handle this."

She turns her back on Rachel, and starts playing with the stuffed chimpanzee.

"Minzi, her mother is on the way downstairs—please hurry!"

Rachel is still holding the toy to her chest, but now Minzi's toy, which is somewhat out of sight, seems pretty interesting.

Minzi hums and makes little noises. Boy, is she having fun playing with that stuffed Chimp—nothing on earth could be more fun.

Rachel can barely see what Minzi is doing, and why that toy is so fun, but it sure seems like it needs some investigating. Her grip on the ratudil loosens. She stretches her neck to try and see better. Why is that toy so much fun? She drops the ratudil and starts crawling over.

"Minzi, her mother will be here in seconds!"

Minzi turns around and, facing Rachel, kisses the chimp, while placing it down on the ground. It is really a cute chimpanzee, maybe the cutest in the world? Rachel just loves that colorful red and yellow outfit it is wearing. She reaches for her new toy, and grabs it gleefully. Minzi darts around Rachel and retrieves the ratudil. Rachel is hugging the cute chimp now—her body starts to fade.

"Good job, Minzi," one of the others say.

"Rachel, honey, what are you doing? I haven't heard a peep from you," her mother calls out, as she comes downstairs on the way to the living room.

Rachel then fades even more from the dimension behind the wall, and in this state, is gently pushed back through the living room wall. She solidifies next to her playpen, still squeezing Chimpy.

"Oh, there you are, hugging your toy. You must really like that monkey, huh?" her mom asks. Then she walks over to the playpen and picks Rachel up.

"Hmmm...I don't even remember this one," she muses. "*Well, she has so many stuffed animals it's possible I don't remember all of them,*" she thinks to herself.

Which, of course, is a much more reasonable thing to assume than the truth—which is that Chimpy is an apport from another dimension hidden inside the walls of her own house.

Chapter 5

[Back to the present time]

Harry and Roger are dragging Big Wally by his feet with the intent of hiding Wally's corpse, and keeping his death a secret. Needless to say, this is not the greatest idea that either of them has ever fostered. Wally weighs a ton and this is no easy task.

"Harry, this is never going to work. It's a terrible idea," Rachel shouts at him.

"Can you please just help us instead of criticizing everything I do?" Harry shouts back.

By now, all the kids have left. Only Harry, Roger, dead Wally, and Rachel, the lone voice of reason, remain.

"I need to stop a second, Harry," Roger says.

Harry sighs, and they both release Wally's feet, which thud to the ground.

"And just where are you going to put him anyway?" asks Rachel.

"We're not just gonna put him anywhere," Harry sneers. "We're gonna bury him nice and deep, so he can't be found. And you better not say anything neither."

"Harry, there were a lot of kids watching," Rachel reminds him.

"We took care of that, Rachel, you were here! We formed a committee, got our story down, and everybody is being told to stick to it."

"Right," Roger agrees.

It was his idea to form the committee, which consisted of three other boys, who were responsible for finding and telling their alibi to all of the other kids who had already left. He felt very adult to be forming committees.

"And you don't think anybody will break down and admit that they saw you and Wally fighting?" Rachel asks.

"They'd better not, or they'll get it even worse," Harry boasts.

"Worse than being dead?" Rachel questions. "How are you going to do that, Harry? Chop them up into little pieces and feed them to rats after they're dead?"

"I told you to just shut up if you're not going to help!"

Harry is yelling, but some crying is also leaking into his voice. He knows he's not being very rational, but can't seem to get his thoughts straight. He is angry, stressed out, scared, frustrated and approaching a nervous breakdown. But he also knows inside that this idea is crazy.

"Harry..." Rachel starts, then pauses while looking at the ground. "I mean, just look at the trail you guys are leaving," she finishes.

There is a distinct dragging trail in the grass and dirt, as well as some blood from where they were fighting. Rachel pleads with Harry to see how foolish they're being.

"And you don't even have a shovel to bury him. And you're going to have to explain where you were today and why you're all bruised to the cops. And they'll know you're lying. Probably some kid has already told his parents what happened before your committee got there."

Harry and Roger are looking at the dragging trail and bow their heads in despair. She's right, everything she's saying, she's right. Probably some kid has already squealed about this incident. And if not, they will. The police will shake the truth out of someone.

Wally is really heavy and Roger has had enough of dragging him.

"She's right, Harry," he finally admits. "This isn't going to work."

Harry is about to yell at him but finds that he doesn't have the strength. This is never going to work and he knows it. He sits on the ground with his hands covering his face and starts to sob.

"But what am I gonna do?" he cries. "He was a big, mean bully and I was just trying to protect Timmy and stand up for him. I was just on my way home. I shoulda never came over. Shoulda just kept walking," Harry whines.

Rachel walks over to him and puts her hand on his back.

"You're going to have to tell the truth. Everybody saw it. You were just trying to stick up for Timmy."

"Not just Timmy—all of us," Roger says as he walks over and joins Harry on the ground. "Wally was a terror to all of us. And finally, somebody brave like Harry shut him up real good."

Once the sobs begin, it's hard to hold them back. Harry breaks down and says,

"But...but...I never meant..." he is bawling now. "I was just...trying..." and his body shakes with uncontrollable sobs.

"We're all behind you," Rachel says soothingly and puts her hand on his back. "It was just in the heat of the battle."

"Every kid here will tell 'em what a great guy you are," Roger adds. "And what a mean bully Wally was."

The three of them stay there for a while as Harry cries, shakes, then gradually stops.

"You think everybody will say good things about me?"

"Yes," they both say together.

"And mean things about Wally?"

"Yes."

"Uh, huh."

Harry sniffs a little and wipes his nose with his sleeve.

"Ya think they'll put me in jail?"

There is a long pause, then Rachel says, "Not like a regular jail, anyway. A juvenile home, for kids."

Roger adds, "And probably not for too long—maybe just a few months? After all it was self-defense."

"Well," Rachel was about to disagree, then changed her mind.

"Well, Wally started it by picking on Timmy," Roger says.

"Yeah—I had to do something," Harry insists.

Rachel nods her head, "I know. We were all glad that you did. You stood up to him, Harry, when nobody else would."

"That's right," says Roger.

Well, that part is true. The hero in Harry rose to the surface and prevailed when the situation needed a hero. Maybe he got a little carried away, or a lot carried away, but he was in "hero" mode and these things happen. If there wasn't a big bully in the first place, then there would have been no *situation*. But when Harry's friends need saving, he comes through, even at great cost. It would be a trait that would follow him for the rest of his life.

You don't mess with Harry or his friends without paying the price.

Chapter 6

It is seven months later. Harry is having a difficult time adjusting to his new life in a juvenile delinquency institution. Unfortunately, his worst fears had come true at the trial. Although he had plenty of character witnesses who testified what a bully Wally had been, and that originally Harry was simply defending Timmy, there was no getting around the fact that Harry had gone a little crazy.

"You were sitting on top of him (Wally), punching him, while he was begging for mercy?" the DA had asked him.

"I don't know," Harry answered truthfully.

"You don't know? How could you not know? Weren't you there, sitting on top of this boy, punching him?"

"Yeah, but I don't know if he was begging,'" Harry replied. "I mean, I don't remember him begging."

"All the other children who testified said he was begging you to stop, and that you had to be pulled off of him in the end."

"I don't know," Harry whined. "I was just kinda zoned out—din't hear nothing, just kept punching him."

"Even when he was still, lying there, not defending himself in any way?"

"Yeah."

"And did it ever occur to you to stop, that you had already won the fight, and that you could be killing him, or seriously injuring him?"

A hush fell over the court room when this question was asked. Nobody stirred. Harry had to think back in his own mind to when the incident happened, trying to remember what he was thinking at that time. He was doing his best to answer all the questions honestly, and this was an important one.

The DA was waiting for an answer. So was everyone else. The silence was deafening, as Harry rolled his eyes and looked up, thinking... thinking.

"No sir," he finally said.

"No? The boy wasn't moving, and you just kept on punching him in his head? And it didn't occur to you that you should stop?"

"I wasn't thinking about what I was doing," Harry admitted. "I was just trying to make Wally see how it must have felt to Timmy, when he was beating on him. *I never meant to kill him. Just to teach him a lesson.*"

Well, after that, the case was really over. The sincerity in Harry's voice rang loud and clear, as well as the remorse. He was a hero who got caught up in the fight, and just went overboard. It's true, he was standing up to a bully that had needed to be dealt with for a long time. The jury totally believed Harry's story about "zoning out" and not really understanding what he was doing.

In his closing statement, the DA admitted that Wally had been a trouble maker, a bully, maybe not a very nice kid. But Wally had a family, and he was only 13. Plenty of troubled teenagers go on to turn themselves around, and become good people, and contributing members to society. But, because of Harry's wrath and lack of self-control, Wally would never get that chance.

The jury and judge were both sympathetic. Nevertheless, there had to be some kind of punishment. Harry was eventually sentenced to live in a juvenile detention facility for boys until he turned eighteen. At that time, he could file for probation, and his behavior for the last five years would determine how much longer his sentence would be.

Chapter 7

After two years, Harry has adjusted quite well to his new life and is popular with most of the boys at the Juvenile Delinquency Center (JDC). It is June, and a beautiful, sunny day greets all. Harry and his roommate, Wendell, are cleaning up and getting ready for this morning's inspection. But something seems wrong with Wendell today. They had been sharing a room for the past 18 months and Harry knows Wendell inside and out. He couldn't have asked for a better buddy.

Wendell may be a little bit on the shy side, but he is a loyal friend with some interesting hobbies. He is a whiz with computers, and also has quite a talent for drawing and painting. Harry was blown away when Wendell finally shared his portfolio with him.

Some pieces depicted remarkably realistic space scenes with alien worlds, planets, comets, and even life-like beings that might dwell there. Others showed binary stars circling each other, and black holes consuming a galaxy from the inside out.

Harry's favorite was a battle scene on some fantastic alien landscape where these horrible, lumpy-looking beings, were in a fight to the death with other alien-looking creatures from all over the galaxy. The art work and colors on these beautiful creations was just amazing. Wendell's surrealistic scenes were both spooky and fabulous at the same time, and made Harry feel alternately both scared and excited, as he often found himself lost in time while dwelling on them.

Wendell was usually cheerful and pleasant to be around. But not today. He is dolefully making his bed for the morning inspection.

"What's wrong, Wendell? Are you worried about inspection?"

"No."

Wendell is squaring the corners while making his bed.

"What's up buddy?" Harry asks.

But Wendell doesn't feel like talking and only gives a one-word reply, "Nothing."

"Fine," Harry says.

Wendell shoots him a look. A strange look. Harry is not sure what to make of it. He's never seen Wendell look so...strange...scared...no, more like disturbed or worried. He opens his mouth to try again, when just then the head master's inspection unit arrives.

"Okay, boys, step back."

Harry and Wendell step back as the morning inspection commences. Harry whispers to Wendell, "Are you hiding something?"

Wendell shakes his head, "No."

The beds are checked, as are the dressers, under the beds, everything looks clean and put away, as usual. Both Harry and Wendell have been pretty good at obeying the rules and keeping their room up to standards.

"Okay, boys, off to breakfast you go."

On the way to breakfast, Wendell opens up.

"I had a dream about you, Harry. Not a very good one."

"Is that all?" Harry says. "Just a dream?"

"Yeah, but it was pretty real-like. You were fighting for your life with someone and losing."

"Man, I get weird dreams all the time, Wendell. They're just dreams – they don't mean anything."

"I woke up scared for you. You've got to stay out of fights."

"I have," Harry exclaims. "What are you talking about? I haven't had one since I've been here. Ever since...Wally (he has a hard time saying it), I've been totally under control. I'm not gonna ruin anything for myself."

"What if you're provoked?"

"I'll laugh it off and walk away. I'm not doing anything that's gonna make me stay here any longer than I have to."

They stop walking and look at each other.

"That's good to hear," Wendell finally says.

"Hell, yeah!" Harry exclaims, "You can count on that. And do me a favor, will ya buddy?"

"What's that?"

"If you're gonna dream of me fighting, dream that I'm winning while you're at it."

They both share a laugh at that and continue on to breakfast.

The two of them arrive at the large cafeteria where the rest of this morning's JD's are eating breakfast. They choose the same table they've been sitting at for the past few months. A big kid with red hair sits down with them.

"Hey, Rusty."

"Tsup, Rusty?"

"Morning," Rusty says.

And something about the way he's speaking, even though he spoke but one word, it was evident that something was also wrong with Rusty. Very wrong. Rusty also looked...disturbed...strange, almost mortified. Apparently, this was a day for people feeling bad.

Their table quickly fills up with their friends. Rusty continues to look down at the table. The other boys are all staring at him.

Finally, Harry prods him, "Rusty, what's wrong?"

"I don't wanna talk 'bout it."

"Okay, bud, chill as long as you want."

Rusty mutters something.

"What?" Harry asks.

"He just disappeared," Rusty, whispers to himself, barely audible, but they heard it nonetheless.

Everyone is silent, staring at Rusty.

"Rusty?"

But Rusty is practically trembling now. Then he takes a deep breath, tilts his head back, and tries to calm himself.

"I gotta deal with this," he tells himself.

Rusty sighs, looks at his friends, "All right guys—I've got something to tell you. You're not gonna believe me but I swear it's true."

"We'll believe you, Rusty."

"Yeah, we will."

"But even if'n ya don't, ya can't tell nobody what I'm about to tell yuz."

"We won't!" they chime in.

Rusty has piqued their interest. Now they have to know.

"I know what happened to Sammy."

Dead silence.

The one and only escape.

Everybody had heard about it a few days ago. And everybody had expected Sammy to be found quickly, dragged back to juvie, and then severely punished. But that was three days ago and still Sammy hadn't shown up.

Now he was a hero to them. Getting out and not being caught for three days was quite an honor. The staff didn't even mention his name anymore, and refused to take any questions about his whereabouts, which were obviously a cause of great embarrassment to them.

That Rusty knew something which no one else did was not only astonishing, but also, very dangerous. The silence was deafening. You could hear a pin drop.

"I wuz out with him that night."

They're all amazed.

Nobody had ever heard of a successful escape from this institution. And especially, anybody that did escape, coming back again without being noticed. It's unbelievable. But they all instinctively believe Rusty, having a feeling that what's to come next is even more astonishing.

"He wuz always braggin' so much 'bout how he could come and go as he wants. That he had a way out and in. Well, it turns out he wuz tellin' the truth."

"But why would you come back here?" one of them asks.

"Well, just let me finish."

"Yeah, dill hole, let him finish!" someone else says.

Rusty continues, "So anyways, I din't believe him either. But just for fun asked him if I could join him on a breakout. He gets this look in his eyes and asks me if I'm serious. He's whizperin' and lookin' around like to see if anybody can hear us. He started to creep me out, tell ya the truth.

Anyways, I tell him I'm serious an' he tells me to meet him by the front office after lights out. I wazn't gonna go, but I just had to. So later that night, Sammy then shows me this locked door at the front office, and opens it."

"How?"

"Where'd he get the key from?"

"I didn't say he had a key, he picked it. In like nothing flat, with these two pointy pins he had with him."

A murmur of appreciation runs through the audience at this.

"The door led to an office, with another door that led down to the basement where there wuz another locked door. And Sammy picked that one too. And then we went aways down, like in a tunnel, and came up on the outside."

"Wow!"

"We were like, across the street, outside the fence. We coulda went anywhere we wanted to."

"That's great, Rusty. Are you gonna show us these doors?" one of the boys asks.

Rusty shoots him a look.

"No. It's not safe out there!"

"Why not?"

"Hey, who's tellin' this story? Ya gonna let me tell it, or maybe I should just drop it?"

"No, please don't!"

"Yeah, c'mon Rusty, we have to know what happened to Sammy."

"Then let me finish with no more interrupshuns," Rusty demands.

"Now where wuz I? Oh, yeah...so it's already dark, like 11 or so, and we're jus' gonna take a walk around the block or somethin' and then come back. An' I know you're gonna ask me *'Why come back?'* so I›ll just tell yuz now so ya won›t interrup' me again. We wuzn't ready to make a break for it yet. You morons don't get that you jus' can't get out and then you have it made. Ya have to plan, ya have to have some money and a place to go to. Sammy an' I figured we would make a break for it soon, as soon as we got some plans, but it wazn't gonna be that night."

Rusty pauses. Nobody says anything. They are hanging on his every word.

"So, we're walking down the block. Me and Sammy. We're walking side by side. And...and..." Rusty stutters and stops.

Nobody says a word. Rusty tries again.

"So we're like walking. And he's laughing at how smart he is and got so good at picking locks. And I'm looking at him, same as I'm looking at you guys right now."

Another long pause.

"And?" somebody says.

"And, and then, and then he gets all faded-like, like he's only half there. I'm lookin' at him, same as I'm looking at you right now. An' he's all wispy, like a ghost. An' he keeps like thinning out, and then just disappears!"

A bewildered hush falls over his audience.

"What do you mean, Rusty? Like he takes off real fast?"

"See? I knew nobody would believe me. But it's true—he just disappeared, vanished. He wuz talking and then jus', faded out and was gone. Right in the middle of talking."

Complete silence. Then, Cory speaks up.

"Rusty, it was dark. He could have taken off and you didn't see him, maybe?"

"Did you hear what I said before? He was talking, then right in the middle of talking, he stops talking and disappears!"

At this, a cold chill creeps up Harry's spine. Harry isn't normally one to get spooked so easily. But something is nagging at his memory and he can't quite put his finger on it. It will come to him later—stories that Rachel used to tell him, that he never took seriously.

Disappearing, going through walls, stuff that he never gave too much thought about because it was silly and she was probably just imagining it, since, after all, she was very young and certainly didn't remember it correctly.

The boys look at each other in shocked silence. Nobody is going to challenge Rusty again. Finally, Rusty gets up, visibly frustrated and out of sorts, almost weeping. As he leaves, Rusty is mumbling, "he jus' disappeared, jus' disappeared, and if it could happen to him..." and he trails off.

Later that day, something happened to Harry that was also, well, spooky would be the best word for it. Nothing to do with disappearing, but something that would continue to haunt him for years to come— the mysterious seven letters.

There had been a light drizzle starting in the evening, and the windows of Harry's bedroom were a little fogged up. The first time it happened, he chalked it up to just a strange coincidence. Still, it was quite odd that the rain and the fog should leave such a distinct trace of letters on his window: G-O-Z-O-D-T-N

And then they washed away, and Harry wasn't even sure he ever saw those cursed letters in the first place.

Chapter 8

It had been over five years since Wally died on the playground of an elementary school on Long Island. Since then, there was no shortage of new, anti-bullying rules, in the surrounding districts. Nevertheless, there was also no shortage of bullies at Jackson High School where Rachel was now enrolled, along with her soon-to-be science partner, Sherman Lester Hollingsworth.

Sherman is short, overweight, awkward, not very good at sports (except for billiards), has poor social skills, but he is exceptionally bright. He has had his share of bully encounters during his school years, and, regardless of any new rules to ward off bullies, he attracts them like flies.

Rachel and Sherman shared a science class together. Although they knew each other, they never really had an occasion encouraging them to speak to each other, or to get to know one another. That was about to change.

Sherman is on his way home from school, minding his own business, cutting through the athletic field, when Chad and his friends decide to have a little fun with him.

"Sherman, Sherman," Chad sings in a taunting voice.

Sherman looks over and sees Chad with his girlfriend and some of his football buddies, ignores him, and walks on.

"Hey, what's the rush, bud?" and Chad and his friends quickly block Sherman's path.

"Leave me alone!" Sherman demands.

"What, you don't want to talk to me? I'm just trying to be friendly," Chad lies.

Chad's entourage snickers, watching the confrontation take place with glee.

"You think you're so smart don't you?" one of the other boys taunts.

"Yeah, but he won't let anyone cheat from him."

"Yeah, he puts his arm up so we can't see his answers. I saw him do that."

"What are you, too good for us?" Chad scolds him.

"Just leave me alone and do your own work!"

Sherman tries to step around Chad, but Chad pushes him.

"Maybe I don't want to leave you alone?"

They stare at each other.

"What are you going to do about it, geek?" Chad threatens.

Sherman tries again to get around him, and Chad blocks his path.

"You want to get by, you have to pay the toll," Chad demands.

"I'm not paying you anything!" Sherman insists.

"Then you ain't going nowhere, buddy!"

"Yeah, well if I'm not going nowhere then I'm going somewhere, since that's a double-negative," Sherman retorts.

"Oh yeah, well how about if I double-negative your face?" Chad threatens.

Chad's friends all laugh at this.

Sherman quickly moves to the right, but Chad blocks him.

Sherman fakes one way and then tries to go the other way, but Chad deftly blocks him again. The kids all laugh. Sherman's imminent beating is quite amusing to them.

"Nice try, buddy, but like I said, you have to pay the toll to get by."

"Let me by!" and Sherman tries forcefully to get around the big moron.

This time Chad doesn't just block him, but pushes and trips Sherman, and he falls down to the ground. Chad's friends giggle at Sherman's helplessness.

Little do they realize just whom they're dealing with. Sherman has had encounters with bullies many times, and finally put his brain to it, and came up with a solution. An incredible solution that probably not too many teenagers on the entire planet could fathom.

Sitting on the ground, Sherman removes his backpack and reaches into it. He takes out what appears to be some sort of small electronic device with a button on it.

"Whatcha got there, Shermy?"

"I'm warning you—all of you. Stay back or you're going to regret it!"

They all laugh.

"Is that so?" Chad sneers.

"You know what, buddy? I tried to be friendly, but seeing as how you're so rude—you just lost your backpack and that thing."

Chad approaches him...and...Sherman reaches out with his finger poised and hovering over the button.

Chad bends over Sherman with the intent of snatching the device from his hand, but Sherman is too fast for him and the button is pressed.

An ungodly, high pitched squeal emanates from the device, causing everybody in the direct vicinity to drop to their knees with their hands desperately clutched tightly over their ears.

It stops Chad dead in his tracks, and he too falls to the ground grasping his poor ears.

Sherman turns it off for only a moment—just for a few seconds—while he quickly reaches into his backpack to put his headphones on. Sherman flips the switch on his headphones and turns on the anti-noise filter. And before Chad or his buddies can get to their feet, he turns on the device again.

Now they are practically screaming, their hands pressing hard against their ears.

"Turn it off!" they beg.

Sherman stands up and surveys his tormentors, now rolling around and suffering on the ground. He smiles and takes it all in. Yes, this is good. He never had any doubts about it working, he had already tested it many times, but only on himself, and just for short amounts of time. There would be no permanent damage, just temporary agony.

"Well-deserved agony", he thinks to himself.

He notices Chad's girlfriend writhing around on the ground, her hands pressed tightly against her ears, probably not even aware how her skirt had come up revealing her lace panties. Hah, hah, what a sight. Sherman's smile spreads wide across his face. She deserves it. They all do.

Finally, he walks away and continues on his way home, leaving the device on. He isn't bothered by it with his headphones securely in place. As he gets further away, the noise and the pain quickly diminish, allowing everyone to recover. When Sherman is far enough away, safely out of sight, he turns it off.

From a distance, many of the other students, including Rachel, had noticed something strange going on over at the athletic field. A few of them were now coming over to investigate. Why were people rolling on the ground and holding their heads? But by the time Rachel gets there, the ungodly squelch is gone and Chad and friends are standing up again.

And after the story was told, nobody would dare to bother Sherman again. It wasn't worth the risk, messing with a mad genius. Who knew what he might conjure up next?

Chapter 9

Harry has been participating in some of the sports programs that the JDC (Juvenile Delinquency Center) has to offer. He is one of the biggest kids there and dominates in basketball, using his size and girth to his advantage. Tony is almost as big as Harry and doesn't take kindly to Harry's aggressive antics on the court.

Tony and Harry usually find themselves on opposite teams and guarding each other, which is the situation in the current game going on right now. Harry would love to show off his new dunking skills, if he gets the chance.

Tony's team shoots and misses. Harry's team gets the rebound. Harry tears down court, and the ball is passed to him. Only Tony stands between Harry and the basket. Tony does the best he can to plant himself in front of Harry's path, while Harry makes a break for it. He runs right over Tony, leaps up, dunks it in, and hangs on the rim for an extra second or two before dropping to the ground with a big smile on his face.

He extends a hand to Tony, who is still on the ground, to help him up. Tony bats it away, stands up, and gets right in Harry's face.

"Who the fuck do you think you are? That basket doesn't count, that was charging!"

"What? You were still moving!"

"I was planted!"

"You were moving!"

"Fuck you!" and Tony pushes Harry.

Harry pushes him right back.

Both teams crowd around the two of them. Wendell rushes in between Harry and Tony.

"Don't get into it, Harry – it's not worth it."

"I have to defend myself, bro. He started it."

Tony is also wary of coming to fisticuffs and getting written up. He has another idea.

"I'm not gonna get into it with you here. I'll see you here tomorrow, in the ring," and he gestures to the makeshift boxing ring in the back.

"Me an' you are going to have a match, and coach Norton will ref."

"That's fine with me!" Harry exclaims.

Wendell sighs with relief.

The boys split up and go their own way. The game is over.

Wendell says to Harry, "I thought you were going to laugh and walk away if you're provoked?"

Harry doesn't know what to say. His adrenaline is still pumping and without a fight to use it, he's left in a state of anger and frustration.

He shoots Wendell a look and walks away, muttering *"it's not so easy to turn it off."*

The next day Harry and Tony find themselves facing each other with 16-ounce gloves on, head gear, and even some body padding that coach Norton was able to dig up. He's not about to allow anybody to really get hurt.

"Remember boys, no blows below the belt or it stops immediately,"

They both nod yes.

"We're going to do three rounds of ninety seconds. Try to pace yourselves," he advises.

"Now shake hands, go to your corners, and wait for the whistle."

Harry and Tony bump each other's gloves and go to their corners.

The boys that came to watch, everybody from the basketball game and then some, start cheering for their favorite.

The whistle blows and the two boys rush at each other and start pummeling. There is no dancing around or defensive tactics whatsoever.

The crowd goes crazy—they are loving it.

Neither Harry nor Tony care about blocking punches, and so continue to go full force at each other for about a minute; heads down, arms pumping, putting everything they have into every punch. It doesn't take long before they both slow down.

Coach Norton blows the whistle after 90 seconds, and Harry and Tony go to their corners, exhausted and sweating.

After a minute of rest, the whistle blows, and the two pugilists go at it again, albeit quite a bit slower than the first round. The action dies down considerably, as their friends cheer them on.

"Come on, Harry, get him!"

"Don't let up, Tony, teach him a lesson!"

But the boys, ignoring the coach's advice to pace themselves, can barely finish the second round.

By the end of the third round, both Harry and Tony have had it, and can barely throw another punch. Coach Norton mercifully blows the whistle at 50 seconds and declares the fight a draw. The crowd cheers the decision.

Neither Harry nor Tony got hurt—just exhausted. But the experience actually starts a friendship of mutual respect between the two of them.

Coach Norton goes over to congratulate the exhausted fighters.

"I want you to know that you both did great, gave it your all, and I'm very proud of you."

"Thanks, Coach."

"Yeah, thanks."

"The fact that you were both smart enough to restrain from fighting on-court during the game, and came to me with this idea instead, shows a lot of growth and maturity."

"Well, actually it was Tony's idea," Harry admits.

"Well, that's great, Tony, and also great of you to agree, Harry," Coach Norton says.

"Yeah, thanks," Harry replies.

A couple of drops of sweat drip from Harry's chin. They are both still out of breath.

"Listen, I saw some good stuff out there," Coach Norton says. "Not too much good boxing really, but a lot of heart from both of you."

"Thanks, Coach," they both say.

"If you're interested, I could meet with you fellows a couple of times a week and teach you how to box? I was Golden Gloves myself when I was a kid."

"Really?" Harry asks.

"That would be great!" exclaims Tony.

"It's my pleasure," says Coach Norton. "Glad to give my time and energy to some fellows who are smart enough to know when to use their heads instead of their fists."

And so, a friendship forms between Harry and Tony instead of a feud.

Harry and Tony turn around a path that was leading to nothing good, to a path of friendship, learning, and growth.

Chapter 10

Sammy slowly opens his eyes. He is groggy. Is this a dream? It sure seems like it. He is looking out at a surreal scene which doesn't register as possible.

His mind is all foggy trying to make sense of recent events.

He was just talking to Rusty after a successful escape from the institution. He remembers things suddenly getting quiet, and then, Rusty seemed to dim.

Then, a blackness—not sure for how long—and suddenly, he is here.

He is on a table of sorts, strapped down by...colors?

He can kick his feet a bit, and they seem to pass right through the table, which is somewhat translucent. As a matter of fact, even his body is not completely opaque.

Nothing makes sense.

Unless...it's a dream? So, that's it then—it must be a dream. But if so, it's sure a strange one.

Sammy struggles to rise from the barely-there table, but can only raise his head.

There are rings of colors encircling his body: blue, red, green, gold, white. They shimmer and spin. Kind of pretty, actually.

But they are somehow restraining his dream body from any movement, except for his neck and head, where there are no circles of light.

He is too confused to be frightened just yet. But that will come soon enough.

Out of the corner of his eye, he can just barely make out a figure, or two figures, standing next to a large screen on a sort of podium. They seem to be communicating with each other, but he only hears humming.

"What's your analysis, Minzi?"

"Not so good, Tsedo, not looking very good."

"I thought so. We did the right thing."

Tsedo is apt to agree with her. Abduction was never to be taken lightly, but in this case, he was inclined to go with the option that kept Rachel alive. Although, what to do with the abductee afterwards was always a problem. It's hard to put people back into their own reality after snatching them from it. That experience alone might lead to many other unforeseen events, which could cause ripples in the original future path—something they always try to avoid. Tsedo shrugs this thought off. They'll think of something.

Should I get the others?" he asks.

"Not yet. Let me finish this projection and finalize the analysis."

Tsedo looks at the shimmering, twisting screen with Minzi. There are patterns of lines, circles, dots, and shapes, all interacting with each other. Streaming across the top of the screen is a constant scrolling of numbers.

"Look at this one," Minzi exclaims.

She fiddles with some controls, then looks disappointed.

"Wait—I'll need another pass over him."

Minzi turns and drifts towards Sammy, with some kind of instrument in her hand.

Sammy's heart starts racing. He knows this is a dream, but nevertheless, he cannot move or get away as this ethereal being approaches. And it's carrying something, and pointing it at him. He's got to wake up.

Sammy thrashes against his ghostly restraints to no avail.

The monster (Minzi) hums and cackles at him.

Now the terror starts.

"He's awake and experiencing anxiety," Minzi comments.

"Put him back into stasis then."

"I'd like to, but we need him awake just a little while longer, to get more accurate probabilities. If we're going to alter his life path we've got to be sure," Minzi replies as she waves the instrument over Sammy's body.

"*We already did alter his life path,*" Tsedo thinks—he doesn't want to say this out loud. What they're doing is too important to be distracted by trivialities.

Sammy sees shreds of color coming out of the tool the monster holds over him. The rings around him are now moving up and down his entire prone body. He feels no pain, just a sense of heat, and maybe a tiny bit of pressure. Nevertheless, it is terrifying.

"*Wake up, Sammy!*" he bellows to himself. "*It's just a dream, wake up!*"

Minzi is pressing buttons on the wand-like tool.

Tsedo is looking at the screen, "Oh, I think I see what you mean."

Minzi is now waving the wand over her terrified patient, "Hold on, just one more pass and then I'll put him out of his misery."

The shreds of light form strings and completely surround Sammy from top to bottom. He starts to scream.

"Okay, okay, that should do it."

She presses another button and the strings dissipate. They are replaced by a flood of softly-colored rings, which completely envelope Sammy. His heart slows down, his eyelids grow heavy, and his terror abates as the sedation goes to work. Finally, he is asleep.

"Okay, let's see what we've got," Minzi says.

The two of them peer into the monitor as it pulses and glows.

"There—look at that," Minzi exclaims.

The monitor is showing them events, probabilities, risks, and calculations of Sammy's probable future. One thing stands out as a certainty.

"No matter what path he takes, they all lead to alcoholism," Tsedo says.

Minzi sighs and says, "Not just that, but he will be a violent drunk. He could very well end up killing someone, either by accident or in a fit of rage."

"It's in his blood," Tsedo agrees. "He never really had a chance. He was born into it by his parents, or his father anyway, and his grandfather. He never even met them— grew up in an orphanage before ending up in the institution. But addiction is in his genes."

"I know," Minzi laments. "It's not very fair. Many earthlings are born into a dismal situation. But this one will interact with Rachel, and, in all probability, will do her great harm."

"I can see that. We can't let that happen."

"No, we can't," Minzi agrees.

"Something has to be done."

"I guess we should let the others know."

"Okay. I'm going to transmit these findings to the rest of the group."

And with that, Minzi presses a button which could result in Sammy never waking up again.

Chapter 11

Harry has been struggling to get a good night's sleep for quite a while. Once again, Wendell is awakened by his roommate's groaning.

"Harry?" he calls out in the dark.

No response.

Harry is still asleep, but is tossing and turning, and groaning something awful.

"*Harry!*" Wendell calls out louder.

Still no response. The groaning gets louder.

Wendell gets out of bed, turns on the light, "*Harry—wake up!*"

But Harry doesn't wake up. And what Wendell sees now, scares him.

Harry is having a nightmare. He is drenched in sweat, gasping for breath—his arms stiff at his sides twitching back and forth.

"*Harry—wake up!*" Wendell shouts, and shakes him by the shoulders.

Harry's eyes snap open. He takes in a giant breath, and then starts panting.

"Oh my God!" he exclaims.

"You were having a nightmare, it looked like," Wendell says.

"Yeah, I was."

"A pretty scary one?"

Harry doesn't say anything. Still recovering, he looks at his trusted friend and nods.

"Want to talk about it?" Wendell offers.

Harry sits up and drapes his legs over the side of the bed. Then he stands up, walks over to the window, and looks out at the black night.

"I was...trapped in something," he finally says.

"Trapped?"

"Or, more like, confined. I couldn't move. I was in a small space and couldn't even move my arms or legs."

"Yeah, you looked all stiff."

"And I couldn't breathe either, just barely."

"Yeah. Well, it was just a dream, Harry. Like you told me, nothing real."

"Thank God for that," Harry exclaims. "Damn, it seemed so real. Wonder if it meant anything?"

"Yeah, I wondered that too, but you told me everybody has crazy dreams," Wendell says.

"Yeah, I guess so."

He turns from the window and paces back and forth, trying to recover the details of his dream. But it fades fast. All he really remembers is being trapped, and struggling to breathe.

The terror of it was very real—too real. Yes, it wasn't just that he was scared, it was so much more. This was all-encompassing, full-blown terror. He doesn't want to think about it anymore. He walks around a little, and finally goes back to his bed.

"Damn, the sheets are all wet."

"So are you, bro. You're all sweaty."

"Yeah, you're right."

"Why don't you change your clothes?"

Harry changes his sheets and gets into new sleeping clothes. He puts his sweaty shorts and tee shirt in the hamper.

"Sorry to wake you up, Wendell."

"No, that's fine, don't worry about it. You good, now?"

"Yeah, I think so. I'm gonna turn off the light now, okay?"

"Sure, if you're ready."

"Okay. Gonna see if I can get back to sleep. Hope I never have that one again," Harry says, referring to his dream.

"Just think about something pleasant before falling asleep," Wendell suggests.

"K. G'night, Wendell."

"G'night, Harry."

Harry flips off the light and crawls back into bed, trying to think of something pleasant. He finally settles on thoughts of him and Rachel, and when they might meet again. That makes him smile.

There's a full moon out, and Harry stares out the open window as he falls asleep. He can just barely see dark, wispy shapes—the clouds blot out the moon now and then as they drift by. Funny how they hide the moon in shapes.

Something odd begins to take place.

Harry stares incredulously as those shapes take on a more distinct outline and begin to resemble letters. First an N, then Z, then G, there they are again: N-Z-G-T-O-D-O.

He must be dreaming.

But his eyes are opened.

He shuts them tight and refuses to open them again until the next morning.

Chapter 12

Harry had done a good job keeping out of trouble during his time in the JDC. His incident with Tony, avoiding a confrontation and settling it in a supervised manner, had not gone unnoticed by the board. He was also popular with the other kids, and good friends with Coach Norton. When it came time for his review, the board was happy to inform him that he would be released on his 18th birthday—now only a few months away.

The headmaster enters the study hall where Harry and some of the boys are studying.

"Harry, your parents are here to see you."

Harry puts away his books and jumps up. This should be a great visit.

"Hello, son," his father smiles at him.

"Harry!" his mother exclaims, her arms wide open for a hug.

Harry embraces both of them warmly and sits down in the visiting room.

"Hi, Mom. Hi, Dad. It's great to see you."

"How have you been, honey?" his mother asks him. "You look wonderful!"

Harry had grown into a fine young man. Although still a teenager, he now stood over six feet tall and had been faithfully following an exercise regime which included lifting weights and swimming. He was developing broad shoulders and a muscular physique.

"I'm fine, Mom. Can't wait for my birthday, when I get out of here and can move back home with you guys."

"We're all ready for you, son. Your room is waiting for you. Or, you can even have your sister's room if you want. It's a little larger."

"Won't she need it when she comes back from college?" Harry asks.

"Yes, of course, she will," his mother jumps in. "Dad, we can't just give away Jill's room like that."

"Well, if she's living with her boyfriend, I don't see why not?"

They bicker about this a little bit. Finally, Harry interrupts and says, "No, I want my old room back—I can't wait."

"Good," his mom says, "then it's settled. We can't wait either."

After five minutes of small talk, Harry's Dad confesses, "Harry, we brought you a little surprise."

And like a vision in a dream, a security guard escorts Rachel into the visiting room. It's an unusually warm April day, and she looks positively stunning wearing a yellow sundress, which compliments her long blonde hair and high cheek bones.

"Rachel!" Harry exclaims.

"Hi, Harry," and she rushes to him and gives him a big hug.

"You really look great! What a pretty dress," Harry says.

"Oh, you think so? This old thing?" and she does a little spin and can't help smiling at his appreciation of her beauty.

"You're looking awfully good too," and she runs her hand through his thick brown hair.

"You've gotten so big, Harry!"

Harry starts to say "You have too," but that wouldn't be right. Instead, he says,

"You have...grown even more beautiful."

That worked just fine. Good save, Harry.

The four of them chat for the remainder of the hour. Now during this whole time, Rachel is dying to tell him the news about her new friend, Sherman. But for some reason, she's not comfortable with spreading the news about Sherman's anti-bullying device with parents. She has grown closer to Sherman, and they are working on a science project together. She wants to tell Harry about this, but prefers to do so in private.

The one thing that they both love to talk about with each other is their new-found interest in astronomy. Two years ago, Harry's institution had received a telescope from an anonymous donor. The JDC made it available to all of the kids to sign up for viewing sessions of the night sky. Both Harry and Wendell fell in love with this, and spent many nights peering out into the universe.

Likewise, when Rachel's father saw her interest in science, he encouraged her to join him on the roof and showed her how to spot Orion's belt, the Big Dipper, Mars, Saturn, Jupiter, and any other heavenly bodies that were in the night sky during the current season.

Rachel also took every science, physics, and astronomy course that came her way during her high school years. She was fascinated with black holes, quasars, singularities, dark matter, string theory—she couldn't get enough of it.

Rachel was anxious to have Harry meet Sherman and see how smart and quirky her new friend was. The three of them could be wonderful friends and learn so much from each other. Well, that is, if Sherman didn't say something so rude or insulting that Harry would reject him.

Sherman did have social problems. She even suspected that he suffered from Asperger's syndrome (a mild form of autism characterized chiefly by significant difficulties in social interaction). Yet, she was confident that she could help bridge any gaps between them. After all, Harry would immediately see that Sherman was no threat to their relationship. It was his brain that she admired, that's all. As a matter of fact, Sherman didn't seem to notice girls at all.

When the visit was over, she never really had the chance to tell him about Sherman because, well, there was just too much going on with Harry's parents there. Likewise, Harry had a confession as well—the haunting seven letters. But he didn't feel comfortable revealing that yet either. Both topics would have to wait until he got out and he could talk to Rachel privately.

Chapter 13

Rachel and Sherman had become good friends. As a matter of fact, Rachel may have been Sherman's only friend. Although there was never any debating that Sherman was truly brilliant, he was practically a social pariah. He just didn't get people. Besides the possibility that he may have a mild form of Asperger's Syndrome, he also suffered from occasional panic attacks when he was younger, and still exhibited signs of neurosis. Sometimes God gives gifts in one area and withholds them in another.

Rachel and Sherman were working on a science project together. They had known each other all through their school years, but it wasn't until they found themselves in the same science class that their friendship began to develop.

Rachel garnered a lot of attention from the boys in high school. She was turning into a beautiful woman with curves in all the right places. Although she had many opportunities, she had rejected all attempts to be anybody's girlfriend. Ever since Big Wally's death on the playground, she felt a certain connection to Harry, and could sense that he felt the same way.

Sherman however, was completely oblivious to Rachel's beauty, and to girls in general. Actually, Sherman was oblivious to people. Yet he was glad to have found a friend he could talk to. He didn't even notice Rachel's gender at all. He only noticed that she was kind, and didn't make fun of him or treat him as an oddity the way many of the other kids did.

"We're going to need more ammonium dichromate [$(NH_4)_2Cr_2O_7$]," Sherman announced, as he carefully molded the paper mâché around the metal frame volcano they had been working on.

Rachel writes down, *more ammonium dichromate [$(NH_4)_2Cr_2O_7$]*.

"Okay, got it, Sherman."

"Rachel, can you please brace the model here, you'll need to use two hands, while I angle it at precisely forty-five degrees."

Rachel complies as requested while Sherman proceeds to lay the strips on exactly as he thought they should be.

"Oh, darn, this side is coming out too lumpy," Sherman complains.

"Sherman, does it really matter that everything has to be so exact? I mean, the fun thing is when the volcano erupts."

"Indeed. But need I remind you that our grade is not strictly based on *the fun thing* but on a weighted value based more on the science behind the demonstration? And I intend to get it exactly right, if you don't mind."

Rachel had, by this time, grown accustomed to Sherman's quirkiness. Yes, he could be arrogant at times, even pompous, but he was harder on himself than anyone else. She knew he didn't mean to be condescending—it just comes out that way. She lets the comment slide without a retort, and simply goes on to the next problem that needs to be solved.

"I'm still wondering what we're going to use as a fuse, Sherman?"

"Magnesium strips," comes the instant reply.

"Magnesium?" Rachel wonders aloud. "Won't we need a blow torch to light it? Why not just use a standard fuse?"

"We could," Sherman agrees, "but magnesium ribbons can ignite just from a lighter, and they put on a much more dazzling display than a regular fuse."

"Won't we need to give everyone goggles? It's extremely bright. Couldn't it be blinding?"

Rachel was no slouch when it came to science. Unlike most teenage girls, she was much more interested in physics, astronomy, calculus, and understanding how the world worked than she was in boys. That may not have been the case if Harry was available, but since he wasn't, science had been her boyfriend for the time being. Rachel looked up to Sherman for his brilliance and their shared fascination of how and why things work the way they do. And Sherman needed her, as his only true friend, although he would deny that he needed *anybody* if asked. Sherman's social inadequacies and self-absorption desperately could use some outside help.

Sherman was unconcerned whether or not members of his audience might go blind. If he warned them not to look at the burning magnesium ribbons—and they chose to ignore his warnings—then he could not be blamed for their carelessness, and disavowed himself from all responsibility.

"We'll just tell them not to look directly at it," Sherman declares.

"But what if some do anyway?"

"Then it's their loss. We will give out sufficient instructions and if they don't heed our warnings, then whatever happens after that is their problem."

Sherman's insensitivity to others is astonishing.

"Sherman, please think this through. Somebody stares at the burning magnesium for too long, goes blind, and sues us, and the school, for all we're worth."

"Yes, but we would win the law suit because we could prove we gave an adequate warning."

"Maybe, but even so, how about the poor person who went blind? Not to mention the cost and trouble of fighting such a case in court."

Sherman is silent for a moment, weighing the risks of what may result by using magnesium ribbons, instead of a standard fuse.

"Well, like you said, we could have everyone wear goggles."

"Yeah, but they couldn't just be goggles. They'd have to be heavily tinted. And what if somebody looks right at the burning magnesium without putting them on?"

Sherman was going to say, *"Well then it's their loss,"* but could see where that statement would lead to. Finally, he acquiesces to Rachel's common sense.

"Okay, fine Rachel, we'll use a standard fuse to ignite the volcano," Sherman says, not without a touch of indignation.

"*Whew!*" Rachel thinks. She actually won an argument with Sherman, and may have saved somebody's eyesight in the process.

Chapter 14

It's the day of the science fair. There are booths galore set up all throughout the gymnasium with many interesting exhibits on display. Sherman and Rachel have plenty of competition in the form of: robotics, animatronics, synthesized art, music exhibits, astronomy—lots of cool stuff.

After the first two hours, and a dozen successful performances, Sherman decides to take a break and check out some of the other booths. As he strolls through the exhibits, one in particular catches his eye. There is a large, cylindrical, funnel with marbles circling around and around, finally falling down the hole in the middle. The marbles exponentially increase their speed until they are nothing but a blur of color, before finally falling through. It is a black hole exhibit.

"May I try?" Sherman asks.

"Yes, please, go ahead," and the student gives him a marble to drop into the display.

Sherman drops the marble in. It starts at the outer edge and begins to circle around the perimeter of the funnel. Sherman is totally absorbed in watching the demonstration take place.

"You see, this is the event horizon..."

"I'm fully aware of that!" Sherman snaps at him. He doesn't need anyone else to explain science to him. After all, they might get it wrong. Then he would have to take the time to explain why they're wrong, and he didn't have the time to teach lesser students the error of their ways.

After Sherman's outburst, the student steps back with a frown on his face, thinking *"Who is this jerk anyway?"* He glares at Sherman, but Sherman doesn't even notice. He's too busy watching the marble as it circles faster and faster while descending towards the hole in the middle.

Rachel has also stepped away from their booth, temporarily suspending their volcanic eruptions. She looks over Sherman's shoulder at the marble on its journey. Along with this main exhibit, there are also charts, graphs, and equations laid out around the booth illustrating the physics of what happens at the center of a black hole, or at least some theories.

Rachel sidles next to Sherman and they both watch as the marble rattles down the funnel and closes in on the center hole. It is now moving so fast that it becomes just a blur of color. Rachel nudges Sherman.

"Sherman?"

He is a little startled by her voice. Didn't even notice her presence before.

"Oh, hi."

"Have you looked at these charts?" she asks, pointing to them.

As the marble finishes its journey and falls through, Sherman finally looks up and sees what she's referring to. He's instantly intrigued.

"Ohhh," he mumbles, his attention now focused on deciphering the science.

As a mass approaches infinite density and time slows down relatively, there may be a point where linear time ceases to exist. Sherman has an epiphany. The chart shows that the region of space surrounding the black hole would be vibrating at enormous speed. What if one were to match those vibrations? Would it be possible to breach the dimensions of our own continuum to a neighboring one?

Something is there which has never been fully understood, buried too deep in theoretical quantum physics, and therefore, never exploited. As Sherman's brain struggles to glean this concept, he intuitively grasps that there must be a way to do this, and solving this riddle would open up the doors to traveling through Hyperspace. The seed of Sherman's life's work has been planted.

Chapter 15

It's been a busy but rewarding day for Rachel. She loved the science fair and was captivated by some of the other exhibits, especially that black hole one. She thinks it was very inspirational to Sherman's work, and thoroughly enjoyed the conversations she had with Sherman afterward. Wouldn't it be wonderful to someday travel the stars without limitations? To shoot from one planet to the next, and observe different life forms, like on Star Trek? How far off was mankind from this dream?

Would they have to make rules, like the prime directive, which forbids the advanced species from interacting and altering in any way the future of the inhabitants? She thinks about this.

What if she were the captain of a ship, zooming around the universe, and able to help save lives on other planets? Would it be the right thing to do?

Who knows? What if she saved the life of a Hitler-like being who grows up and wreaks havoc on his/her fellow beings? And for that matter, what if she knew a planet's future was doomed because of a certain individual? Would killing or removing that individual be wrong if it benefits the rest of the world?

It's a few minutes before midnight and Rachel is getting ready for bed.

"Maybe a quick glimpse of Saturn first?" she thinks.

She goes over to peer through her telescope, already pointing out at the night sky, and quickly finds Saturn, its beautiful rings on display.

Now, while she's completely engrossed in this task, little does she notice the faint, but colorful rings of light, hovering and spinning above her head. Behind the wall, in another dimension, Tsedo is scolding Minzi.

"For God's sake, Minzi, wait until she goes to sleep. She's liable to see it!"

"Nonsense," Minzi retorts, "she's completely occupied and those spinning disindrils are so faint to her eyes as to be almost invisible."

"Still, why not wait until she's in bed?"

"Because I can get a little more data while her brain is occupied with Saturn than I can when she's sleeping," Minzi replies.

"You know it's been over 15 years of their time and we can never fully map her, or anyone," Tsedo reminds her.

"We have to strive to be as thorough as possible, Tsedo. We need her awake for just...a few more moments...aah, good!"

As Rachel fiddles with the focus of her telescope, the purple ring hovering above her head splits into three: gold, red, and blue, and they quiver in mid-air before gently floating up and down over her body. The information being transmitted includes her blood type, her levels of every kind, sugars, red blood cell count, DNA sample, and all forms of bio-data that go into making Rachel who she is. Yet bio-data makes up for only half of the examination.

The other half of the information that the rings transmit is much more interesting. It is the consciousness of Rachel, the part that can actually share their world. It is not limited by any physical boundaries or physical matter—just pure thought and vibration existing through five dimensions.

This race, the Trinollians, exists outside of linear time and has the ability to see all time as one stream. They can foresee that Rachel is headed for extreme circumstances and dire situations which will bring her to the brink of what's humanly possible. The Trinollians know that her success or failure will affect many races and species too numerous to mention. Rachel has a purpose and must, at all costs, succeed.

The rings fade and dissipate seconds before Rachel steps back from the telescope, her examination of Saturn and its moons are done for tonight. Tsedo and Minzi upload the data and fade out of existence from behind her wall. Rachel swats the light switch down and slips under the covers.

Just then the phone rings.

She looks at the clock. 12:01, a minute after midnight. Who could be calling?

Then she realizes what day it is, and smiles.

"Hello?"

"Hi Rachel, guess who?" Harry taunts.

"I know—Happy birthday, Harry! I figured it was you."

"Well, I'm glad you didn't forget."

"Forget? How could I? It's all we've talked about for the last two weeks," she laughs.

"I know it's late. I'm sorry if I woke you up—I didn't, did I? But I'll be home in just a few hours."

"I know. I can't wait either Harry! I'm so happy you'll be free again."

"Yeah, so much Rach. I've been waiting so long. Now I can start my life again."

That's a nice thing to hear. It's exciting—to start one's life again.

"And what will you do?" Rachel asks.

"Well, anything I want to, I guess. Go to college...maybe study science...take some courses in astronomy, I suppose."

"Yeah," Rachel muses, "me too...probably."

They're both quiet for a moment. Then, "Harry?" Rachel asks.

"Yeah?"

"I want to introduce you to my friend, Sherman."

"Oh? Who's that?"

"His name is Sherman Hollingsworth. We're partners on a science project. He's really smart and has all kinds of insights into physics and cosmic theories. I think you would find him pretty interesting."

Pretty interesting? What was Rachel talking about? Here they've been waiting for this day for years and all this time she had another interest, somebody else she likes, a possible boyfriend? No, it can't be. He knows her. She can't possibly be romantic with someone else. Besides his name is Sherman Hollingsworth. Not likely a girlfriend stealer with a name like that. More likely a geek, he figures. Harry changes his attitude.

"Okay, sure, I want to meet him," he tells her, "but I'd love to see you first."

"Of course, silly. What time do you get released?"

"Less than nine hours, 9 a.m. My folks will be here to take me home, and then I'm planning on stopping over your place after I get all my stuff settled in."

"Well, don't you want to spend some time with your parents first?"

"Yeah, of course. I'll be home most of the day. I'll come by in the late afternoon."

"Can't wait," Rachel says.

"Me too. Bye Rach."

"Bye Harry, see you tomorrow."

Harry hangs up his phone, turns out the lights, and settles into bed.

Wendell is looking at him and says, "So this is it. This is our last night together, huh?"

"Yeah, I'm going to miss you, bro. But it won't be too long before you get out too, right? Just another six months?"

"Well, I have a hearing coming up, but if it goes well I could be getting out sometime in the fall. Yeah, maybe 6 or 8 months."

"It will be great to see you on the outside," Harry says.

"Will it ever," Wendell agrees.

Then...

"Harry?"

"Yeah?"

"Remember the story Rusty told us about Sammy disappearing?"

"Yeah, who wouldn't?" Harry answers.

"Did you believe it?" Wendell asks.

Damn.

This is one subject Harry does not feel like discussing. Especially late at night. He's had enough spooky things going on in his life lately. Harry had always felt like he has a touch of ESP, or more than a touch, but does not trust whatever it is that sends him the information, and would rather it just go away.

And that disappearing Sammy story really spooked him. It reminded him of something he couldn't quite put his finger on.

"Yeah, I guess I do," he admits to Wendell.

"Did you ever hear any more of that story or talk to Rusty about it?"

"Uh, no, not really. Why, did you?"

"Yes."

A chill creeps up Harry's spine. Harry doesn't want to know, but can't help himself.

"What did you hear?" he asks.

"Well, a few days after he told that story, me and Joey were leaving the cafeteria when Rusty comes shuffling in, pale and sweaty."

Oh, no. Harry does not like the sound of this. He doesn't want to hear it. But he doesn't say anything. However, he does turn the lights back on. He especially doesn't want to hear this story in the dark. Wendell sits on the side of his bed looking at him and continues.

"Well, we hadn't seen him for breakfast, and now he almost completely missed lunch. So we asked him what's up? And he doesn't say a word, just looks right through us."

Wendell pauses, waiting for Harry to ask him what he means.

Harry would rather Wendell would shut up and just let him go to sleep. He doesn't need to hear ghost stories right now. But he doesn't say anything.

Wendell goes on anyway: "So again we ask him what's up, why'd you miss breakfast anyway? And Rusty looks at us and we can barely hear him, but he says he saw Sammy last night!"

Harry's got to ask, "What? Rusty went out again, alone?"

"No," Wendell says.

"No?"

"Rusty says he saw him in his dreams, but it was like, real."

A flood of relief washes over Harry.

"Oh, for God's sake, Wendell, you were spooking me out! Everybody dreams weird things now and then. I don't want to hear anymore!"

"No, Rusty swears it wasn't totally a dream. Sammy came to him and tried to tell him where he was and Rusty was like, not totally sleeping anymore. You shoulda heard him tell it."

"Wendell, I'm getting out tomorrow and leaving all this behind, I don't wanna hear it anymore."

"But I'm telling you..."

Harry flashes a touch of indignation.

"No, you're not! I'm going to sleep now Wendell, and so are you. Look buddy, I'm thinking about going home, seeing Rachel tomorrow, please, just go to bed. After tonight the next time we see each other we'll both be outta here."

That shakes Wendell up a little.

"You mean you're not gonna visit me after you're out? I've still got plenty to go."

"Oh, yeah, you're right, of course, I will. I didn't mean that. You've got me all rattled buddy. Yeah, I'll visit you, even bring you a file in a cake if you want. But let's just both go to sleep now, okay?"

Wendell smiles at his file in the cake joke. "Yeah, okay. Well, I was going to say I don't think Rusty is in his right mind, not completely anyway. But that's not your world anymore. Never mind. Good night Harry."

Harry switches off the lights again.

"No, you're right. It's not my world anymore. And soon enough it won't be yours either. Good night, buddy."

The room is dark and silent, except for the noise of the heater and the sliver of moonlight piercing through the window and illuminating a small spot on the floor a few feet from Harry's bed.

He is staring at that spot as he drifts off to sleep. He imagines he feels a very soft breeze swirling in the dark. Must just be the heater blowing?

And as his eyes close he thinks he sees, or maybe he's already dreaming, letters forming in the dust on the floor under the moonlight. First a T, then an O, followed by Z, N, D, O, G.

Chapter 16

It's almost four p.m. when Rachel hears the doorbell ring. Finally!

She rushes to open it, and there he is—tall, handsome, strong, and...free.

"Wow! Hi, Harry."

"Wow, yourself. You look great!"

"So do you."

They embrace, kiss, and share a long-awaited moment. Rachel then takes his hand and leads him into the living room.

Harry looks around. It's been a while, but he's been in Rachel's home before.

"Are your parents home?"

"Not yet. They're both working, but my mom should be home soon."

Still holding hands, they both sit down on the couch.

"Man, it's been a long time since I've been in this house."

"Were you ever here before? I don't remember," Rachel admits.

"Yeah, when we were kids. You know, right after the whole Big Wally thing, when our parents were trying to figure out what to do. You guys had us over to, uh, discuss it."

"Oh, yeah, right. I kind of try not to think about that whole situation anymore," Rachel says.

"That makes two of us. But it's over now. I did my time and now I'm free!" Harry declares.

"You certainly are. And so am I."

She looks up at him and runs her fingers through his hair. They share another kiss.

"When did you say your mother was getting home?"

Rachel laughs. She knows what he's thinking.

"Anytime now, sorry to say. She wants to say hello to you too."

They look at each other, happy to be together. Rachel squeezes his hand affectionately.

"Harry?"

"Yeah?"

"I want you to meet my friend, Sherman."

"Yeah, you mentioned that before. Sure, I'll meet him. He's your science partner?"

"Yes, we worked on a project together and he's quite brilliant, and also is interested in astronomy, like us."

"Yeah, okay."

"Well, he's actually interested more in the physics part of it. Sherman wants to study at Stanford or Berkeley next year, and is hoping to get a scholarship at one of them."

"Wow! Well, he must be really smart to score a scholarship at either of those colleges," Harry agrees.

"Um..." Harry starts, not quite sure how to say what's on his mind. "Um...Rach...he's not my competition is he?" he finally blurts out.

"Oh, don't be silly Harry, not in any way, shape or form! Sherman isn't like that at all. He doesn't really have any friends that I know of. And certainly not any females. He barely notices that I'm a girl, come to think of it. He only sees people by what's inside them, and what they have to say. He's very cerebral. Maybe a bit socially awkward, but a good person on the inside."

"Well, that's good enough for me," Harry says, a little bit relieved. "Any friend of yours is a friend of mine too."

I was right. He's a total geek," Harry thinks.

"So, are you okay to meet him at Starbucks later?"

"Sure."

Harry goes in for another kiss.

Just then they hear a car turn into the driveway, followed by a loud bang. It startles Harry and cuts the kiss short. Rachel laughs.

"That's how she announces that she's here."

"That was a backfire? Damn, someone needs to buy her a new car."

#

The coffee shop is a short walk from Rachel's house. When the two of them arrive, Rachel spots Sherman inside and points him out to Harry.

Sherman is sitting at a table with all of his snacks laid out in a perfect line. There are potato chips, a piece of lemon cake, and a chocolate, nutty candy bar. Currently, Sherman is carefully fixing his cup of coffee. He only drinks decaf because he gets too jittery from the caffeine. Sherman must have the creamer and sweetener in his coffee perfectly proportioned. Depending on the volume of the coffee, he estimates exactly how much he needs, and puts it in little by little, continually taking short sips to make sure it's just right. Sherman is so engrossed in this task, he does not even notice Harry and Rachel as they enter.

"He startles easily," Rachel whispers. "Let me approach first."

Rachel walks over to where Sherman is sitting. Sherman doesn't look up or notice. He's still working on getting the half and half just right.

"Hi, Sherman," Rachel says softly.

"Oh," Sherman jumps and spills a little coffee. "Oh my, now I have to start all over again."

"Sorry, Sherman, I didn't mean to startle you."

"Didn't mean to, but did nevertheless. Now all the proportions are messed up, and I have to get a new decaf."

Harry is watching all of this and comes over.

"Here, let me get you another cup," he volunteers.

Sherman looks at him. "Oh, you must be Harry?"

"Harry Stone at your service! Nice to meet you Sherman," and he stretches out his hand.

"Hello, Harry Stone. I'm Sherman Hollingsworth. You may have heard of me, a 4.0 at Jackson High? I'm sorry, but I don't do handshakes. Too risky. Salutes are much safer—no skin-to-skin contact," and Sherman gives Harry a sloppy salute.

"Okay, I understand, no problem," Harry returns the salute. "Let me get you that coffee."

"Decaf, please," Sherman requests. "And a medium one, not large. I would have to recalculate the proportions of additives."

"Right."

Rachel sits down with Sherman.

"So how are you doing?" she asks.

"Oh, fair today. So this is your friend from prison?"

"Not prison, juvenile detention."

"And he's a killer, if I remember correctly?"

Rachel sighs. She has already told him the whole story. Sherman just does not take to meeting anybody new—or people in general, actually.

"It was a horrible accident and he was defending a smaller boy from being beaten up by a big bully. He's really a great guy. Please give him a chance, Sherman. Talk to him about astronomy, he might surprise you."

"Well if you say so, Rachel. You're one of the few people I trust. So... don't let me down."

"I won't. Who else do you trust?"

"Hmmm?"

"You said I was one of the *few* people you trust. Who else?"

"Oh, well, let's see. There's, um, my mother. And,..." this is a hard question for Sherman. "Well, actually I don't totally trust my mother. I'll have to back track on that. She's made some bad decisions here and there. Like trying to get me to play sports when I didn't want to. And insisting I learn to swim, which didn't work out very well. Oh, well, there's math. I trust math completely. And science...and..."

"No, math and science don't count, Sherman. I'm asking you what other people do you trust?"

"Well, let me see..."

Sherman is still pondering this when Harry returns to the table with his coffee and sits down.

"Here you go, buddy!"

Harry is trying to be friendly. But calling Sherman "buddy" is the wrong thing to do. Sherman gives him a disapproving look, but thanks him for the coffee.

"Thank you, Harry, that was very decent of you. I mean, I know it's not expensive and I could have just as easily bought another one myself, but I appreciate the gesture."

"Happy to do it, buddy!"

"But please don't call me buddy anymore."

"Oh, okay, sorry. Do you have a nickname?"

"None that I like. Sherman is fine. Or, Mr. Hollingsworth will do nicely too."

"Sherman," Rachel exclaims. "Don't be rude!"

"Hey, that's fine," Harry says. "I understand. A person has the right to be proud of his name. No nicknames from now on."

"Thank you, Harry. You do seem to understand."

Harry is winning him over, slowly but surely.

"So, I understand you're interested in Hyperspace?" Harry asks.

And with that question, he opens up a door to Sherman's intellect and friendship—the floodgates are raised.

Sherman's demeanor changes immediately and you could almost see a glow emanating from him as he takes a position of lecturer.

"Well, as you probably already know," Sherman starts explaining, "the idea of Hyperspace was first postulated in the 1940's in science fiction by Isaac Asimov. It was then alluded to as another dimension of space, but co-existing with our own universe, whereby a breach may be made from one to another by various methods that could effectively open a link or a jumping point as it's sometimes called. Parts of this theory may soon be proven correct, at least as far as alternative dimensions that either don't have the same restrictions regarding faster-than-light travel, or, the distance covered in the alternative dimension is much shorter than the corresponding points in our own universe. Now, if one were to find a way to create enough energy to open a jumping point..."

Sherman is off and running. Harry detects the slightest sigh from Rachel, indicating that they are both now trapped for however long Sherman's pontificating will continue. But Harry also sees how happy Sherman has become, truly enjoying talking about this subject matter. Harry is somewhat captivated by Sherman's enthusiasm and knowledge of this pretty much unknown area of what used to be science fiction, but is now becoming science fact—at least according to Sherman.

Rachel has heard it all before. Although Sherman could sometimes come off as being condescending (to put it mildly), she also holds a fascination of the subject, and understands that she may very well have befriended a person who may well be on his way to being one of the foremost authorities on interdimensional travel.

The implications of Sherman's work in this field could turn out to be one of the most astounding discoveries of mankind. Sherman has theories that he is working on (backed up by a new term he invented, nanophysics), that could not only open the door for space travel beyond our own solar system, but could possibly even stretch across galaxies. It is feasible that someday Sherman's name could become as famous as Isaac Newton, or even Albert Einstein. She believes she is seeing the birth of history-changing events in the course of human understanding, and of our ability to shape the universe in which we live.

During the course of the afternoon, Harry becomes convinced that Sherman is some kind of savant. Is he possibly in the company of somebody destined for greatness? There is no doubt that Sherman thinks that about himself. He has revealed to Harry and Rachel his ten-year plan of obtaining a PhD in physics, and then finding a job at NASA, or possibly JPL in California—which ever will allow him access to a laboratory with the greatest amount of resources in which to test his theories of Hyperspace using nanophysics.

"I'm hoping it will become a standard in the curriculum of most colleges that specialize in science and physics," Sherman says convincingly.

"I think you might have something there," Harry concedes.

"Think?" Sherman is somewhat offended.

"I mean, I think you really do have something there," Harry corrects himself. "It's just very abstract, at least to me, at this point."

"Would you like to see the math to back it up?" Sherman volunteers.

"Well, I, um..."

"I can't draw it out for you right here, but if you want to come over my house I can retrieve all my material and we can go through it from the beginning. Shouldn't take more than three hours," Sherman says jubilantly.

"Oh, well, um, you see...Ow!"

Rachel gave him a kick under the table.

"I mean, yeah, sure, I'd love to."

"Really? Oh, that would be grand! But why did you say Ow?"

"Oh, um, I just got a crick in my calf," Harry lies.

"Oh, yeah, I get them too," Sherman admits.

"Can we set it up for later this week, Sherman?" Rachel asks.

"Certainly!" and they make their plans.

On the way home, Harry confesses to Rachel, "I'm not sure I'm so crazy about going to his house and listening to more lectures, Rach."

"I know. He's hard to take sometimes. But I really think he's on to something and maybe you and I together can work on understanding some of his calculations that support his theories?"

Yes, Rachel has a good point there, Harry thinks to himself. That vibration stuff, jumping points, alternate dimensions, nanophysics

Sherman called it. Actually it was pretty interesting. But quite a challenge to understand.

It was also a challenge to be in Sherman's presence for so long. He could be rude and condescending. And so arrogant! But he's real. He's not hiding anything. That's the way he is, and he doesn't even try to change himself to suit others or fit in.

That part of Sherman was kind of endearing. Kind of a rare quality to find in people—those with no filter whatsoever.

Whatever they feel, they put right out there without any attempt at changing to fit into the world better. And Harry knew, just by pondering this thought, that that was a big part of Rachel's friendship with Sherman. Rachel doesn't really judge. She just lets people be who they are.

As Harry and Rachel walk back to her house from the coffee shop, Harry is overwhelmed with good feelings. He looks around at the beautiful day. He takes in a deap breath and smells the fresh air. It's wonderful.

Just being free. Being next to her. Smelling her. Talking about things.

"So?" she asks. Rachel is still waiting for an answer. He looks at her on this beautiful day. Her hair is blowing in a light breeze. This is what life is all about. He hoped it could be this way for a long time to come.

"Yeah, sure, we'll go together."

So he takes her hand as they walk together, chatting about Sherman and his science and what it could mean—just enjoying being together. Both hoping nothing will ever force them apart again.

Yet, even as they are taking in one of life's wonderful days, there in the sky are five planes stacked next to each other, spelling out some advertisement. It's crazy, but even after a few minutes, when all the other letters have faded, Harry can still clearly see the haunting letters which failed to dissipate much: T-O-O-Z-D-N-G

And as those cursed letters finally start to fade, he could swear the double O's flatten out and sneer at him.

Chapter 17

Back at Rachel's house, Harry sits down while Rachel makes them something to eat.

On the other side of Rachel's bedroom wall, in another dimension, there's a remarkable event going on that holds the destiny of a boy Harry used to know at the Juvenile Detention Center.

The Trinollians have a process for returning the victim to his/her own world if the ripples of the abduction are minor. Sammy's fate lies in their hands now, as they discuss the options of what to do with him.

He remains in stasis, blissfully unaware of his life being judged by alien beings. The very essence of who Sammy is, now being examined to determine his chances of ever returning to earth. Unfortunately, it's not looking too good.

The head of the abduction committee is Elder Randallt who has seen over all of the abduction cases in the last 10,000 earth years—a meaningless time measurement from their point of view. He telepathically communicates a clear picture of the consequences involved in letting Sammy return to his life.

Tsedo and Minzi, along with the rest of them, nod their heads in agreement. Sammy had no real connections, (not even a family since he was an orphan) who would miss him if he never returned. And yet, if he did return, his life of alcoholism would surely come into fruition. It would be a difficult and miserable struggle for him. Sammy's proclivity to alcoholism was inherited from his father and grandfather. So was his rage, which eventually, would most likely harm those around him.

There was a high probability that Rachel's life-path would be negatively affected by Sammy.

"We could return him if he's handicapped," one of them suggests. There is a murmur of approval at this.

While it's true that physically impairing the poor victim before returning him seems like a sadistic and cruel thing to do, the Trinollians think it is better than robbing the individual of the rest of his life altogether. And, by being handicapped, the person might even be forced to learn humility, as well as to be reliant and thankful for other people's assistance. The same people that he might have hurt may instead become his helpers during his life. This situation would be mutually beneficial, as it would result in the most growth for all involved.

"His impairment would have to be severe enough to prevent him from ever having the ability to really hurt someone. He's going to live with rage and bouts of violence his whole life," one of them says.

This discussion goes on and on, not everyone is in agreement. It would be nice if the final verdict was unanimous, but Elder Randallt has the final say. However, he will hear every single opinion on this matter before making a decision.

Will they put Sammy in a wheel chair the rest of his life, and if so, how much movement do they allow him? Will he be a Paraplegic or a Quadriplegic? Will he have a straw in his mouth to control the wheel chair or be able to move it with his wrist? Of course, any victim that is returned after an abduction, especially one that results in a debilitation of some sort, is also give a false memory to explain how the debilitation occurred.

Now of course, however they acquired this right to interfere with mankind's progression, well, that is for another story. Clearly they felt they were anointed to look over other planets and act in their own best interest. This did not fare too well with the victims of their abductions, which, thank God, were rare. Nevertheless, poor Sammy was under their magnifying glass now and totally at their mercy.

Blinding Sammy is also an option that is suggested.

Yes, it seems cruel, but it has to be considered—everything has to be considered really. If the Trinollians are to take the chance of returning

Sammy to earth in a disabled state, what would be the fairest way to do it? Would he have a better life if blind, or partially blind, but he could walk and have arms that work? And if he was partially blind, how much would it have to be to ensure that he relied upon others for help so that he couldn't possibly fight or hurt anyone?

Sammy sleeps softly nearby, blissfully unaware of the horror that awaits him.

Chapter 18

Back in Harry and Rachel's reality, it's the following day. They show up at Sherman's house ready for anything. Well, ready for...patience, more than anything else. Patience and tolerance—along with putting up with Sherman's arrogance. This, in exchange for the prize of a healthy and informative discussion about nanophysics, and a look at what could be the next astonishing step in technology for all of mankind.

Before she rings the bell, Rachel cautions Harry again, "Now remember, we're likely to be scolded for being late but it's just his attention to details. He doesn't mean to be condescending, it's just that..."

"Oh, he means it all right," Harry counters. "I get the feeling he gets a kick out of correcting or proving other people wrong."

"Yes, well all right, I guess that's true," Rachel admits. "But, he's my friend and I put up with it because the pros greatly outweigh the cons in this case."

"I get it, Rachel. Don't worry. I won't slug him or do anything but turn the other cheek at his rudeness—haven't I so far? I've learned a lot of tolerance during the past few years."

"Perfect," Rachel says and rings the bell. *"Because you're gonna be put to the test,"* she adds under her breath.

Harry heard it but just smiles and doesn't say anything.

The door opens.

"Hello, Rachel, and you must be Harry," Sherman's mother says as she greets them with a warm smile.

"Yes, it's a pleasure..."

"Mother, please dispense with the formalities and bring them right up here. We have a lot of my work to go over and they're already ten minutes late," Sherman calls down at her.

"Shermy, don't be rude!" his mother scolds him. "Why don't you answer the door yourself then?"

"Mother, I am indisposed at the moment. Please show them to my room and I'll be right there."

Sherman's mother makes a face and rolls her eyes, then turns back to Harry and Rachel.

"Please won't you come in? He'll be with you in a moment. Can I get you something to drink?"

"No thanks."

"No thank you, Mrs. Hollingsworth."

She shows them to Sherman's room and opens the door.

"He'll be right here. Please make yourselves comfortable and call me if you need anything," Sherman's mother says.

Rachel sits on the bed. Harry takes the chair beside the desk.

"Thank you."

"Thank you, Mrs. Hollingsworth," Rachel says.

This is the first time Rachel has been in Sherman's room and, of course, it's the same for Harry. Sherman's room is large, neat, and in perfect order. There is no clutter, and everything seems to have a place where it belongs. There are two bookcases that line the walls, filled to the brim with books and magazines. There are storage containers all lined up neatly inside an entertainment center, and a filing cabinet on the floor. On the wall, there are pictures of Albert Einstein, Richard Feynman, Nikola Tesla, Stephen Hawking, and a slew of other prominent scientists and mathematicians. Harry doesn't see one personal photograph of Sherman or his family anywhere.

There is a large desk with two computer monitors and a notebook labeled "Nanophysics by Sherman Hollingsworth" next to the mouse pad. Harry opens it and starts to read.

"Hey, look at that," Rachel exclaims. She stands up and walks over to a closed door on the side of the bedroom wall.

Just then, Sherman walks in.

"Hi! I trust you had no problems finding my house?"

"No," Rachel says, "Hey Sherman, what does this door lead to?"

Sherman was about to scold them for being late, but instead walks over and opens the door.

"It leads to this!" he exclaims, and shows them a beautiful bedroom with a pool table in the center, taking up the entire room. The balls are racked and the cue ball sits at the opposite side of the table, ready to be played.

"Hey, Sherman, you play pool?" Harry asks.

"Oh, maybe a little," Sherman lies. "Do you?"

"Yeah, sure I do," and Harry walks into the pool room and examines the cue sticks in the rack. "Can I take a shot?"

"Go ahead—you can break."

"You mean you want to play a game?"

"Maybe just one. Straight pool—you have to call all your shots," Sherman says.

Rachel is astonished to learn that Sherman has a hobby like this. Not even a hobby, a sport.

"Sherman, you never mentioned this before."

"Well, you never asked."

Harry chalks up the cue stick and positions the cue ball slightly to the side, draws back the stick, and sharply thrusts it forward. He gets a decent break and one ball goes in the pocket.

"Hah!" Harry exclaims.

"Good shot," says Rachel.

He then lines up his next shot and calls it out, "10-ball in the corner pocket."

He takes his next shot but misses by centimeters.

"Darn."

"My turn," Sherman says.

Sherman quickly analyzes the table. "5-ball in the side pocket."

He deftly sinks the shot, putting a touch of English on it so that the cue ball retreats back a bit after hitting the 5-ball in. It is readily apparent that Sherman is very good. His stance, his form, his shot—Harry recognizes the air of a confident opponent.

"Thirteen in the corner," Sherman announces.

Boom—another perfect shot as the 13-ball disappears from the table.

"Seven in the corner."

Boom—the 7-ball drops in the pocket.

Sherman struts around the table, quickly lining up and sinking shot after shot. Some of his bank shots are extremely clever and well-executed. He practically runs the table. The final score is 13-2.

"Where did you learn to play like that?" Harry asks.

"From Tesla," comes the reply.

"Nikola Tesla?" Rachel asks.

"The one and only. And I know he's dead, of course. But he was a pool shark and inspired me to take up the game."

"I think that's fantastic," Rachel exclaims.

"Me too," Harry agrees. "Great game, Sherman. I hope we can do it again sometime?"

"I don't see why not. Would you mind racking the balls, Harry, and putting them back into place?"

"Yeah, sure," Harry knows why he's being asked to do this—because the 'loser' racks, However, he politely remains silent.

When everything is put away, Sherman leads them out, closes the door, gestures for them to sit, and picks up his "Nanophysics by Sherman Hollingsworth" notebook.

Despite the arrogant tone, what Sherman has to say that afternoon is intriguing. Actually, it's more than just intriguing. It's compelling, and extremely thought-provoking. Harry could see why Rachel struck up her friendship with Sherman. He was interesting, and had a genuine love and excitement for his work.

It's no wonder Sherman has some quirks. Harry's first impression of him, that of a savant, was accurate.

Sherman begins the session by repeating the discussion of how parallel dimensions could exist in an alternate continuum. Using a white board, he begins writing equations to represent mass, and the vibrations that surround the mass, which hold it in its current reality.

"We can explore the proof of these equations using nanophysics, but the concept is that these equations can be thought of to represent an object, like a spaceship. If we could accurately forecast how this ship is held in its current dimension, by the quantum physics that make up matter including the spin and vibration of the sub-atomic particles, we could then calculate and possibly manipulate the essence of the object as it exists in its current reality by raising the vibrations of the core region of space that surround it to match those of a parallel dimension."

"How do you know that the vibrations would need to be raised and not lowered?" Rachel asked.

"Good question! Most likely they would have to be raised because otherwise the parallel dimension would be visible to us and breach our continuum. But, I could be wrong about that. There may be dimensions existing below our vibratory rate that we can't detect for other reasons."

"The same way that we can't hear sounds that are too high or low on either end of the spectrum?" Harry asks.

"Yes, kind of—excellent analogy, Harry!"

The three of them were really getting into it. Sherman continues,

"Therefore, my theory postulates that once the core vibrations are in sync with the vibrations of a parallel continuum, jumping points will appear forming an interdimensional bridge. The matter contained in the enveloped core would then be able to slip in and out of hyperspace. As long as we have control over the vibratory core it would be possible to cross into a second dimension where the distances between objects fold, resulting in closer proximity to each other."

Sherman's enthusiasm is contagious. His audience is captivated. After a dramatic pause, he continues.

"The cosmic speed limit, that of light (roughly 6 trillion miles/year), would no longer be a barrier. Even traveling across galaxies would be possible!" Sherman exclaims, holding up a finger and pointing to the sky for dramatic effect.

However, as Sherman continued to pontificate, it became apparent that even if the science panned out to be true, the technology to test his theories didn't exist today. Unless a grant or government-funded program was put in place, the proof of concept could be a long time coming.

It was actually Sherman who admitted this towards the end of his lengthy dissertation, ending it on a rather blue note.

"Oh, Sherman, don't sound so sad about that," Rachel sympathized. "That's how it is with many scientific breakthroughs. We each have to stand on the shoulders of our predecessors and it may take generations before a theory like this is proven or applied."

"Many of Einstein's theories of relativity weren't proven until long after he died when our generation finally had the technology to test them," Harry finishes.

Sherman knew what he was talking about. He was well aware that many of Einstein's theories of relativity were not proven until after Einstein was long dead.

This was not acceptable. He needed to see his work funded and tested in a laboratory. Sherman had a strong intuition that altering the vibrations of a region of space and slipping through to the next dimension could be solved in years, not generations. He felt he was close enough to be able to prove his theories in less than ten years if given a high-tech laboratory.

"I am going to solve this if it's the last thing I ever do," he says indignantly.

Sherman's resolution is to be commended even if it is not realistic. When he is in the zone—look out!

The group is silent for a moment.

Then it occurs to Harry that Sherman might be just the right guy to help him with a little problem he has been having for the last few years.

"Hey, Sherman?" Harry asks.

"Yes?"

"I was wondering if you might help me solve a puzzle I've been working on recently?"

Sherman was all ears.

"Why, yes, of course! What is it?"

"Can you tell me what words you see from these letters?"

And Harry writes down: N - T - O - O - Z - G – D

Sherman looks at the letters for five seconds, furrows his brow, and then declares,

"Well, I'm not sure, but I know that it's not from God!" he jokes.

"Yeah, I thought of that too, but it has a Z in it," Harry replies.

"The Z is used to separate the two words. It's Zed, the last letter in the alphabet. In this case, the space between the two words," Sherman asserts.

Harry stares at the letters he wrote, the letters that have cursed him for so long. "NOT GOD" is kind of a scary message. He feels a chill creep up and down his spine. "Sherman, are you sure?"

"Why yes," Sherman assures him. "Your letters say NOT GOD. Where did this puzzle come from?"

Rachel looks at Harry with the same expression. She never heard of this before. What was he going on about?

"Oh, it's just something I saw in the paper, like a jumble to solve. I never realized the Z was just a space."

"Yes, it is," Sherman reassures him.

"Okay, thanks, Sherman."

"My pleasure. Thank you, both of you, for coming over."

They say their good-byes, including good-bye to Sherman's mother, and finally leave. On the car ride home, Rachel asks Harry, "What was all that NOT GOD stuff?"

"Well..." Harry is not sure he wants to broach this topic.

"Well," he starts again, "how about if I tell you about it later?"

Rachel can see something is wrong, but thinks it would be best to wait for him to be ready. She doesn't want to force it. But, Lord, she is curious.

"Okay, whenever you're ready, Harry."

"Thanks, Rachel."

Harry is thinking about this. He wants to tell her about the ghostly seven letters but, well, not yet.

"What is going on with me?" he thinks to himself. *"Am I being chased by the devil?"*

All this time Harry had thought he had a touch of ESP. He had always felt a strong and special connection to the universe and to nature, which he treasured. As a matter of fact, he had come to believe that he had a special relationship with God—or something out there—that protected him and warned him of things.

The last thing he wanted to hear was that it was "NOT GOD". That scared him. If not God, then it must be the devil or a demon, or something sinister. Maybe something that was trying to inhabit him and take possession? It gives him the creeps.

They drive on in silence with Rachel patiently waiting, hoping he would reveal the secret, and with Harry wanting to, but just—well just not yet.

Chapter 19

The next few months, are very pleasant for Harry. Of course, he loves being home, being free. His relationship with Rachel is blossoming more than he could have hoped for. And, even his friendship with Sherman is something he's glad to have.

But Harry dreads the nights. Well, not the nights so much when he's awake, it's going to sleep that scares him.

He is plagued with scary dreams. Phantom dreams. Ghostly, weird, unpleasant dreams. NOT GOD dreams.

One of them is recurring and it is, well, a *nightmare* would be the best word for it.

Harry dreams that he is in bed sleeping. The house phone rings and wakes him up. He answers it, says hello, but nobody is there.

Well, that's not exactly true because he can hear breathing. And somewhere within that raspy breathing, his name is called out. There is also another word after his name, but he can't quite make it out. "Harry...dnnn," something like that.

Harry leaves the phone off the hook, and walks out of his house with a flashlight.

He goes around back and shines the flashlight towards his bedroom window. Look at that. How weird. There is a telephone line coming out of his window from the second floor. It loops down and goes over the back fence into their neighbor's yard. He climbs the fence and follows the telephone line.

The line continues on and on, and Harry follows it through the streets, in the dead of night. For some reason, walking is becoming difficult, but he presses on.

Harry notices that the telephone line seems to pulse now and then. It's hard to see, in the blackness of the night, but it almost seems alive. It is taking more and more effort just to walk. He keeps his head down and continues to place one foot in front of the other, totally focused on following this mysterious, throbbing, telephone line.

Just then, there is a flash of light behind him—a car is coming. It's coming fast. He bolts to the side of the road.

It races by and somebody throws something out the window. A child's block set, with letters on them, scatters onto the street. He shines his flashlight on the blocks one by one. Six letters this time: D-O-G-T-N-O. The Z has been omitted for some reason. The NOT GOD message is now very clear, although the letters are all mixed up, as usual.

Harry tries to move faster and, for a moment breaks, into a jog. But it's so difficult. His feet become heavy. The street has changed texture and now it's soft and mushy. Harry's legs are getting stiff, but he continues to try and run, following that blasted telephone line. He senses that there is some answer to be found at the end of it. A sense of desperation washes over him.

He turns a corner to find that the telephone line now leaves the road and heads up a hill, over a small fence into—a cemetery.

The night gets even darker. His beam of light follows the phone line weaving between tombstones until, at last, it comes to an end. Well, no, not exactly an end.

The telephone line leads right down into a grave.

He shines his flashlight on the headstone—can't quite make it out—then it becomes clear. Sammy McPearson. The one kid who escaped from Juvenile Detention—and then disappeared.

He stares at the line leading down into the grave.

The line is pulsing now.

The dirt starts to move.

He can hear his name being called, muffled and scratchy, from below.

There is a dead something, now screeching his name, from within the grave.

He turns around and wants to run away. But he can't move. The ground is now like thick mud and refuses to let him take a single step.

A cold wind whips across his face and the headstones start to wiggle and shift.

And then, a bony hand darts out from the grave and grabs his ankle. From just below the dirt he hears the screeching clearer now:

"Harry, DNNNNNN!"

Harry wakes up in a cold sweat.

His heart is racing and his clothes are damp. He looks around his dark room. Every shape seems to be alive. He tries to calm himself and succeeds, slightly, by taking deep breaths.

"It was just a dream, just a dream," he tells himself.

He looks at his bedroom window. There is no telephone line leading out his window to the cemetery.

But...wait. Is there something there? It's hard to tell in the dark room.

He is *not* going to investigate. He *will not* go over to that window and look out. *No way!* Harry remembers a story he read one time where a boy went to investigate spooky sounds. He looked out the window, and the sky was filled with Night Gaunts—vaguely human-shaped creatures with horns and barbed tails. They were flying around in the still of the night, almost soundless, looking for victims.

As legend has it, if you but look at a Night Gaunt and it sees you looking at it, you become instantly hypnotized and brought under its spell. It then owns you, and can use you as a herald. The rest of your miserable life will be spent looking for things for your Night Gaunt to devour.

No sir, Harry is taking no chances. He's just going to go to sleep and wake up tomorrow morning, and everything will be normal.

Harry shuts his eyes tight and pulls the covers up over his head.

And then he NEARLY JUMPS OUT OF HIS SKIN WHEN THE TELEPHONE RINGS!

Chapter 20

Sammy McPearson walks out the back door of his beach house and looks out over the ocean. It's a gorgeous, beautiful day. There are a few puffs of clouds dotting the clear, blue sky. The surf is gentle, the water is warm, and the tide is high. It is picturesque—just a perfect day.

How did he come into all of this? His past is blurry.

Sammy is quite happy with his surroundings. He feels content—no, even content is an understatement. He has a feeling of serenity like he's never felt before. But his memory is foggy, and this bothers him.

Sammy walks in bare feet on the soft sand towards the water. He stands ankle high in the tepid surf as he looks out over the horizon. So beautiful—but it doesn't make sense.

Peaceful scenes like this are so contrary to the chaos that Sammy usually surrounds himself with. Sammy intuitively knows that this is all wrong.

Don't question it, the voice says.

Just take it all in and be happy.

No need to question it, just accept it.

But Sammy isn't built that way.

For all his faults, the one thing that remains consistent in his character is that he is honest with who he is. Sammy accepts and likes himself regardless of his faults. He knows that he has a temper, curses like a sailor, can be a bit brash at times; but all that doesn't make him a bad person. He just sometimes, well always, wears his emotions on his sleeve. Unlike others, he doesn't put on masks or try to pretend he's ever something other than the person he really is.

But, how did he get here? With a house on the beach and all these beautiful things? He doesn't remember buying them. After all, he's only 17.

This must be a dream.

Yes, it certainly has dream-like qualities. But, it's so solid. It just seems so real.

Of course, Sammy has no idea what stasis is, and the Trinollians did a pretty good job diminishing his memory of being abducted and examined. He will remain here until they make their final decision about how to return him, if indeed they ever do.

They continue injecting subconscious suggestions into Sammy's mind in order to keep him happy and content with his new reality, instead of fighting it.

"Just accept it, don't ruin it," the voice in his head says.

And why does he have a voice in his head anyway? It's not that he doesn't have a conscience, it's just that it never speaks up that often. And if this is a dream, why is there something telling him not to question it?

Sammy doesn't like to be tricked, and he has a faint sense that this is exactly what's happening. He desperately wants to wake up from this dream. He tries to rouse himself by pinching his arms and legs, but gets no results. He balls his hand up into a fist and punches himself in the stomach. Nothing. He tries slapping his face. No luck. His surroundings haven't changed at all and still seem very real.

Sammy walks along the beach, smelling the salt water in the air, and thinking. Well, if this is a dream, he wonders if he might find some beers around somewhere?

It was a rare occasion when the boys back at juvie were able to sneak their way into the headmaster's office where the booze could be found. But boy, did he enjoy it when he could. The taste of alcohol on his tongue, the way it made him feel warm inside, and happy on the outside; and for a while you could forget all of your troubles and just dwell in a blissful state of inebriation.

Hey, that's right, the institution and all the guys there—Rusty, Wendell, Harry and the rest. What...how...he fights against the fog in his head trying to remember.

He got out, didn't he? He and Rusty were on the outside, walking down a public street, right? He thought so, but his head was so foggy he couldn't really remember anything after picking the locks and opening the doors that led outside.

Sammy's memory of actually walking in town, at night, and then disappearing, and finally coming to on Minzi's examination table—this memory has been expertly suppressed.

Nevertheless, Sammy has a strong intuition that something is not right with his current world. He knows that this dream is different somehow. And, although everything seems beautiful, it is actually pretty scary. Because he can't wake the hell up and has a feeling that something else is in control.

Sammy is getting angry—something that comes pretty easy to him. His temper quickly escalates his mood to furious and frustrated. He storms back to the beautiful beach house. Maybe he should just trash it? That would show *them*, whoever *them* is.

He kicks over a chair. Then he goes into the kitchen and smashes a dish.

"Fuckin' wake up, Sammy, wake the fuck up!" he shouts.

He kicks the refrigerator. Hey, wait—his own refrigerator? If it's his, then...

He swings open the door and his anger immediately abates.

Beer—his refrigerator is stocked with beer. Wow! Maybe he's not so anxious to leave this dream after all?

He takes out a six pack and gets started. A half hour later, and well into his second sixer, he's feeling pretty good. The alcohol feels like home to him, even though he's not had very much experience with it.

"Thish plashe ain't so bad after all," he says out loud.

Sammy gets up and decides to take a little tour of his dream house. He goes into the bedroom and notices a phone on the night table.

And through his inebriated eyes, he's not sure, but it looks like there are colorful rings hovering around it. What an unusual sight. Pretty though. The colorful rings gently float and shimmer around the phone. It's a rather old phone—a landline.

"Now leshts shee—who can I call?" he thinks.

Chapter 21

Harry holds his pillow tight over his ears. The blasted phone continues to ring.

Then...it stops...and he hears his father talking.

"Hello, who is this?"

"Do you have any idea what time it is?"

"I don't know what you're saying. You're drunk—go dry up and don't call this number again!"

Harry sighs with relief.

Just a wrong number.

Just a coincidence.

A bad dream, followed by a wrong number, and his imagination got the better of him.

That's all it was.

Chapter 22

It's the next day, and Harry and Rachel are meeting Sherman at the coffee shop to hear some exciting news that he wanted to tell them in person.

Usually, walking to the coffee shop with Rachel, or walking anywhere with Rachel, is one of the most enjoyable times of the day. But today Harry has decided to confide not only his NOT GOD issue, but also wants to let Rachel in on his dream/nightmare last night.

"So, what do you think this exciting news might be from good ol' Sherman?" Harry asks.

"I think it has to do with a scholarship. Knowing Sherman, he probably got a full one to some prestigious university."

"Oh, yeah? You're probably right. Good for him. Have you heard back from any colleges yet?"

"Not yet," Rachel says, "Have you?"

"Nothing yet, it's still kind of early."

They continue walking, hand in hand.

Harry finally decides to broach the subject.

"Rachel?"

"Yes?"

"You know that jumble Sherman deciphered, the NOT GOD message?"

"Yes?"

Rachel holds her excitement but she is *extremely* interested. She's been waiting patiently for this confession.

86

"Well," he pauses. "I'm not sure how to put this."

"Just say it, Harry! Start at the beginning and just tell me."

"Okay, at the beginning. Well, you see...I..."

"Yes?" She urges him on.

"Well, for years I've seen this jumble of letters. On my window from the rain and fog. In the clouds. In my dreams. I've always felt I had a touch of ESP, and that maybe somebody up there is looking out for me?"

Rachel nods her head at this. She kind of feels the same way. She vaguely recalls a connection to her imaginary friends when she was little.

"But ever since I found out what the letters mean...I mean...that's the *last* thing I wanted to hear!"

"Yeah," Rachel agrees softly. She doesn't want it to be not from God either.

"I mean, if it's not from God, then who are the messages from? The devil? A demon? What else could it be?"

"An angel?" Rachel suggests. "After all an angel isn't God."

"I don't think an angel would just say 'NOT GOD.'"

Rachel tends to agree with this.

"Yeah, probably not. But it doesn't really have to be from the devil either. It could be coming from your subconscious."

Harry doubts this.

"I don't know Rach...and...and, you see...I had this dream last night."

"Yes?"

"It was pretty scary."

"Okay. What? Please tell me."

Harry pauses again. He wants to tell her.

He decides to make it short and get to the point in order to tone down the actual horror that it really was. He tells her briefly about the cemetery, the muffled "Harry, DNNNNT" screeching, and the wrong number phone call that followed after the dream was over.

"Wow!" Rachel exclaims. "That really is scary. And creepy. It gives me chills just hearing it."

Rachel crosses her arms in front of her, thinking, then...

"Are you reading a Stephen King book right now?"

"No."

"Dean Koontz?"

"No."

"Horowitz?"

"No, I'm not reading anything outside of science stuff right now that Sherman keeps assigning to us," Harry exclaims.

"I don't know Harry. I think the phone call at your house was just a coincidence. After all, your father said it was some drunk dialing the wrong number. How would this Sammy guy even know your number?"

"Yeah, I guess so," Harry agrees.

But what he's thinking is, what if it really was Sammy? Because Sammy *does* know his number. It's easy to remember. It spells G-W-E-E-D-I-N. Harry had mentioned this once in juvie when they were making up words from their phone numbers. It wouldn't be hard to believe that Sammy could remember that one. And Harry's last day was also common knowledge long before Sammy disappeared. Sammy would know that Harry would be living at home by now.

He hasn't yet told Rachel about Sammy disappearing. Maybe another time. He doesn't feel like continuing this subject.

"Well, thanks for telling me Harry. It is kind of scary. I'm not sure what it means, maybe nothing, but I'll be with you all the way no matter what."

That really hits home with Harry. He needed that.

"Thanks, Rach, I needed to hear that."

They embrace, glad to be together. Ready to face whatever the world throws at them. And it's a good thing, because the adventure they're about to go on would blow the minds of even the strongest, most courageous people ever to walk the earth.

They take each other's hand, and continue their walk to the coffee shop. Totally unaware of the excitement, and horrors, that await them.

Chapter 23

Rachel had guessed right. Sherman was excited to announce that he had received a full scholarship to the University of Berkeley, in California.

"They are one of NASA's largest recruitment centers," Sherman brags.

"That's really great, Sherman," says Rachel.

"Congratulations, bud! That's a great accomplishment," Harry adds.

Sherman shoots him a look. He doesn't like to be called "bud". Harry knows what that look means. He just likes to rattle Sherman a little now and then. For God's sake, he needs it.

"I guess you'll be going up there soon?" Rachel asks.

"Yes, they're flying me out next week, as a matter of fact."

"Are you going to bring them up to speed on your nanophysics?" Harry asks.

"Well, Good Lord, Harry, that would take years, and they still wouldn't understand it. But I'll bring my notebook, and a video I'm making, explaining my theory at a rudimentary level."

To Sherman, "rudimentary" in this case, means to dumb it down to scholars and professors.

They all talk about going to college.

Harry's choices are limited, having a murder on his record, and a weak substitute diploma he earned from juvie. In contrast, Rachel's choices are wide. They would love to go to the same college, but Rachel was hoping to go to a good university. It would mean their relationship would be severely tested.

Sherman offers his opinion.

"Your education is your treasure, at least the way I think of it. It helps forge the right path for your career, and steers you on your life path as well."

Harry agrees.

"I know Sherman, I'm not disputing that. Rach, you know that I would never want to stand in your way of getting a top-notch education. I'm just gonna miss you so darn much."

"Well, I haven't received any word yet on anything," Rachel says.

"But you will soon enough," Harry says. "If you get into any Ivy League universities—I don't want to stop you. Or, any college for that matter. I don't want to stand in the way of your education or career... but...I just don't want to lose you."

Harry says this straight from the heart. No embellishment is needed. And, it really doesn't need even to be said. Their feelings for each other are evident. Nevertheless, Rachel melts at hearing it.

She looks up at him with tears in her eyes and smiles, "No matter where I go, we'll still see each other Harry. And, I'll always be your girl."

It's what Harry needed to hear.

Chapter 24

[13 years later]

So, what happened during the last thirteen years?

Unfortunately, the Trinollians are really going to do a number on Sammy. They plan to return him to Earth in a crippled and debilitated state, thinking it's the right thing to do. And it's going to happen soon— well, relatively speaking.

While Sammy is in stasis, time practically comes to a halt for him. He can't feel the passing of it, and it doesn't really flow the same as it does if you're in the normal, physical dimensions of Earth.

The Trinollians will not perform their ghastly operation on Sammy until Rachel's future solidifies into a certainty, and they know for sure she will be going on a trip that will change the future of mankind. At first, they thought they could just keep Sammy out of Rachel's life long enough until she leaves on her mission, and then return him to earth. But Sammy's path is so strongly intertwined with Harry and Rachel— and so destructive to others if he were able-bodied—they thought it was best for him to lead a life that was dependent on others, instead of risking the possibility that he might destroy or damage many innocent lives.

Many may rightly question who put them in charge of judging humanity and interfering when they see fit? Well, to answer that completely would take another book (as yet, unwritten). However, the shorter answer is, that the Trinollians were once on the same level as humans are in this story, and took a wrong turn down the path of self-indulgence, fear, and technology.

While there were many wonderful things to be gained by ever-increasing technology, they also manufactured terrible weapons of mass destruction that were simply off the charts, and eventually wiped out most of their own race. After thousands of years, giving their planet a chance to heal, rebuilding and repopulating, they finally evolved back to where they had once been, and this time did not make the same mistake.

Eventually, evolving even further, many of them wanted to share their gifts and higher technology to what they called "emerging species." Their intentions were only to help others stay on the right track, and not destroy each other, as they had once done.

It was difficult to find humans that they could communicate with subconsciously, and extraordinary to find someone like Rachel, who not only possessed the proper subconscious elements, but had such an important part to play in mankind's history. The Trinollians knew of Sherman's work and projected how it would alter the course of human history, but they couldn't touch Sherman's mind. It was completely sealed to them. The same could be said of Harry.

But, Rachel was reachable. And they were taking no chances with an out-of-control, "I'm sorry but I was drunk", Sammy, that could alter her path.

Anyway, other things that have happened during the last 13 years...

Wendell and Harry continued to keep in touch with each other once in a while, but have mostly gone their separate ways. Wendell pursued his love of art, and Harry went to a junior college, then matriculated to a university, where he graduated with a Bachelor's of Science degree in Astrophysics. Harry then got a full-time job as a lab assistant and continued to take classes at night, eventually obtaining a Master's Degree in Astronomy.

Harry has grown a lot, both physically and intellectually. He played some sports in college, and was on the wrestling team, as well as track and field. He was well-liked by most because he had an easy-going manner, and was known to stick up for his friends, or anybody, if he saw them getting harassed.

He was respectful and pleasant to everybody as long as they gave him the same back. But don't ever get on his bad side. Harry possessed a dark side that was best to remain hidden, unless circumstances were so dire that extraordinary, almost superhuman, qualities were needed to survive.

Harry and Rachel's relationship withstood the test of time and distance. Through hard work and perseverance, Harry went from a community college, to a university, and then on to grad school where he earned a master's degree in astronomy, eventually landing a job as a research assistant for one of the professors. After that, he got a job teaching astronomy while continuing to do his own research. The strange dreams and haunting letters had dropped out of sight for years at a time, but never completely left him. Even now, these things continue sporadically, and have actually increased in frequency during the past few months.

Rachel excelled throughout her college years, earning a bachelor's degree in mathematics (in hopes of trying to understand Sherman's work) and, like Harry, a master's degree in Astronomy. She and Harry are now living together not far from the University that he works at on Long Island—S.U.N.Y. Stony Brook. Rachel is a rising-star scientist working at Grumman Aerospace in Calverton.

Now Sherman is the one who really has a story to tell.

He roared through college at Berkeley, California obtaining a Ph.D. in physics in just six years.

He set the entire physics department ablaze with his theories on nanophysics and hyperspace. He was the number one candidate recruited by NASA in his final year at Berkeley, and has been working there for the past six and a half years.

Sherman has been "in the zone" for quite a while, devoting all of his time and energy to solving the vibratory sub-space equations that would enable him to create, or find, jumping points. Towards the end of his college years, he made substantial breakthroughs and began to get noticed in the science community.

At this point in time, Sherman is known far and wide within the space program at NASA, not only for his theories on hyperspace and nanophysics, but also for his rudeness and savant-like personality. His superiors all put up with it, understanding that in order to get to the prize, they have to put up with Sherman's idiosyncrasies.

Using NASA's labs, Sherman has devised computer simulations that are extremely convincing in showing that he is on the right path with regards to breaching hyperspace, and give much weight to his papers on nanophysics. Most of his peers now think that he is on the cutting edge of something absolutely phenomenal.

Whereas before NASA had their sights set on a manned trip to Mars, Sherman's theories have totally ripped apart any limitations of space travel within our own solar system, or even our own galaxy. If proven correct, breaching hyperspace would be the biggest breakthrough in physics ever—even exceeding Einstein's relativity theories. Sherman regularly hosts lectures and discussion groups, where he displays his latest computer simulations depicting interdimensional travel.

Sherman had been trying to get Harry and Rachel a job at NASA to work with him on his theories of hyperspace. The three of them had continued to keep in touch over the years. On a few occasions, Harry and Rachel had flown to Florida to see Sherman. He had proudly obtained visitor's passes for them, and shown them all over the grounds at the facility where he worked. When Sherman introduced them to his coworkers and bosses, both Harry and Rachel made very good impressions. Sherman's coworkers were actually surprised to see that he had such normal friends.

NASA's Department of Human Space Exploration had allocated a substantial budget to research and explore Sherman's theories. The money was certainly there to employ Sherman's friends, and the fact that he even *had* friends that were qualified, and got along with him, was a big asset. However, while many of the scientists would welcome Rachel with open arms, they were reluctant to hire someone who had a homicide on his record, even if he was only an adolescent when the crime was committed.

On the other hand, those that had met Harry believed that he would be a good addition to the team. After all, some of Sherman's coworkers could relate to being bullied when they were younger. Knowing Harry's story, and understanding the situation that led to the tragedy, certainly weighed in Harry's favor. Loyalty and bravery were highly valuable qualities in any employee, especially those that were training to be astronauts.

It took a few interviews, and eventually Sherman's wishes had been granted. Both Harry and Rachel were offered employment, which they eagerly accepted. Sherman had demonstrated that it would take a team of four to man all of the instruments needed for a test jaunt into hyperspace. A highly-trained and specialized pilot would also be added to the mix, making it a crew of five.

This would be the first voyage of the *Galaxis*, a new space vessel that NASA had built with the intention of being reusable, and kept in operation for possibly twenty years. The *Galaxis* could support up to a crew of seven, including the pilot.

Besides Harry, Rachel, and Sherman—Linda Crebassa, a scientist specializing in quantum physics with emphasis on particle vibratory patterns—would also be joining the team. Linda is a few years older than Rachel and is slender, with long, dark hair, although she wears it up at work. She is one of the more attractive females in her department where the males out-proportion the women five to one.

Chapter 25

When Linda was a little girl, she had a remarkable experience on a field trip to the zoo with her class. There were about sixty children between the ages of eight and ten, and plenty of teachers and parents to help supervise and keep the kids under control. Nevertheless, as often happens, there were a few trouble makers in the group hell bent on mischief that day.

The children made their way throughout the exhibits, laughing at the monkeys, and oohing-and-aahing at the giraffes. They giggled as the huge hippos yawned and displayed their cavernous jaws.

While the hippos held everybody's attention, Tommy Johnson said to his buddy, Dennis, "This is it, let's go!" The two of them ran off unseen to explore the zoo by themselves.

It was only twenty minutes later that Tommy found a breach in an enclosure, and managed to slip through into an unknown exhibit that seemed to be void of animals.

"C'mon Dennis, let's explore," he urged.

"But I don't see any animals."

"Me neither, we're far away from them. The seeing part is way down that way, where the water is," Tommy points out over the grassy field.

"But we don't even know what animals are here. Could be lions."

"It's not lions, we already passed that one. C'mon, don't be scared. We'll just go a little bit to see whatever animals are here then run back out."

"I don't know Tommy," Dennis says.

"What are you, scared?"

"Yes," Dennis admits.

"Fine," Tommy says indignantly. "You go back to the group—I'm going exploring!" he declares triumphantly.

Dennis watches his friend take off in search of the animals that live there. He turns around and heads back to the group.

It's not too much longer when he circles around a bend and hears screaming and shouting.

"My God, how did that little boy get in there?"

"Those tigers are going to eat him!"

Yes, there is little Tommy, way down below on the wrong side of the moat, in the exhibit, standing on a high rock with five tigers cautiously approaching him.

Tommy has never been more frightened in his life. He looks down at the tigers circling below him. Sometimes, misbehaving and going rogue can be exciting. However, there are times when it can be the worst idea in the world. Zoo rules are meant for everyone. Tommy is learning a tough lesson in life. And, this might be the last lesson he ever learns.

Tommy has no way out, and no options. His life is at the mercy of whatever these tigers decide to do to him. He weeps and starts screaming, "Pleeeasse! Someone get me out of here now! I'm sorry! I'm sorry!"

Tommy's boulder sits atop a ledge. One of the tigers easily jumps up on it. The audience gasps.

All of Tommy's classmates and teachers have just arrived, and security is on their way with guns. But they may be too late. The teachers and parents are astonished, and frightened out of their minds. They are about to watch a child get eaten or mauled. And, it's their fault for not keeping a better eye on their kids. The only thing they can do now is pray.

Finally, Linda manages to squeeze through the throng of people and edges her way to the front. She places her hands on the fence separating the audience from the enclosure. Beyond the fence, a long way down, is the moat, and the horrific scene just described. The tiger that jumped up on the ledge is now standing on its hind legs, leaning against the tall rock, where the frightened child is standing and crying. At any instant this scene can become tragic.

"Please don't hurt him, Mr. Tiger," Linda says softly. "He didn't mean anything bad, and he's my friend."

Not one person could have heard Linda's plea over all the commotion. And certainly not the tigers, way down below. But, the tiger on the ledge turns his giant, predatory head in Linda's direction, and looks directly into her eyes.

"Please," Linda says again. "It would make us all very sad."

The tiger lets loose a growl—the crowd gasps again.

"Where is security?" Somebody shouts. "That tiger is about to pounce!"

The tiger returns to all fours and walks on the ledge, turns around, and walks the other way. A second tiger jumps up on the ledge. Astonishingly, the first tiger snarls and chases him back down.

"Oh, no—it wants to eat him all for itself," someone cries.

But that's not what's happening, and Linda knows it.

The tiger on the ledge, again, looks right at Linda. A small smile comes to her face.

"Thank you, Mr. Tiger. Thank you so much."

The tiger pads back and forth on the ledge, not letting any of the other beasts share the platform with him. Zoo security finally arrives. Just before they are about to shoot their animals dead, they give them half a chance to return to their inside cages by firing a loud noise and opening the inside gates.

Amazingly, the tigers take the cue and return to their inside cages. The one on the ledge is the last to go, and finally jumps off to follow his friends inside. Just before going in, he turns and looks at Linda one more time, and roars.

"Thank you, Mr. Tiger," Linda says again.

Not a shot was fired, and Tommy is rescued unharmed. To say that Linda has a way with animals would be a world-class understatement. Linda is an animal-whisperer.

Chapter 26

Sherman, Harry, Rachel, and Linda are all together at the Space Center for the first time. They are being addressed by one of Sherman's superiors, Dr. Vance Bowman, who has just briefed them for over an hour about the risks they face, and lauded their courage in accepting such a mission. They have signed all the necessary paperwork disavowing NASA from being held responsible for any injuries or deaths sustained on the mission.

"As you know," Dr. Bowman says, "we all are greatly appreciative of Dr. Hollingsworth's contributions to NASA, and his choice to become part of our family. Yes, we do consider our employees to be a family in a sense, where everybody looks out for each other, and we depend on one another to follow the rules and respect each other's work, as well as respect each other as individuals. It is this spirit of cooperation and loyalty that I want to convey to all of you, as you will be carrying our name and reputation out into the universe!"

With this bold statement, Dr. Bowman makes a grand gesture waving his arms towards the sky. Somehow it fits and seems right.

The happy team is wide-eyed with excitement, and bursting with enthusiastic smiles for having been picked as the crew of this historic mission. Dr. Bowman continues...

"Dr. Hollingsworth will be in charge of all of you except for the pilot, who will captain the ship and holds the highest of responsibilities, which is, of course, bringing you back safe and sound."

That doesn't sit too well with Sherman.

"Um, yeah, just a question about that?" Sherman interrupts.

"Yes, Dr. Hollingsworth?" Dr. Bowman asks.

"Am I to understand that this pilot, whomever he or she is, has greater authority than me on this mission?"

"That is correct, Dr. Hollingsworth. The captain of the ship, be it in the sea, the air, or even in space, is the ultimate authority. You will all report and take orders from him."

"But what if his orders contradict mine, or are adverse to what I think is best?"

"Then you will stand down and do what he says, Sherman. But he will not be advising you on anything that has to do with your science. He is strictly there to pilot the vessel, and see to it that NASA's mission is running smoothly, safely, and according to our procedures, which will all be laid out in detail and available for your review before being finalized."

"Okay, so I do get a say in how this mission is to be run?" Sherman confirms.

"Absolutely. Sherman, this is a collaborative effort that depends upon each one of you doing your jobs to the best of your ability, and putting the goal of the mission first. Don't get caught up in who is taking orders from whom. This is a team effort, and I assure you that the pilot will not overstep his bounds. Nevertheless, I must have your assurance that you will respect captain Kluco as your commander on this mission, and do what he asks."

Silence.

All eyes are on Sherman.

"Sherman?" Dr. Bowman asks again.

"Okay," Sherman finally says it, albeit reluctantly. "But this captain Kluco must also be aware that I am the authority when it comes to programming our jumping points and all matters concerning hyperspace."

"That goes without saying," Bowman says.

"Well, I would actually like to hear him say it."

You could hear the collective sigh in the room, but Dr. Bowman does not flinch. After all, he's been working with Sherman for a while. Sometimes to unlock the genius, you have to suffer the abuses of their ego.

"I don't think that will be a problem, Sherman. And that's actually next on the agenda. Would you all like to meet your captain now—and take a tour of the Spaceship you'll be calling home?"

"YES!" comes the loud roar.

Chapter 27

The four of them follow Doctor Bowman out the door, and crowd into a golf cart that drives them over to the hanger. Upon entering, they are floored at the sheer size and beauty of the craft that will lead them into space and beyond.

"My God, it's so big!" exclaims Linda.

"And beautiful," adds Rachel.

"It looks so strong," says Harry.

"All this just for a four-man crew?" asks Sherman.

"Well, we build things now with the idea of reusing them," explains Bowman. "There will be other missions besides yours, I'm sure. This vessel can carry a crew of seven, including the pilot. Do you want to see the inside?"

"YES," they say in unison.

They all get out of the golf cart and excitedly follow Dr. Bowman to the ship. The entrance hatch is already down. Bowman leads the way up and into the ship.

"Watch your step—follow me."

As they ascend, they notice a hand ladder surrounding the entire ship. There is a worker on the far side, spraying the outside of the vessel with some finishing touches.

The four of them are now standing inside the ship, astonished, and look around in wonderment. The vessel is just beautiful. They are standing in the bay, the cockpit is in the front, and there is a corridor leading to various rooms in the back.

The walls are sleek, dark blue, and have various instruments and panels embedded within them. There is a viewing window on one side where they will actually be looking out into space, unfettered by lights from Earth. It's simply amazing to think about looking out this window from space and seeing the glory of the universe.

Harry puts his arm around Rachel, as they stand there astonished—their wildest dreams are going to come true.

"We're actually doing this, Rach—going into space—we're astronauts!"

"Oh, it's so exciting! And a little scary too," Rachel admits.

"Oh, come on, we're in good hands," Harry says. "They know what they're doing. Sherman knows his stuff. All the preliminary tests will have passed many times over before they send us up."

"I mean, I wouldn't miss it for the world," Rachel says, "But to think..." she trails off, captivated and awed at where she is and what they'll be doing.

Bowman's voice breaks the spell, "Come on—let's meet your pilot."

He leads them into the cockpit, and there, in the captain's seat, sits the most extraordinary being they have ever seen in their lives.

He is a robot.

His "chair" isn't a chair at all, more like a podium, with arrays of controls and displays. It sits upon a lowered floor so that he can stand while piloting the ship. There is a backing that can slide up from the floor, with a seat belt on it, so that he can strap himself to something sturdy if need be.

He has a somewhat mechanical look to him, even though he was built to be an android. His head is slightly robot-looking, perched atop a neck that can rise up and down. He has metal arms, and extremely agile robot hands/claws, complete with an opposable thumb. Everyone is shocked into silence—totally captivated.

The mechanical marvel turns, raises its neck a good four inches, and introduces himself.

"Hello. I am Captain Kluco. Pleased to make your acquaintance."

Nobody says a word, still taking it all in.

Captain Kluco presses a button and the lower portion of his station rises to the same level as the floor. It's now clear to see that his legs are on small wheels. He engages them and rolls towards our friends.

"A robot?" Sherman gasps.

Dr. Bowman proudly looks at Captain Kluco and announces, "Crew, I'd like you to meet your pilot for this mission, Captain Kluco. The most advanced android ever!"

"But, he's a...robot?" Harry says.

"An android is our pilot?" Linda whispers to herself.

"How..." Sherman starts.

"Captain Kluco is the 10th Generation in our Jupiter Series of auto-pilot mechanicals—the most sophisticated of all models thus far—with the ability to receive and process thousands of gigabytes of information per second. There is nothing else like him on Earth," Bowman proudly announces.

Captain Kluco manages a slight bow, and says, "At your service."

"But he's a robot!" Sherman blurts out. *"You can't be serious. He's in charge of me?"*

As usual, Sherman makes no effort to filter his true feelings. It doesn't really make a difference. Kluco has no feelings that can be hurt.

"Yes, Dr. Hollingsworth, he's in charge," Dr. Bowman says, "And you couldn't be in safer or more capable hands. He has access to every simulation and situation that exists in our database that may come up during your mission. He knows how to react instantly to any emergency. He has artificial intelligence and can grow, both intellectually and environmentally, as time goes on and he encounters and learns from each situation."

Sherman is indignant.

"But he's a..."

"Captain Kluco, come here and let me introduce you to your crew," Bowman interrupts. "I would like you to meet your first in command, Dr. Sherman Hollingsworth," and he gestures towards Sherman.

Sherman backs up a step as Kluco approaches.

"It's your pleasure to meet me, I'm sure," Kluco says with the greatest amount of deference, and bows slightly again, directly in front of Sherman.

"What?" Sherman doesn't know what to say.

Harry and the others stifle a giggle. They are beginning to like their captain.

"We all need to give him a little slack on his conversational speech. All effort has been put first on his technical skills, and I assure you that his speech will greatly improve in the next few weeks," Bowman says.

"It's your pleasure to meet me!" Sherman insists.

"Yes, it is indeed, Dr. NothingsWorth," Kluco replies.

"What?" Sherman exclaims.

The others can't stifle it any longer—laughter fills the ship.

"He means Hollingsworth," Dr. Bowman assures Sherman. "He's never heard your last name before and auto-corrected it to a word that's closest—*Hollings* and *Nothing*. It was an honest mistake, not a snide remark in the slightest way."

"Well, you just admitted he did it on purpose," Sherman retorts.

"Captain Kluco, this is Sherman Hollingsworth, not NothingsWorth, please correct."

"Oh, you have to say it again?" Sherman mutters.

"My apologies, Mr. NothingsWorth. I will auto-correct immediately."

"Hollingsworth, Captain Kluco, Sherman Hollingsworth," Bowman corrects him.

"Yes, sir. Mr. Turdman Hollingsworth, it's a pleasure to make your acquaintance."

Once again, laughter fills the ship—even louder than before.

"Well, this is just ridiculous!" Sherman says.

"It's Sherman Hollingsworth, please auto-correct henceforth. And here is your engineer, in charge of monitoring magnetic core vibrations, Harry Stone."

"Please to meet you, Mr. Harry Stone," Kluco says with no problem.

"Oh, he gets that name right on the first try," Sherman whines.

"And this is Rachel Mannix, in charge of monitoring sub-space activity and synchronizing hyperspace coordination points."

"It's my pleasure to meet you," Rachel says.

"Likewise, Rachel Mannix. It's my pleasure to meet you too," says Kluco.

Again, Sherman whines, "Oh, he has no problem with that name either."

"Dr. Hollingsworth, please!" Bowman scolds him.

"And last, but certainly not least, we have senior engineer Linda Crebassa. She will be in charge of monitoring an exhaustive set of autonomous, diagnostic, and structural activities for this vessel, as well as tracking the particle vibratory patterns relative to the core region surrounding the ship."

"I'm honored to meet you," Linda says.

"It is my honor also, Linda Crebassa," Kluco gets her name perfectly correct.

Sherman frowns at this. *Come on—Crebassa is no easier than Hollingsworth,* he thinks, but says nothing for the moment. Then he remembers something.

"I would like to hear him say it," Sherman demands.

"Say what?" Rachel asks.

Dr. Bowman knows what Sherman is referring to.

"Captain Kluco, would you please state your mission and your priorities for the crew?" Bowman asks.

"My mission is to pilot this vessel on an exploratory journey through multiple jumping points into hyperspace and back. My priorities are to keep the crew and myself safe, and make sure that every NASA safety protocol is followed. In the event of any emergency, I will sacrifice myself for any crew member if necessary, to ensure safe passage for everyone under my command. This is only possible if we are close enough to earth whereby automatic safe-return can be engaged."

That took them by surprise. Kluco just revealed that he will give up his life for anyone aboard the ship, if possible.

Even Sherman is touched by that, for a moment.

"Captain Kluco, please tell me what your duties are pertaining to the science we will be using concerning cultivating jumping points for entry to and from hyperspace?" Sherman barks at him.

"I have no responsibilities in that area, Mr. Nothing, excuse me, auto-correcting, Mr. Turdman Nothing, auto-correcting, Mr. Sherman Hollingsworth of Nothing."

"You see?" Dr. Bowman says. "Names throw him a little, but he's almost got it already. And his mission and responsibilities are clear and shouldn't provide any conflicts with yours, Dr. Hollingsworth."

"All the science is your business, Mr. Turdman, just as you requested," Harry teases.

"Oh, very funny Harry—don't you start!" Sherman scolds him.

The entire crew is full of smiles, except for Sherman, of course.

"Let me show you the rest of the ship, folks. Thank you, Captain Kluco, we will be seeing you again soon," Bowman says.

"It was your pleasure meeting all of me," Kluco says, and again does a little bow and returns to his station.

There are suppressed giggles at Kluco's clumsiness with English. Sherman does not find it amusing at all.

"I don't see how we can trust that thing with our lives if he can't even master English?"

Bowman reassures him, "Believe me, Dr. Hollingsworth, by the time we're ready to launch, Kluco will have learned more knowledge than the total accumulation we've amassed in our individual lifetimes!"

"Well, I very much doubt that," Sherman huffs.

The tour of the vessel they will call home leaves the crew astonished.

Bowman shows them the living quarters, two airlocks, a small exercise room, and even a small kitchen of sorts. Then he brings them back to the main bay.

"It's really fantastic. Thanks for this opportunity," Linda says.

"Thank you also, Dr. Bowman and Sherman, for allowing us to be part of your team," Rachel adds.

"Yes, I second that," Harry says. "It's an honor to be working with all of you and taking part in this mission."

"You're welcome," Sherman replies.

"It's our pleasure to have all of you—such a splendid team! We're expecting great things from this mission," Dr. Bowman declares. "Our first launch isn't scheduled for at least another six months, and we've all got plenty to do if we want to meet that date. This ends our session for today. I'll see you all tomorrow at 9 am."

"Great, thank you so much," says Rachel.

"Thank you, Dr. Bowman—it's been wonderful," Linda says.

They all walk towards the open hatch and begin to exit. But just before descending, Sherman gives a look towards Kluco's station and mutters, "He better have my name right next time or I'm not going!"

Chapter 28

Far, far away, on a distant planet, there is a crisis going on. There exists a highly advanced civilization of an extremely intelligent species that call themselves Xirxonians. They have evolved well-past Earth's technology, but are now on the threshold of planetary genocide.

As their technology evolved, so did their ability to destroy themselves. Many regions of the planet now possess their own nuclear arsenal, as well as gamma-ray weaponry, toxins, chemical warfare, electromagnetic cannons, and even telekinetic individuals that can destroy things using only their minds.

Within the past century, each region (or country) felt it necessary to one-up the rest of their world, until all are armed so heavily, that the first region to launch their weapons would have a distinct advantage. Many of the countries now possess enough weaponry to destroy the rest of the world several times over.

This situation has caused a fear of too many trigger-happy countries—nobody wants to be the last one, or even the second or third one, to enter any type of war, because there would most likely not be a chance to launch any type of counter-attack, since the first attack by the enemy would be overwhelmingly devastating.

#

Sammy wakes up to another gorgeous day. He grabs a beer from the fridge and heads out to sit on the front porch. It's warm, but not too hot. There is a lazy breeze blowing. He stares out at the beautiful scenery. The gentle surf of the fake ocean instills peace and serenity.

The Trinollians are watching him on a monitor.

"Poor guy," says Tsedo. "Just born into an unlucky situation. Never had a chance."

"Has the phone and all other contact items been removed?" Minzi asks.

"Oh, yes, absolutely," Tsedo assures her. "We wouldn't want to take a chance on that again."

"Good," Minzi says.

She looks at Sammy sitting on the porch and feels some sadness for him. Tsedo notices this.

"Having second thoughts?" he wonders.

"If I did, what difference would it make?" Minzi answers. "It's been decided. He'll be returned without legs and this will be enough to prevent him from doing harm to others."

"I know," Tsedo agrees. "And I don't like it either. But I suppose the Elders know best?"

"I suppose too," Minzi says. "It's a shame we can't alter his tendencies instead. Like, make him allergic to alcohol or something like that?"

"Yeah. Well, I hear they're working on it, but messing with a human's DNA is quite complicated."

"Well, he can still have a good life," Minzi says. "And so can those he comes in contact with."

"Yeah, I guess you're right."

"Is everything ready to go for the amputation?"

"Not yet. Do you want me to start preparations?"

"Yes," Minzi says, "Please have him prepped and properly sedated."

Back in his alternate reality, Sammy tosses his empty beer into the trash and heads over to the fridge to get another one. He cracks it open, takes a swig, and then goes back outside and sits in his beach chair.

He thinks he is in a dream. He is a little buzzed and in a good mood, as he looks out at the fake ocean. After a little nap, he goes back inside and stands before a mirror, admiring himself.

"I've put on some muscle, look at those calves and thighs!" he says out loud, looking at his reflection.

Chapter 29

[Six months later]

Captain Kluco is at his station. He has been through exhaustive training that no human could possibly endure. However, Kluco's processing speed and memory banks can consume gigabytes of data in seconds. The amount of knowledge that Kluco has gained in the past few months has been incredible. At this point, he is probably the most knowledgeable pilot in the world. And now, his abilities are just seconds away from being tested.

The final countdown has started: T – 30, T – 29, T – 28....

On board, and securely strapped in their seats towards the back of the cockpit are: Harry, Rachel, Sherman, and Linda. Each of them is taking it all in. They are about to launch into space and test the most astonishing theories in the history of humankind—Hyperspace.

If successful, this voyage will go down in the history books as a turning point in mankind's understanding of the universe. This would be an amazing achievement, never before broached—a journey into another dimension and back.

The results could be astounding. The concept of looping realities, multiple dimensions each containing their own laws and geography, could all become science fact rather than science fiction. A temporary bridge could be built to establish a conduit between continuums. The speed of light would no longer handcuff man to his own solar system.

Darting around the universe and visiting other planets could become a reality.

The crew can barely contain their excitement, strapped into their seats, seconds away from lift off. Well, except for Kluco, who has no emotions.

But wait, there is something going on with Harry—something is not right. He is sitting back with his eyes closed, and, he seems to be... trembling. Not from excitement, but from...something else...something peculiar and distressing.

Small beads of sweat form on Harry's brow as the countdown continues: $T - 20$, $T - 19$, $T - 18$....

From somewhere in the back of his mind, those haunting letters have started up again. This time, they are spinning as if they are on a carousel. Only six of them now, going around and around, trading places. It's funny, but ever since Sherman correctly deduced the "Z" was a space, his visions frequently omitted that letter. It's like, once the puzzle is solved, there is no need for the riddle to remain.

But if that's the case, then why does he keep seeing these mysterious letters? And although his visions had greatly decreased in the years following Sherman's decryption (NOT GOD), in the last six to twelve months his visions have increased.

This is especially true within the last two months. Harry has been seeing those letters all over the place; his dreams, his thoughts, once in his alphabet soup.

Now the letters tumble and twist and rearrange themselves inside Harry's mind.

And grow larger.

And larger still, and bolder.

The letters suddenly lock into place, displaying a configuration never before seen. Harry's heart skips a beat, and he gasps.

After all this time, thinking they had the puzzle solved. Sherman had been wrong. It wasn't *NOT GOD* after all.

Finally, the real message is clear to see.

The letters say: *DONT GO*

Well, it's a little late for that.

And now, the letters shatter and explode, and Harry knows that he will never see them again.

Because he's strapped into his seat, three seconds away from blasting off.

T – 3, T -2, T -1, LIFT OFF!

He's going.

Chapter 30

The monstrous spaceship blasts off into the heavens. It's a beautiful launch. The weather is clear, and all systems are working perfectly.

The crew is silent as each one puts on their bravest face to cope with the g's of the launch. (G force, or gravity force, is the measure of the force of gravity on the body during the acceleration of lift-off.)

Up and up the rocket soars—through the troposphere, the stratosphere, the mesosphere, the ionosphere. And finally, the roar of the engines goes silent as they break through the invisible barrier that we call space.

It's a thrilling moment for our friends as they look out and see Earth receding, now over 200 miles below. Harry gazes out upon the wondrous beauty of our planet, as it takes on the appearance of a mushy, white, blue ball, of clouds and water. He looks over at Rachel.

Rachel looks back at him and smiles. Harry does the best he can to smile back, given the circumstances he has just experienced. He still can't believe it. All this time, the message was *DON'T GO*. And Sherman had convinced him it was *NOT GOD*. Now what was he supposed to do?

Kluco begins communicating the current data with ground control.

"All systems go," Kluco says as he relays their position, speed, and all pertinent data.

Harry is going nuts dealing with the current situation. Although usually a solid, dependable, and reasonable man, his emotional state has never been so stressed.

What should he do? What could he do?

Are they all about to die on this mission?

He's been getting messages for years warning him not to go on this trip, and he just figured that out a few minutes ago. Should he try to abort this mission and make them turn the ship around and go home? It's not like NASA is going to say, okay, everybody just come back, forget the mission, Harry senses it's going to go bad.

Plus, he never told anybody except Rachel about the mysterious letters. NASA might think him psychologically unfit. They would wonder why he never mentioned this phenomenon during his orientation or training. They had asked for "full disclosure," but he didn't want to share the weird things with anyone else, except for Rachel. And, of course, he didn't want to make any trouble for Rachel either. They might ask her if she knew about his weird stuff, and she would have to admit it.

The best thing he can do is to try and make sure this mission is a success by doing his job and letting everyone else do theirs. If there's an emergency, they'll have to deal with it at that time.

He could even be the catalyst to destroying this mission if he were to reveal the *DON'T GO* message. He might spook out the entire crew, causing them distress and instilling fear—which could only exacerbate the situation. What good could possibly come out of it?

So, in the end, Harry decides to keep the *DON'T GO* message to himself. He must contain and not reveal all the upsetting stress that goes along with it as well. He decides to just deal with it by himself, and act as normal as he can.

He looks out the small portal and sees earth receding.

Pretty Earth. All blue and alive.

It almost seems like the planet itself is a being, expanding and contracting as the tides rise and fall.

Breathing.

Harry isn't the only one caught up in these majestic sights. Somehow, looking out at the planet you live on, from space, does something to you. Except for Kluco, they all love their home, and respect it as another living being—with people, animals, and trees all dwelling within it. It's an attitude that most every astronaut before them has shared.

The deep sense of unity and compassion accompanying these thoughts compels us to ask one another: Since we all have to share this world, why can't we understand how organisms that fight each other do only harm to the body as a whole? Why can't we see how our wars, hate, and fear have created malignant lesions upon it? Our relationship with our planet—as well as with each other—should be symbiotic, not parasitic.

The ship reaches its maximum ascent and levels off. Kluco skillfully comes out of full thrust and settles into orbit around the earth. According to plans, they will maintain orbit for about five hours before the first exciting jump into hyperspace.

"Dr. Hollingsworth, please begin making the necessary preparations for our first jump. We will commence in five hours," Kluco says.

"Affirmative," Sherman responds. He is very happy to hear Kluco getting his name right.

"Captain Kluco, how many orbits will we make around Earth in five hours?" Rachel asks.

"About three, since we're traveling at an excess of 18,000 miles per hour," Kluco replies. "And we have to go through every diagnostic test before we can make the first jump."

Kluco opens the con to make an announcement:

"ATTENTION CREW: Please report to your stations for automation testing. Dr. Hollingsworth, you will be supervising all items pertaining to jump point parameters."

"Yes, Captain Kluco," Sherman says. He loves hearing that he'll be in charge of something. It's the first time Sherman used that term, *Captain Kluco*. Sherman is warming up to him.

Harry, Rachel, Linda, and Sherman take their posts and get down to work.

Rachel smiles at Harry. She's loving this.

Harry does the best he can to smile back. He's not going to tell anyone about his demons right now.

Chapter 31

Minzi is going through a checklist too, when she sees Tsedo approaching her.

"They want to know if you'll be starting the amputations soon?" Tsedo asks.

"Yes. I'm just finishing up going through my instruments. You can tell Pacbaer to prepare the anesthetic and to bring in the patient after he's been properly sedated."

#

In the meantime, Sammy is enjoying a swim.

When the alcohol wears off, and he's able to think clearly, the creative and intelligent part of Sammy comes through. He has found that he can build things in this weird dream.

Sometimes, if he concentrates long enough and is able to focus his thoughts on one thing, like a hammer or piece of wood, he can bring the item into existence. The smaller the object, the more likely it is to appear.

Sammy was able to visualize and build all kinds of objects and toys, but his pride and joy was his train set. One by one he visualized the tracks, then each car of the train, then the conductor, the people, and even the tunnels it would go through. Then Sammy decided most of its passengers would be females, and dressed them provocatively.

Why not? It's his dream—kind of.

The "kind of" part bothers him.

He very much wants to wake up or escape in some way. He feels the "wrongness" of his environment. No matter how pleasant and beautiful it is, he wants to be free and in the normal world. He is convinced that there is something keeping him in this strange dream, and he feels trapped. In his thoughts, he refers to this unknown entity as *them*. Sammy hates *them*, and wants to get out. He just doesn't know how.

Sammy has also noticed that his refrigerator is never out of beer. In a funny way, that bothers him too.

If he wants to drink that's his business. He doesn't need *them* to influence him to drink all of the time. After a while, constant inebriation was not so wonderful after all.

Sammy very much enjoys swimming, and the great feeling that goes with being young, strong, refreshed, and even being sober feels good too. It's almost as if the *voice* (the invading thoughts that sometimes come into his head), and the infinite supply of beer, are pushing him to desire a more balanced state of normality.

When you have everything, suddenly, you don't want everything.

Chapter 32

Linda stares out the portal window next to her station as their vessel completes its third orbit around Mother Earth. She is struck by the shape of Earth as seen from space.

It's irregular, more like an oblate spheroid than elliptical, or oblong. And, Linda is also struck by the sheer beauty of it. It's remarkable how the oceans blend together to make up most of the pretty, blue color.

It is her home—all of their homes. Linda will be glad to return to it after a successful mission.

Their vessel is almost in position for the first jump. Kluco makes an announcement.

"Attention crew, this is your captain. We are approaching our destination for the launching of our first skip. Dr. Hollingsworth will you..."

"Yes!" Sherman jumps in immediately and starts barking orders.

"Mr. Stone, I need the last ten minutes of magnetic core vibrations. Miss Mannix, please transmit hyperspace coordination points on my mark. Miss Crebassa..."

"Dr. Hollingsworth, wait. We're not there yet. I specifically said *we're approaching.* Just be ready."

"Roger that," says Sherman, trying to sound official. "How long until we get there?"

"Six minutes and 23 seconds," Kluco says. "But wait for my command before starting up the sequence."

"Aye aye, Captain," Sherman responds.

This is it. The excitement of the crew is bursting through the roof. *"We're really doing this,"* Rachel is thinking.

She can't stop smiling and looks over at Harry, who smiles weakly back.

Their first jump, or skip, will be the smallest one. They will enter Hyperspace for a mere 10 seconds and exit at a point that should be almost half a million miles away from where they entered. That's like traveling to the moon and back in 10 seconds. It will be a remarkable achievement, and will instantly ensure a front-page article in *Science Magazine,* and most likely world-wide mention in the news. Sherman would win his coveted Nobel award in science and become famous. He would be sought after for interviews, talk shows, speaking engagements—it would be everything he ever dreamed of.

Depending on the results of the first jump, Sherman will adjust and calculate at least two more. The second skip will span millions of miles, and then, the third will cover billions of miles, landing close to the orbit of Pluto.

It is not without some trepidation that NASA and Doctor Bowman had agreed in allowing Sherman to exercise so much control when it came to calculating and laying out courses for each jump. Originally, they wanted much tighter control on all aspects of the mission. But, truth be told, nobody was able to completely follow Sherman's equations, especially when he introduced nanophysics into them. Eventually, they had all decided that in order to ever launch such a fantastic mission, there would be some elements that would simply require a leap of faith in trusting Sherman's equations.

After all, every mission had risks. They had hoped to mitigate this with Sherman by having the most advanced, autonomous robot ever created at the helm. Pilot Kluco had been versed in thousands of emergencies and emergency procedures. He was able to make adjustments and maneuvers much more efficiently than any human being ever could.

Six minutes later Kluco announces, "Attention crew—we are ready to start our first jump. Please confirm that you are strapped in, and all systems are go."

Sherman, Rachel and Linda immediately respond, "Yes, Captain—strapped in, ready to go!"

There is a slight pause, and then Harry joins in, "Roger, Captain. Strapped in, all systems ready."

Kluco contacts mission control, "This is Captain Kluco to mission control. We are ready to commence with our first skip. All systems are go."

Mission Control responds, "Excellent Captain Kluco. You may proceed."

Kluco points at Sherman, "Dr. Hollingsworth, on my mark."

"Ready," Sherman replies.

Kluco, "Engaging warp engines, now," He flips a switch. "Dr. Hollingsworth, go!"

This is it—the moment everyone's been waiting for. And Sherman can't help but ham it up a bit, "Engaging Hollingsworth Hyperspace drive—Now!"

Sherman flips a switch, and then Kluco presses a button.

WHOOOSH! The ship rockets forward and then disappears.

#

Back in Minzi's lab, we see Minzi and her assistant preparing Sammy for surgery.

"Okay, we are all set to begin. Pacbaer, is the anesthesia ready?" asks Minzi.

"Yes, all ready."

"Can you please secure the patient and begin administering the anesthetic?"

"Yes, right away."

Pacbaer goes into the area where Sammy is being kept in stasis. Sammy's body is in a tube with a flood of colors weaving up, down, and all around it. The tube is also filled with a type of gas/liquid that further keeps the body from aging or changing in any way.

She presses a button and the liquid is quickly drained from the tube. Pacbaer then enters a series of commands. The colors dissipate, and then vanish as the tube opens.

Pacbaer levitates Sammy out of the tube, hovers him over to the operating table, and then lowers him. Sammy's body is then "strapped" in again by the colorful rings.

Sammy, of course, is completely oblivious to what is about to happen. As a matter of fact, his mind is having quite a moment right now in its virtual playpen, where he is currently standing atop of a small platform, maybe 15 feet high, about to dive into the water. He bends his knees and springs up and out, soaring into the air, then looking down at the spot where he will land. And, as he makes his descent, with his arms stretched out in front of him in perfect form, the most incredible sight manifests right before his eyes.

A huge spaceship appears in the water directly below him. It is shimmering and seems to blink in and out of existence. It disappears for a moment while Sammy is falling towards it, and then reappears the next instant, and closes around him.

#

Pacbaer finishes strapping Sammy's body in, begins the anesthetic, and pushes the table over to where Minzi is stationed at the operating site.

"Thank you, Pacbaer."

"You're welcome, Doctor."

Minzi, presses some controls on the podium and Sammy's legs rise up in "amputation" position.

"Okay, here we go!" Minzi exclaims.

A horde of others, including Tsedo, are watching Minzi's every move from a station above. Minzi takes her scalpel instrument, raises it, and just as she's about to make the first cut, she gasps in astonishment as Sammy's body vanishes from the operating table.

Chapter 33

Inside the *Galaxis* something very odd is taking place.

The entire crew is experiencing a strange sensation as they are temporarily removed from normal space-time. Things seem to stretch, and stop, and start again. Their surroundings become dream-like.

Amazingly, unbeknownst to any of the crew, Sammy's body materializes in one of the cabins in the back. He is beside himself in confusion, thinking he must be having a dream within a dream somehow. He is too bewildered to speak at the moment, wondering if this might be yet another trick by *"them,"* or has he left *"them"* completely behind?

Within the ship, the entire second deck is stretching, while the first and third decks contract. The occupants feel a complete loss of physicality, and a jarring sensation of electromagnetism overwhelms all of their other senses.

As the ship lingers in this new dimension, Kluco's voice can be heard barking out orders, or possibly just coordinates. It's hard to tell, as his voice has slowed down, becoming much lower. His words are stretched out and cannot easily be understood.

And then, it's over, as the ship comes out of hyperspace and enters back into the four dimensional constructs we are familiar with: length, width, depth, and linear time. The crew is shaken up, and somewhat discombobulated, but coming out of it.

Kluco, the least affected, scans their current location.

"Dr. Hollingsworth, you better take a look at this."

It takes Sherman another few moments to adjust, but he manages to unstrap himself and joins Kluco at the helm.

"Good Lord!" he exclaims.

"This isn't quite what we expected, is it?" asks Kluco.

"No, I think it's much better."

"But our first skip wasn't supposed to take us this far. And we're not on course anymore."

"Bygones," says Sherman. "It's worked far better than anyone could have expected. We've gone further than Saturn in just ten seconds! It's already an incredible success and a historic mission."

"It won't be a successful mission until the entire crew is returned safely," Kluco reminds him.

Sherman ignores that remark. In his mind, they have accomplished the most important part already, proving Sherman's theory correct; that a ship can enter and exit Hyperspace with a live crew and travel unheard of distances in just seconds.

"All I have to do is relay the sub-space wormhole signatures recorded, and recalculate and synchronize the electromagnetic vibrations surrounding our vessel, and we'll be close to our target in just one more jump. The distance we've covered is fantastic!"

"But are you sure you can trust your equations to land us closer to the target and not skip us further away?"

"Mr. Kluco, please leave the science to me," Sherman assures him.

They are so far from Earth that there is no way to ask mission control for approval. Kluco is forced to allow Sherman to lead the way, hoping that things will work out.

Meanwhile, nobody is aware that they have gained an extra passenger. Sammy is now sitting on the bed in one of the extra cabins, still trying to make sense of things.

He stands up, and cautiously walks from one end of the room to the other—feeling the walls, the desk, the chair, the bed. Things feel very real. Not like a dream at all. If anything, things have become more solid than they were before. What is going on?

The crew is barely recovering, when Kluco announces, "Okay, everybody please remain strapped in. We are now attempting our second jump through hyperspace. According to Dr. Hollingsworth, this will get us back close to our original coordinates."

WHOOOSH! They're off again.

Chapter 34

"Minzi—what happened? Where did your patient go?" cries Tsedo.

There are quite a few Trinollians who had come to watch the surgical procedure of removing Sammy's legs. A step this drastic was never done in haste, or without unanimous consent from the Elders.

Never before had a patient vanished from the operating table. It was the first escape in history for the Trinollians. Minzi is awestruck.

"I don't know—this has never happened before!" Minzi exclaims.

"The only way something like this could happen," begins one of the elders, "is if he escaped from stasis. If his consciousness were to find its way to another continuum, then his body would follow."

"How is that possible?" someone asks.

"I didn't think it was," the Elder admits.

Another Elder speaks up, "There must have been interference— some outside help of sorts."

"I don't see how," Minzi says.

"Where's your earth contact right now?"

"Rachel Mannix? She's in a space vessel...Ohhhh no."

Some of the other Trinollians have also just put it together.

"They breached our dimension," one of the Elders says.

"Even so, how did Mr. McPearson get in their ship?"

This question causes the room to go silent for a moment. Everyone is thinking about how that could possibly happen. Nobody knows.

"Well, can we get him back?" Minzi asks.

Tsedo considers if this is possible. Finally, he admits, "I'm not sure. They're in a vessel traveling thousands of miles an hour through space. And, his return changes everything."

Another Elder speaks up, "We'd have to recalculate what effect another abduction would have."

A second Elder is shaking his head, and then says, "No, first we would have to recalculate what his presence alongside this Rachel Mannix would have. Would she still be at risk?"

Silence. Then Tsedo speaks up, "I don't think so."

"Why not?" Minzi asks.

"Because all of Mr. McPearson's problems revolved around alcohol consumption," Tsedo replies, "That's no longer a possibility. There is no way he could obtain any. Without that possibility, I think we can safely predict that he won't be prone to violent outbursts that would result in harming someone else."

"There might be other things that could happen that would set him off."

"Yes, to be angry, but not violent—I don't think. At least not to the point of hurting someone else," Tsedo says.

"I think you're right," Minzi agrees. "Every projected violent incident we saw occurred when he was inebriated and out of control."

There are murmurs and mumblings. The Trinollians have never before been in this situation, and have no protocol to go by. Finally, the senior Elder speaks up.

"I don't know if we could catch them in their vessel even if we wanted to. But if we did, we would have to abduct him right out of the ship, which would most likely have serious ripple effects. We could then be endangering all of them, as well as upsetting their mission. We could be the cause of changing Ms. Mannix's path!"

The Elder's wisdom is spot-on. He is absolutely right, and everybody knows it.

The Trinollians continue discussing the situation. A short time later...

"Then it's settled," the senior Elder says. "If fate has somehow intervened in Mr. McPearson's life to the extent that he was able to leave stasis, we must admit to ourselves that there is still a lot that we don't know, and let things run their own course."

"Most of us were uneasy with abductions anyway," Tsedo admits.

"But we're only trying to help them by eliminating the worst threats," another Trinollian exclaims.

"But maybe we're making things worse?" the Elder says.

"That's why we run projections!"

"Which don't always account for everything. I think we should reconsider our own goals, and our proclivity for interfering."

"But we're only trying to save them from the same fate that our planet suffered. It's an honorable goal!" one of the Trinollians insists.

"Honorable yes, but there are consequences of trying to help by abduction and ridding earth of beings that we see as harmful. Maybe it's better to let them go through their own history unaided?"

No doubt. It's hard to play God and get it right.

"Sammy McPearson will remain free," The Elder states. "And, there are to be no further abductions for the time being. We must reexamine our pattern of interference."

For the first time ever, a human escapes from their clutches.

Chapter 35

The ship arrives at its new destination, and once again the crew must recover from the hyperspace romp. Kluco, always the first to recover, scans the instruments. He stares at them in disbelief. This can't be right.

"Dr. Hollingsworth, I need you to take a look at this. Come over here."

Sherman is a little slower to recover, but is making his way over.

"Okay, Captain, I'm here, what is—GOOD LORD!"

Sherman and Kluco are looking at their current space coordinates in utter amazement.

"How can this be?" Kluco says.

"We've left the Milky Way? This is an incredible breakthrough! My modified calculations are astounding," Sherman exclaims.

"This can't be right," Kluco says. "Let me run a diagnostic."

But Kluco finds nothing wrong with the instruments. Everything is working perfectly.

"Dr. Hollingsworth, your calculations can't be trusted to get us anywhere near our target," Kluco insists.

"Oh, it's just a little glitch. I can fix it," Sherman says confidently.

"But we've left our galaxy!"

"Yeah, but not by too much. According to these readings, we're in Andromeda, just one galaxy over," Sherman says, trying to act like it's not a big problem.

"Only one galaxy over? But that's over two million light years, Dr. Hollingsworth."

"I know. Isn't it grand? Who could have ever envisioned it?" Sherman says proudly.

"Dr. Hollingsworth, we may all spend the rest of our days in space trying to get back. Even me—and my lifespan is 10,000 years," exclaims Kluco.

"Oh, don't be such a drama queen," Sherman scolds him. "We've skipped this far, I'm sure we can skip back. I just have to make a few adjustments."

"Left our galaxy?" Harry can't believe what he's overheard.

"What?" Rachel exclaims. "How can that be?"

"Wait, did you say we're not in the Milky Way anymore?" Linda can't believe it. "How can this be? Maybe our instruments have been affected?"

"No, I've run diagnostics. All instruments are working perfectly," Kluco confirms.

"What have you done to us?" Rachel cries, "Can you get us back?"

All three of them unstrap themselves and join Harry and Kluco at the helm in utter disbelief and confusion. They all start talking at the same time.

This makes Sherman very nervous. He likes to be the center of attention, but they've got it all wrong. This has been an astonishing proof of concept for mankind. It's the dawning of a new understanding of our universe and how it works. This mission has introduced and proven a new dimension of physics. Science has taken an astonishing leap forward. Sherman begins to lecture them.

"Now be quiet and hear me out!" he shouts. "This is a time for celebration, not condemnation and foolish questions."

"Foolish questions?" Harry shouts at him. "You think that..."

"What the hell is going on here?"

The entire crew gasps in utter amazement as Sammy enters the area. He has only a damp pair of shorts on. There is complete silence, and total bewilderment.

"Oh my God!" Rachel exclaims.

"An intruder, how is that possible?" Linda asks.

"Where did you come from? Identify yourself immediately," demands Kluco.

Harry is staring at Sammy in total bewilderment and confusion. Harry opens his mouth to say something, then closes it, then opens it again. He simply cannot believe his eyes.

Yes, he recognizes Sammy. He recognized him immediately. Because he looks pretty much the same as when Harry last saw him, like a seventeen-year-old kid. The same kid who vanished into thin air all those years ago, according to Rusty. How can this possibly be?

"S-S-Sammy? Is that really you?" Harry says.

Now it's Sammy's turn to gasp in amazement.

"Hhh...Har...Harry? Harry Stone? From JDC? How..."

Sammy can't even finish the sentence. He is stunned.

Harry is incredulous. Sammy is incredulous. Well, everyone is incredulous. How could a human being just appear inside their ship? Exactly what happened during their romp into another dimension?

Harry slowly approaches Sammy, staring at him—he hasn't changed a bit.

"Sammy, you look the same as you did before!"

"Before what? Where the hell am I? How did I get here? How come you're so much older?"

Harry puts his hands on Sammy's shoulders. He wants to make sure it's not an illusion.

"Sammy, what happened to you? The last anybody heard of you, Rusty said you vanished into thin air. And where are your clothes?"

"Rusty? Is he here too? What the hell is going on Harry? How did you get so big? How the hell did I get here?"

Sherman steps forward, "This is simply incredible! Fantastic really. Everybody, this is one of the most important moments in human history. And you're all very privileged to be here to share it with me."

"Sherman, do you know how he got here?" Rachel asks.

"I think I might."

"HOW?" Linda, Rachel, and Harry all yell at the same time.

"He hitched a ride on our ship when we entered an alternate dimension during our last skip."

Complete silence. They have to digest this. They are all trying to take in what Sherman just proposed. Hitched a ride on their ship when it went into Hyperspace—fantastic!

"But how did he get inside here?" Linda asks.

Sherman approaches Sammy.

"Sammy. Can you tell us what you were doing immediately before you found yourself on our ship?"

"Well, I...Hey, who th' fuck are you, anyway?"

"I must tell you that I...and also my crew, don't appreciate your vulgarity," Sherman scolds him.

"Oh, you DON'T, huh?" Sammy starts up.

Harry puts himself between them.

"Hey, chill, both of you! Sherman, let him tell his story. That's just the way he talks."

"Well we don't have to tolerate..."

"Dr. Hollingsworth, please do not speak for me or our crew. I am the captain of this ship and I will interrogate our intruder," Kluco rolls forward towards Sammy.

Sammy stares in disbelief.

"What the...?" He backs up two steps and looks Kluco up and down.

"You're a friggin' robot?"

"I am Captain Kluco, and yes, I am a robot of sorts—although an extremely advanced one. I am also in charge of this ship and this crew."

"Whoa!" Sammy stares at Kluco, the mechanical marvel. He has never seen anything like Kluco before. He can easily see that Kluco is robotic, but the movements and the speech, and even his personality—Sammy is amazed at the technology.

"Sammy, how is it that you haven't aged?" asks Harry.

"Since when? A few days ago? How the hell did you get so big and older?"

"Sammy, what's the last thing you remember?" Sherman butts in.

Kluco looks at him. He thought he had made it clear to Sherman that it was the captain's job to interrogate the intruder. But it's a good question and Kluco would like to know the answer too. He allows Sherman to get away with it.

"Well, I was swimming. I mean, I was dreaming that I was swimming. It seems like I was in a long dream. I had a beach house, and a fridge full of beer, all the time—it never ran dry. But after a while, I din't feel like always being drunk."

"You had a refrigerator that was always full of beer?" Harry asks. "So you were dreaming?"

"Yeah, that's what I said. It had to be a dream 'cause, I mean, I had this beautiful beach house. And an ocean to swim in, which I really liked. And, I was...diving. Yeah, I was diving from a ledge...yeah...that's what happened. And then, suddenly there was this ship. I mean it was *this* ship, the one we're all in now. It just appeared out of nowhere, blinking on and off. And I dove right through it and landed in a room in the back. And then I heard talking and came out here."

Sammy folds his arms in front of him. He could use some dry clothes.

Harry sees this and says, "I'm going to get you some clothes buddy—hold on," and leaves to get Sammy something to put on.

Kluco is convinced that Sherman has it right, and says "We shared the same dimension with him during our jump."

Sherman doesn't want to let someone else explain and interrupts Kluco.

"Somehow, this person was in an altered state, whereby he entered a different and adjacent dimension. When my equations triggered the jumping points, this enabled both our ship, and Sammy here, to temporarily share the same space/time coordinates. And when we came out of it, Sammy was enveloped in our core vibrations, and came back with us!" he finishes triumphantly.

Linda and Rachel stare at Sherman with mouths open. They are astonished, but also, convinced. The explanation seems plausible. Yes, it's amazing, but it does explain things.

Harry returns with some clothes for Sammy. He also heard everything that Sherman said and is trying to make sense out of it.

"Sammy, what happened on that day you left the center with Rusty?" he finally asks.

"Yeah, I'm not sure. It's all so foggy. I think Rusty just disappeared? It wasn't that long ago, just a few days."

"Sammy, it's been about 13 years," Harry says. "At least for us. Not for you though, you look the same."

"How can that be?" Sammy asks incredulously. Then, Sammy remembers something and exclaims,

"Hey, I tried to call you from that dream!" Sammy suddenly remembers. "I think your old man picked up and yelled at me."

"WHAT?!" this hits Harry so hard that he nearly falls over. His heart is racing now. Rachel goes over to him.

"Oh my God, Harry, you were right! How can that even be?"

"What are you all talking about?" Linda shouts.

Kluco sees how things are getting out of hand and realizes that he must take some type of action before this overwhelming confusion turns into hysteria.

"Dr. Hollingsworth, everyone, I want you to return to your stations. We're going to have to make another jump. Harry, escort our intruder to the bed in the room that he came from, and secure him the best you can with whatever is available."

"But, what will happen to Sammy?" Harry cries.

"I don't know," admits Kluco.

"What will happen to me smart-guy?" Sammy asks Sherman.

"I'm not..." Sherman starts, then changes his answer. He does not like to ever admit that he's wrong, or doesn't know—if possible. Instead, he speculates, "Well, if you stay enveloped in our core vibrations, meaning this ship, I imagine you'll stay here throughout our skip."

"Huh, what's a skip?" Sammy says.

Just then, the ship's emergency system flickers on and off. The lights dim for a moment, the instruments spike and then return to normal.

In the distance can be seen tiny white dots that seem to be getting larger and larger.

"Kluco, what just happened? Is there something wrong with the ship?" Harry asks.

"That was the emergency notification system!" Linda shouts. "Captain Kluco what's causing it to go off?"

"Checking. Everyone, please get to your stations. Mr. Sammy, please secure yourself to the bed in the cabin that you arrived in as best you can. Unidentified vessels are approaching."

"WHAT?" cry Harry, Rachel, and Sherman.

"Three vessels are approaching us. We've got to go—now!" Kluco tells them.

"Engaging warp drive. Dr. Hollingsworth—go!"

Sherman begins, "Engaging Hollingsworth Hyper—"

BANG!

Their ship shudders and rocks. All of its occupants are jolted, and strain against their straps.

"Dr. Hollingsworth—engage Hyperspace, now," Kluco demands.

"I already did—it is engaged," Sherman exclaims. "What was that loud bang, Captain?"

"I'm not sure," Kluco says, "but I think we may be caught in a tractor beam. I'm going to reinitialize. Shutting down and restarting..."

"Captain Kluco, hurry!" Harry urges him.

Kluco is ready to try again, "Engaging warp drive, Dr. Hollingsworth—go!"

Sherman, "Engaging Hyperspace Launch."

Just for a moment, the ship jolts and shakes. But just as quickly, it stops. The lights dim, and the engines shut off. It is dark and eerily silent. All of our friends look up and around, straining to see each other. They can see a little out the viewport, and...there is something there.

They are surrounded by three alien vessels. Each one is only half the size of their ship, but they are sleek, fast and maneuverable. These ships are armored with a vicious array of weapons. As of yet, the weapons are not powered up.

All three alien vessels have synched up and tripled the strength of the tractor beam. They have gained enough control to completely disable the *Galaxis*, which is now floating dormant in space. Suddenly, the *Galaxis* gives another jolt and starts moving. It is being towed, completely under the control of the aliens.

Kluco immediately begins reviewing thousands of emergency situations that he has in his databanks, looking for a similar situation and best procedure to follow. He opens up a channel,

"This is captain Kluco of Earth. We come in peace. Can you understand me? Come in pl—"

"WE ARE THE GLARBS!" a terrible gruff alien voice fills their ship.

"YOU ARE OUR PRISONERS. WE WILL BE BOARDING YOUR VESSEL AND TAKING IT OVER. DO NOT TRY TO RESIST OR YOU WILL BE DESTROYED!"

"Get us out of this, Kluco!" Harry shouts.

"Captain, *do something*!" Linda pleads.

"I am. I am processing," Kluco replies as he darts through the cabin.

Suddenly, the ship is filled with a terrible smell and the air burns. The horrible Glarbs are materializing right before their eyes.

"Get them!" Sammy cries, as he unstraps himself.

Harry does the same. Their intent is to rush the aliens and fight them to the death, if necessary, to regain the ship from these monsters. But, as the Glarbs are materializing, at the same time they fire a spray from their belts that fills the air and makes it almost impossible to move.

Harry tries to attack. However, the harder he tries, the more resistance he's met with. He cannot effectively advance on them—it's like walking in thick mud.

Sammy manages to stand up, takes a step in their direction, and then cannot move. The others suffer the same fate, except for Kluco, who managed to hide just before the Glarbs materialized.

Our friends are reluctantly docile and immobile as the lead Glarb approaches each crew member, and uses some type of gun to implant a magnetic chip attached to a metal plate into their bodies. The chip goes under the skin, and the metal plate is visible outside the skin. They implant two of these into each member of the crew—one in the chest, the other goes into the thigh. Mumbled shrieks of pain can be heard from the crew, as one by one they are branded in this manner.

Up close, the Glarbs are indeed terrible. They are somewhat humanoid, except that their body looks to be plagued by tumors and lumps growing every which way. Their skin is scaly, sort of gray/green, with lesions, and scabs, and bumps growing out of other bumps.

Their teeth are pointed and grimy. Their breath is revolting. As the head Glarb embeds the last crew member with the chips, he sneers at them, laughs, and declares, "HA, HA, HA—That should do it. You are now our prisoners for life!"

"We are the Glarbs, and you are our prisoners," the leader announces through their universal language translator.

"You will be able to move soon, but do not attempt to escape or be uncooperative in any way, or you will get this," and he presses a button on a remote that he is holding. The entire crew, except for Kluco, receives a painful shock from their new implants, and falls to the ground, writhing in pain. The leader releases the button and the pain stops.

Harry looks at his tormentor with eyes of unbridled hate. But he realizes he must wait for the right moment. There is no way to fight these things right now. Hopefully, an opportunity will present itself.

Rachel lets out a soft whimper. Harry is able to turn his head a little. He looks at Rachel, and then looks about, and sees the paled and defeated faces of his shipmates—their eyes are filled with terror and fear. Nobody can hurt his friends without suffering the consequences. He swears to himself that he will make these Glarbs pay dearly for this. But for now, the only thing any of them can do...is obey.

Finally, the effects of the spray wear off. One by one, each crew member is able to move and gets up. But they are extremely wary of their horrible metal plates. Nevertheless, Harry dares to speak up, *"What do you want?"* he demands.

"Shut up!" the leader answers, and points the remote at Harry and taps it for one second.

Harry yelps and falls to his knees, as surges of electricity emanate from the new chips embedded in his body.

"You don't ask questions, I do. You listen and obey from now on. Got it?" the lead Glarb says through his translator.

Harry hates this thing with all his might, but wisely stays silent, for now.

"I am Gritzel, the Commander—and your owner. You will come back to our planet with us and be slaves for the rest of your lives," Gritzel explains, "which will be very short if you do not cooperate," he finishes.

"Go to hell!" shouts Sammy.

Gritzel points the remote at him and Sammy drops to the floor, writhing in pain. Harry tries to rush Gritzel, but again, finds himself on the receiving end of the device, and is forced to join Sammy on the floor, in agony.

"You will obey, or I will kill you one by one as the rest of you watch."

Sherman, Rachel, and Linda are frozen with fear. They say nothing.

"Who is captain Kluco?" asks Gritzel.

It's at this point that they all realize that Kluco managed to hide, just before these disgusting things materialized. At least, if one of them is still free, there's a much better chance to be saved.

"I am," Harry lies.

"You? You're the same one who announced that you come in peace?" Gritzel mocks him. The other Glarbs all snicker derisively.

"Come in peace, *Hah!* You'll be coming in pieces soon enough."

Gritzel's crew roars in laughter at this.

"Zrigo, scan the rest of the ship for life forms."

Zrigo finds none.

"No other life forms beyond this area, sir."

"Then so be it. You're all coming to your new home now!" Gritzel commands.

He presses a button on his belt, and our friends look at each other in utter amazement, as their legs and stomach fade away, followed by the rest of their body.

But Zrigo's sensors didn't detect Kluco's presence as a biological entity, and he remains on the ship—alone.

#

The loathsome Glarbs and their prisoners materialize on the Glarb ship. The gang is thrown into a small room.

"Don't do anything to make me press this button anymore," warns Gritzel, "or it might be the last thing you ever do. We're towing your ship and taking it as a souvenir."

Gritzel leaves, and locks the door behind him. They all look at each other, scared and disillusioned, except for Harry and Sammy. Both of them are pacing back and forth angrily.

"Sherman, how did this happen?" Linda exclaims. "What about all the testing that was done in the last few years? What went wrong? You blew us clear across into another galaxy!"

"Well, no one can pinpoint hyperspace landing points," Sherman defends himself. "And there was extra mass, not calculated. You can't..."

Sammy is pacing around the room, too mad and confused to catch that *extra mass* part. He stops in front of Sherman, turns and yells at him.

"Look what you've done to us, smart guy. This is all your fault!"

"Now everybody STOP IT!" Harry shouts even louder. "This isn't going to get us anywhere, attacking each other."

"We've got to work together and figure things out," Rachel adds.

"What is there to *goddamn* figure out?" Sammy rants. "We're captured, and have these damn metal plates sticking out of our skin!"

"I know it looks bad," Sherman says, "but Kluco is still on our ship. He'll get us out."

"How? With these stupid metal things on, we can't even fight them!" Sammy shouts.

Harry is thinking now of that "DON'T GO" message. If only he had listened. All of those years thinking it meant NOT GOD. Because of Sherman. And now this mess.

Well, Harry thinks, *I'm just going to have to fight our way out, that's all there is to it. I'm going to rip these metal plates out of us, fight these damn Glarbs, and get all of us home again.*

"I'll get us out, don't worry," he says with grit determination.

Everyone looks at Harry. The way he said it gives everyone a little hope. They could tell that he meant what he said.

Harry is as mad and as determined as he's ever been in his entire life. But he knows that they have to play it cool for now.

"Listen, we've got to act like we've given up and decided to obey them. Just for now. There's going to be an opportunity for us to strike. I don't know when, but it's going to happen. And when it does, we will kill these things if we have to, get back to our ship, and *we will get home!*"

#

Back at NASA, a deep sense of worry and gloom now hangs over mission control. Dr. Bowman is consulting with the scientists and engineers regarding the disappearance of the *Galaxis.*

"What was their last known location?" Bowman asks.

"Just outside the orbit of Saturn, sir."

"And then they attempted their second jump?"

"Yes, sir. From all indications, they successfully breached hyperspace a second time. But we have no indication of their exit point, or if they ever exited at all."

Dr. Bowman thinks about this.

"They probably exited at a point so distant that we might not receive any communication from them for hours."

"There's no way to know, sir. It could be days, even months."

"You think they left our solar system?"

"Possibly. If they got to Saturn in seconds, well, they could be anywhere in the galaxy. Maybe even another galaxy? Anything is possible."

"Please continue to scan for the *Galaxis'* signature, and notify me any time of the day or night, when you hear something."

"Understood, sir."

"Well, at least we know that Sherman's theories worked, there is that," Dr. Bowman says. "We were able to confirm, after the first jump, that breaching hyperspace is possible."

"Yes, sir. That's a fantastic step forward for all of us—for science!"

"Yes, it is. We just have to be positive and hold out hope that Captain Kluco will get them back again."

Chapter 36

On planet Xirxon, things have not been going so well. The weaponry and the tension between countries has reached a feverish pitch. Governments have put more and more focus, and more money as well, into detecting a first strike, or first launch, or first thought attacks (if possible) from an enemy country. Even though the leaders of each country world-wide swear they would only strike in self-defense, what if any of the early-warning detection systems malfunctions just once, detecting a false signal?

One of the largest countries on the planet has been holding regular "think tank" sessions, trying to come up with a way to steer clear of planetary genocide. A worldwide agreement to disarm and destroy a good percentage of the weapons of mass destruction is what is needed. But most likely this will never occur. The leaders would be too suspicious that the plan was a ruse and that their nation would be left vulnerable.

But if things just keep progressing the way they have been, a false alarm will eventually occur. When it does, it's possible that it could trigger a major mishap that could destroy life as they know it.

In the event that such a catastrophe could really happen, the scientists are experimenting with building a virus that could enter a dead body and reanimate it, possibly even renew real life into it, if the body was well-preserved and hadn't been dead too long. They will get to work manufacturing tens of thousands of these viruses, hoping that if the world's population was wiped out, they could preserve their species.

#

Harry and the gang have been left alone and locked in a room for a few hours. Suddenly, they hear footsteps approaching, and then the door opens. Three Glarbs enter the room, two with trays of food. The third one, named Zrigo, is carrying a folding table and a large bag containing prison clothes for the new slaves-to-be. The shorter one carrying the food tray is Ditzin.

Zrigo tosses the clothes on the floor.

"Put these on later, and leave your rags in the corner. You won't need them anymore."

The folding table is then set up in the center of the room, and Ditzin proceeds to lay the food out. Surprisingly, the food looks and smells pretty good. There is some meat that looks similar to chicken, and some greens. The Glarb vegetables are a little bit rough, but not too bad. There is also some grain type of food, and plenty of water.

Ditzin is atypically cordial to them, unlike his comrades. He uses the word *please*, which sounds strange, coming from a Glarb.

"Please accept our hospitality, and try to get used to your situation," Ditzin explains. "You will be with us for the rest of your lives and there's nothing you can do about it."

"That's what you think," Harry mumbles to himself.

"We have scanned you, and have prepared good nourishment for you, please eat. We will be arriving at our planet soon and you will need strength," Ditzin warns them.

"You'll never hold us—we're gonna kill all of you and take your ship!" Sammy shouts.

"Sammy!" Harry scolds him. But it's too late.

"The slave will learn to remain silent," Zrigo says, and taps the remote in his direction

Sammy immediately falls to the ground in agonizing pain.

"Maybe we'll get a third chip for you?" Zrigo threatens.

The Glarbs leave the room, locking the door behind them.

"Sammy, now's not the time! What good does it do?" Harry admonishes him.

"Well, when is the time?" Sammy answers, still on the floor. "We've got to do something!"

"I'm not sure, but we'll know it when we see it. When we catch them without that damn remote, I guess," Harry answers.

#

The Glarbs have landed the vessel on their home planet. Gritzel, accompanied by two guards, opens the door where the gang is being held.

"Stand up," Gritzel commands them. They stand, and Gritzel barks out, "One behind the other, in a line."

One of the guards then chains them together by their feet and necks. They are marched out of the room and through a corridor, to the back of the ship. A hatch opens and, following Gritzel and his two guards, they exit the vessel. The rest of the Glarbs march behind them.

"No talking, or else," they are warned.

And so we see Sherman, Harry, Rachel, Linda, and Sammy, all being escorted down the ramp and onto the alien world of Glarb. They are all wearing their dull, brown, slave outfits that those who are "owned" must don for the rest of their lives. That way, it is immediately apparent to anybody who looks upon them that they are of the lowest class. Their purpose is only to serve others. Their lives are unimportant, and can be extinguished at the drop of a hat.

The air smells different. But at least they can breathe without any apparatus. However, they are having a little difficulty walking, as if they were heavier. Perhaps this planet is a little larger than earth and has more gravity? Or, it could even be the psychological effects of walking with torture chips embedded into your skin, as well as being chained to your friends by your neck—a constant reminder that your free will has been handed over to your captor.

Our sullen group marches onward, ever cooperative under the auspices of their hated implants. They gaze out upon this strange, new land, and see all sorts of creatures; large and small, humanoid and reptilian of sorts, bugs and insects that are larger than tennis balls.

They are marched down dirty streets. There are flying creatures in the sky, but not really like birds. They look more like flying globs of bat parts.

There are disease-carrying animals, roaming about looking for food.

There is garbage and rot, and what look like buzzards, only larger, are feeding on carrion right in the street.

There is pollution, and it makes it hard to see the horizon, but it does look like there are mountains in the distance.

It's uncomfortably warm on planet Glarb. And their new slave-uniforms are itchy. There is litter everywhere, and a stench that seems to come in waves.

They have been walking for quite some time, and are now hot and tired, but too frightened to complain. They force themselves to march on.

There is a definite class structure in this world, from the very wealthy to the beggars and slaves. The lower class is easily identifiable, by a dismal, hopeless expression.

Harry can't help but think to himself how bad things look. These damn metal plates with the torture chips. If only he could fight back.

But Harry will play it smart and wait for his chance. He can't afford to make any mistakes and get himself, or one of his friends, injured or killed.

Sherman is walking behind Harry, and is strangely the only one without the glum demeanor. Sherman sees all of this as fantastic, in a way. His wonderful equations jumped galaxies.

And now, captured by an alien race on a distant planet. If it wasn't for being forced into slavery this could almost be fun.

Sherman is intrigued by the metal-plated chips—how completely they control things, how they work, what makes them tick? His fantastic mind is completely engaged.

Chapter 37

On they walk, herded like cattle through the streets of another, smelly Glarb city. They are gawked at, on display, the news of the day, as they are paraded in front of all creatures large and small, grateful to have something interesting happen in their sullen lives.

They are passing through another down-ridden section of town now, and Gritzel shouts out, "Look over there, my monkeys. There's your new home!"

As they get closer, they can see a compound through the fence containing all sorts of creatures which appear to be mostly humanoid. There are many different species, and they are all dressed in similar dull, brown attire. Most of them look miserable—skinny and undernourished. A sense of despair pervades throughout the entire camp.

As they are led into the compound, Harry catches the sight of a mother and child sharing a morsel of food. They both have marks on their skin, as if they had been beaten or whipped.

The Glarbs finally halt the procession and unchain their prisoners.

"Welcome to your new existence," Gritzel sneers. "I hope you enjoy our accommodations. We usually do not get too many complaints," he says and taps his remote while laughing. Gritzel's soldiers follow his lead, and laugh as well. It makes an indelible impression upon our friends, as they watch the gate close—locking them into their new home.

Linda and Rachel look at each other with tears in their eyes, and then embrace, sobbing softly. Harry, who was mad before, is now bursting at the seams with anger and frustration. Sammy is scared and docile for the moment, remembering his painful lesson. Sherman however, is a different story.

He can't help feeling proud of the fact that it was his science that enabled them to end up here. Never mind the fact that they are now slaves to horrible beings on an alien planet. They are *on* an alien planet. Because of *his* equations, *his* science.

Never before has this been done. Other than being enslaved, *it's so damn cool!* He wants to gloat about this, but has a feeling it wouldn't go over very well with the rest of the crew.

The despondent group, except for Sherman, finds a spot to sit and commiserate.

"Oh, Harry, what are we going to do?" asks Rachel. Her voice never sounded so weak and miserable.

"We wouldn't be in this mess if it wasn't for our genius here," complains Sammy.

"You know it's quite probable that this is all *your fault*, Sammy!" Sherman counters.

"My fault? How could it be? I din't do nothing!"

"You mean you didn't do anything. If you didn't do nothing then obviously you did something."

"I ain't done nuthin' I tell ya."

Sherman doesn't bother correcting Sammy's English again. Instead, he strives to reason with the crew and get them to see things from a much more enlightened perspective.

"Now remember everybody, it's true that we're on an alien planet, and forced to be slaves but..." and he holds up his finger to emphasize the truly important part, "we are no doubt the first human beings to ever establish contact with another intelligent species," he finishes triumphantly.

The others look at him with disdain. Not one smile. He tries again.

"We are pioneers of a kind never before seen in our entire existence. We have broken through the barrier of exceeding the speed of light, in a very real sense. We have advanced mankind's understanding of the universe and have unveiled the mysteries of interdimensional travel. All of our names will be immortalized as the first human beings to ever leave, not only our solar system, but to travel beyond our own galaxy!"

Again, the rest of the crew looks at him, now in utter amazement *and* disdain.

"The Milky Way!" Sherman roars. "Surely some of you can see the positive side of this as well? Mankind will forever be grateful for this day! By applying the laws of nanophysics, quantum mechanics, and space-time relativity, we have brought order to Hyperspace and indeed even commanded it. And we all get to share this credit together."

That should do it, he thinks. *I'm unselfishly sharing credit with them for something that I invented by myself.* Sherman expects to hear gratitude from them at this point.

Sammy is really getting riled up. Sherman's speech has infuriated him.

Harry doesn't know what to think. This Sherman Hollingsworth must be from a different planet, or maybe right now he's home? He seems excited, almost happy, in the face of these dire circumstances. Still, there's something almost admirable about it—almost, but not really. It's his fault they're here.

Linda is also getting mad.

"Commanded it? We didn't command anything, it commanded us. You had no idea where we were going to wind up with those hyper-jumps, yet you risked all of our lives just to see if your equations worked."

"I did have an idea where we'd end up, or at least I thought I did," Sherman shouts back. "It isn't an exact science, and I was on the ship too, risking my own life, need I remind you. We all knew the risks and we all signed the waivers."

"But we're millions of light years from home," Rachel exclaims.

"If we jumped this far once, we can jump back again," Sherman says.

"How do you know that?" asks Linda.

"Because the fold doesn't change," Sherman tries to explain.

"What doesn't change?" asks Harry, although he thinks he knows what Sherman means.

"I know what he means," says Rachel.

Sherman starts explaining,

"The fold. When we take a shortcut through hyperspace we enter a new continuum of space-time that folds space and allows us to get from one point to another without traveling the same distance that it would take in our dimension."

He doesn't have a sheet of paper but tries to draw on the ground, using a stick. He draws a large rectangle and puts "A" at the top and "B" at the bottom.

"Suppose we want to travel from A to B," Sherman explains. "We would have to cover this distance," and he scratches the ground with his stick from point A to B.

"Now imagine, if you will, that this is a sheet of paper and you fold it in the middle so that A is on top of B. Well, you can see how the distance you need to travel is much less. Because you entered hyperspace through a fold."

Linda, Harry, and Rachel are right there with him in understanding. Sherman has articulated it so clearly with his example. Sammy is also no dummy. Not as bright as Harry and the girls, but he kind of gets what Sherman is saying. However, Sammy is still angry and continues to vent.

"Well, if you're so smart, then how the hell did we wind up here?"

"None of my calculations took into consideration having a stowaway on our ship, with all that extra mass that you added."

"Oh, so it's my fault?" Sammy retorts.

"Well, it's your mass."

"Listen, I din't ask you or anybody to kidnap me."

"We didn't kidnap you, Sammy, you somehow breached our ship when we went into hyperspace," Harry says.

"But we're not even on our goddamn ship no more!" Sammy shouts.

"Kluco still is," says Sherman. "He'll rescue us eventually."

"How Sherman?" Linda asks. "How's Captain Kluco going to fight an entire planet of these Glarbs?"

"And we can't even resist with these horrible metal chips embedded in us," Rachel adds.

"Well..." Sherman starts. He doesn't want to say too much just yet, but he's been studying their metal-plated chips and thinks he can find a way to short them out. But before he can say a word Harry interrupts.

"This is getting us nowhere," says Harry. "We're all in this together, and like Sherman said, we knew the risks and we all signed the waivers. Let's not attack or blame each other. We're a team, and we've got to stick together and figure something out."

"But Harry, what can we figure out?" cries Linda. "They can electrocute us at the touch of a button!"

"I don't know yet. *But we're going to get out of this,*" Harry promises, more determined than he has ever been in his entire life.

"Oh, Harry, are you sure?" asks Rachel.

"Yes, I promise you, Rachel. I promise all of you—*We're going to get out of this!*"

Chapter 38

The gang has one of the most miserable nights of their lives.

They sleep clumped together in the corner, on the floor. There are bathrooms, of sorts, with areas to deposit one's bodily wastes, but there is no privacy.

There is a makeshift sink that they must share with the other prisoners. It serves as both a sink and shower, by splashing or cupping the water, and then spilling it on one's body.

They haven't eaten in quite a while, and they are hungry and thirsty.

The other prisoners have been wary of approaching them. Maybe they were warned not to? Without the universal language translator that all the Glarbs carry, communication with other species is very difficult, if not impossible.

Their fellow prisoners are indeed strange. From the bizarre to the somewhat humanoid, they all share a few things in common: the metal-plated implants protruding from their body, dull, brown rags for clothes, and a sullen, defeated look. Sherman notes with some interest that there are a few prisoners who have as many as four metal plates embedded into their body. He speculates that is for the ones who have been disobedient more than once. The pain must be terribly agonizing, bringing the victim close to death. Sherman and his friends only have two each, and it is already unbearable.

There are also definite cliques in the camp, and most species seem to stick together. A group of beings with long bodies and short limbs are rummaging through a type of dumpster. One of them turns, and Harry is caught staring at them. The creature's long, greenish face contorts into a grimace. Harry is embarrassed and quickly looks away.

It is implied that to give the illusion of some sort of privacy, beings do not stare into others' personal space. Harry and friends have a lot to learn about their new home and neighbors.

The Glarbs enter the compound with some carts of food. They leave most of it out near the front gate, where the quickest prisoners are rewarded. Soon there is a crowd fighting for food.

But the Glarbs have a special cart that they're saving for Harry and his friends. One of the soldiers points in their direction, and the food cart is brought over to them.

"Earthlings, here is some nourishment."

Again, it is evident that some research was done on their biology and what they eat, because, actually, the food looks great. There is something that looks like chicken, and some type of grain or bread. There are some Glarb fruits and/or vegetables. The food smells pretty decent—even enticing.

Hesitant at first, but too hungry to resist for long, they all dig into it. It feels so good to fill up one's belly.

Some of the other beings look over and take a few steps in their direction. The Glarb soldiers give them a dirty look and they stop dead in their tracks, back up, and look away. Apparently, the meal is just for Harry's group.

The Glarb soldiers return a little later and are pleased to see the food cart is completely empty.

"You have enjoyed your meal, yes?" the lead Glarb observes.

"Now you will come with us and start your day. The females will go with Kreezling here. You two follow Gruggin. And you my big friend, we have special plans for you. You will follow me," he says to Harry.

Our friends reluctantly obey—commanded into obedience by their despised implants.

The five of them are led off in three different directions to start their lives of slavery.

Chapter 39

The *Galaxis* has been deposited in a large airstrip type of field, with many other captured vessels. Kluco remains inside, still undetected. He has no weapons, and no ideas at the moment as to how to save his crew.

He hears noises outside. The Glarbs are circulating through the airstrip, going in and out of vessels, looking for valuables. Soon they will be boarding the *Galaxis*.

Not only is Kluco fearful of being captured and possibly deactivated, or worse—scrapped, he is also afraid that the Glarbs might strip the ship, or damage it in such a way so that they can never take off again. Things have never looked so bleak.

#

Kreezling leads Rachel and Linda inside a large, dirty building. It looks like a combination office and living type of arrangement. Some rooms look somewhat domestic with places to sit and sleep. Other rooms seem like laboratories where there are Glarbs working on various projects using alien types of computers, microscopes, and other equipment that is unidentifiable.

The women are given cleaning equipment, and led to the domestic waste rooms (the bathrooms). Rachel is indignant.

"I will *not* spend my life cleaning up your crap," she begins then suddenly stops, realizing what she is risking.

Too late. The remote is pointed at her and the button is pressed. She goes straight to the floor as the implants do their job, shooting painful electric surges through her body.

After a few agonizing seconds, the lead Glarb deactivates it. Rachel is still twitching and now openly sobbing, on the ground. Linda is also in tears, helpless to do anything but obey. The Glarb soldier points his finger threateningly at them, shouts something, and finally leaves them to begin their first day of slavery weeping, and cleaning out the nasty Glarb toilets.

"Oh, Rachel, what are we going to do?" cries Linda.

"Don't worry, Harry will get us out of this."

"*But how?*" She thinks to herself. "*What can anyone possibly do?*"

Chapter 40

Sammy and Sherman are led to a site where other prisoners are busy carrying equipment and setting up tools and machinery. The Glarbs are always building something, and there's much construction everywhere. Sherman and Sammy are given instructions what to load, and are assigned a supervisor. Sammy is indignant, but any thoughts of disobeying are quickly put asunder as they observe another prisoner getting the electro-treatment for dropping something.

Poor Sammy and Sherman begin their new life of slavery. Sherman does not care for physical labor so much, but nevertheless is still somewhat cheerful and on some strange mental high, just for being on an alien planet due to his breakthrough equations that jumped galaxies.

Sherman's mind has never stopped working. He is absolutely fascinated with the implants and needs to take one apart somehow, and look inside. Or maybe if he can't do that, he can set up some experiments and analyze the results? But there is something there to be exploited, he just knows it.

Chapter 41

Kluco remains carefully hidden in his abandoned spaceship. If he were capable of feelings, he would be ashamed, dejected, and in the depths of despair. Fortunately, he is a robot and has no feelings at all.

Kluco has gone from pilot to prisoner in his own ship. By now, he has been thinking and processing, thousands of alternative paths to take, each with its own nuances. He knows that he cannot allow the Glarbs to come inside and loot the ship, nor find, and then subsequently, deactivate him. It would mean the end-of-the-line for any chance of escape for him and his crew. It would mean that the mission failed. And, bad as it seems right now, Kluco has no intention of failing this mission.

Kluco will strive for the rest of his 10,000-year life, if necessary, to bring the *Galaxis* back to Earth with as many alive as possible. But try as he might—after scouring thousands upon thousands of emergencies, processes, and every similar situation imaginable—there is no winning solution.

Kluco is totally outmatched in any type of combat, which it would inevitably come to. Since the odds are so bad, and the risk so great, he has concluded that the best course of action is to stay hidden and wait. The situation will eventually change, opening up a better possibility for succeeding in a rescue mission.

He has considered what to do if any Glarbs board his ship. Killing them is out. He would have to hide. He is confident that if he had to, he could kill any one of them using the element of surprise. But if there's more than two, he would most likely lose. And even if he were to fight and kill anybody that came on board, more would follow to investigate, and eventually they would overtake him. He scours the ship looking for anything possible that might be used as a weapon.

Through the view screen, he sees the Glarbs going through the air strip, investigating other captured vessels. As he's observing this, the answer comes to him.

Kluco has no problems adjusting his telescopic vision to zero-in on...the tag.

As the Glarbs loot ships, they leave a tag with a special symbol on it to show that they have already inspected and looted the ship. If he can make a duplicate tag and somehow affix it to the outside of the ship without being seen, they may bypass his ship, thinking they've already been on board and taken everything of value.

He quickly gets busy fabricating a duplicate tag.

Chapter 42

The Glarb leading Harry to his new activity takes him inside a facility that closely resembles a gymnasium. It is laden with all sorts of equipment to be used for combat. There are alien weapons: swords, serrated knives, mats, shields, spiked balls on a chain. There are also arenas and six-sided rings where other prisoners are engaged in either combat or training.

Two different species are sparring in the center ring. Harry and his guard stop a moment to watch.

One of the combatants is about to strike the other. The second combatant blocks it, and at the same time whips out a jagged tongue and slices his opponent in the neck.

"Wow—what do you think of that, my big slave?"

"I don't like it," Harry replies, "doesn't seem very fair."

"Hah!" the Glarb guffaws, "There is no such thing as *fair* here. There is only winning and losing. If you continue to win, you live, if not, your stay here will be short."

"What if I refuse to fight for your amusement?" Harry tests him.

"You already know what will happen. First, you get to experience the joys of your implants. If you continue to misbehave, then we will torture and kill your friends right in front of your eyes."

Harry is boiling inside. He wants to knock the remote out of this Glarb thing, grab his weapon that he carries at his side (a baton of some sort to pummel others with), and beat this Glarb guard into oblivion, along with any other thing that interferes. Harry hates having to listen to some green-gray, bumpy, stinking, lumpy Glarb threaten to kill his friends—he's not going to let that happen at any cost.

But for now, he has to remain in control. So, he grits his teeth and remains silent. What can he possibly say?

"Follow me and I will introduce you to your trainer," the guard says.

Chapter 43

Needless to say, our friends have the most miserable day of their lives, except possibly for Sherman. Despite the physical labor, Sherman is still awed and excited about being the first humans to ever leave the galaxy, courtesy of his work. Strangely enough, even the physical labor has made him feel good. He never had much of an exercise routine in his life, and although he's tired and a little stiff, it feels good, and he feels like he's getting stronger. Sherman never had the good feeling of sore muscles after a workout because he never had a workout. But now he has, and he kind of likes it.

Throughout the day of loading and carrying and performing construction, Sherman had plenty to think about. He has formed a hypothesis about the implants. The entire time he was working his mind was fully engaged wondering how the implants work, and how to test them. He still has more calculations to do, but feels that he is on the verge of yet another breakthrough. So many breakthroughs coming from that wonderful brain of his. He is proud and excited.

The group is back in their compound now, and they have been brought dinner. Once again, the food is not bad. For whatever reason, maybe it's the Glarb's research, they have all been fed well during their time as prisoners. For a short time, this helps a lot, until the hopelessness of their situation sinks in once again.

Harry has shared his day of training with the others. Rachel is alarmed and worried.

"Oh, no, Harry! They're going to make you fight other prisoners?"

"Yeah, it looks like that's what's coming."

"What are you going to do?"

"Fight, I guess. If I don't they give me the juice," Harry says, and taps the implant on his chest. "And if I resist, they're going to start coming after you guys."

"Oh, Harry, we've got to get rid of these implants."

"I'm working on that," Sherman announces.

They all look at him.

"Go on," Sammy urges him.

"Well, it's a little early to tell, but I have noticed that there seems to be no grounding, and I'm pretty sure there is a metallic substance just millimeters beneath the outer coating of the metal plate."

"Meaning...?" asks Harry.

"Meaning there might be a way to short-circuit the metal plates if we could expose the metal."

The others look at Sherman with renewed interest.

"How?" Rachel asks.

"Not sure yet, but..."

"You better damn well be sure, buddy," Sammy shouts. "If you so much as breathe sideways they zap you! We both saw it today, going on all the time."

"And they'll implant a third one in you if you're a repeat offender," Linda adds.

"It's true," Rachel says. "We both saw a couple of unfortunate beings with three, and one with four, in them."

"I know, I saw it too," Harry agrees.

"Well, I should probably keep my theories to myself for a little longer then, if you don't mind?" Sherman says. "I've still got a ways to go, but I do think I can figure out a way to short-circuit these chips."

Sherman's words give hope to rest of the group. It helps.

"We appreciate you working on it," Rachel says.

Chapter 44

Back on planet Xirxon, exactly what was feared had transpired. A false alarm triggered an emotional response, and one country launched their arsenal of deadly weapons against another country. This triggered a chain reaction of fear that eventually destroyed the life on their planet. Each country thought that they had no option but to try and get the other guy before the other guy got them. The explosions on the planet sent many objects flying out into space, including thousands of those reanimation viruses.

#

It is the next day and Harry is being trained. His trainer is a big, tough Glarb called Phyllis.

Just kidding. His name is Torka. By many, he is known as "Torka the Terrible." He is mean, ugly, and ruthless, but he is also a very good trainer. Torka takes pride in being known to have the best fighters. It's largely because of him that Harry and his friends have been fed so well. Torka sees a lot that he likes about Harry, and thinks he may even be able to win the tournament. He feels that he may have a champion on his hands and pushes Harry to the limit.

"Letz me show yerz how itz dun," Torka instructs, as he takes Harry's arm and twists it. "Now letz me see yerz getz out."

Harry uses all the strength that he has, but cannot pull away. Torka has complete leverage and twists it more.

"No, earthlingz, yerz cantz reliez on yerz strengthz alone. Yer must learnz the sienz of fightzing. If yer arm is twisted thiz way, follow it with yer head and then roll, and itz untwisted."

Harry gets it immediately, and tumbles forward, instantly relieving all the pressure and he can now pull away.

Despite being a slave and forced to be obedient through electric implants, there are some aspects of his training that he likes. He likes the physicality of it. He likes the sport of fighting; when to use strength, when to use leverage. He enjoys the science behind the moves that Torka shows him. Harry knows that he is becoming a much better fighter than ever before. He will need all of this when the right opportunity comes along.

"When yerz opponent turns hiz back ta yer, yerz do thiz," and Torka snaps a choke hold on Harry from behind, but does not apply too much pressure.

"Yerz don't need t'be strong once yerz in thiz puzition, it's all lev'rage," Torka explains as he cuts off Harry's breathing in an instant, and then releases it.

"Seez howz I'm controlling yerz with juz a small squeeze? I dunt hafta sqeeze hard and uze up my enerzy. Yerz opponent is in terrible trubble juz from thiz. From here, yerz can kill him juz by holding the squeeze fer a minute," he lets Harry go.

Harry is shaken up but does not allow Torka to see it.

"Go aheadz anz tryz it on thiz," and Torka gestures towards the dummy they've been using.

Harry does not get it completely at first, but with Torka's help, soon masters a killer choke hold. How he would love to try it out on Torka. But there are always security Glarbs standing around with those damn remote controls.

#

It is a few days later and the gang is reluctantly getting accustomed to their daily chores. The life of slavery and forced labor is taking its toll on them, and they are finding it difficult to see their escape coming anytime soon. They wonder what is going on with Kluco. When will he rescue them?

The only thing they have to look forward to is congregating at the end of the day when they can be together and talk, and maybe construct a plan. They are still alive and healthy. They are being fed fairly well. They are anxious to hear Sherman's latest theories about the implants.

Sherman is repeating his latest hypothesis.

"I'm pretty sure that if we were able to expose some of the metal beneath the outer coating of the metal plate, and touch another metal object to it at the same time they triggered the remote control, the implants would short out and possibly become damaged enough to remove."

"But what would happen to us?" Harry asks.

"We might feel a second of pain, but then they would short out," Sherman replies.

While they are all talking, another prisoner has been watching them from afar. He creeps around the camp, hiding behind objects, getting closer and closer to our crew. He manages to get close enough to hear them by hiding behind some trash dumpsters. He adjusts his universal translator, eavesdropping on their conversation.

"I would definitely give up a second of pain to be free of these horrible things," Rachel exclaims.

"Me too," says Linda.

"In a heartbeat," says Harry.

Sammy is shaking his head, "Yeah, but even if it worked, they would just gang up on us and put 'em in again. Probably we'd get three or four and then they'd turn on the juice."

"Correct," says Sherman.

"We would all have to revolt at the same time," Harry says.

"We would get just one chance to make our escape," Linda adds.

"Also correct," says Sherman.

"But, at least we have a plan," says Rachel.

Linda is getting excited, "At least it's something we can hope for!"

Harry adds, "We're also assuming that our ship is still intact and that Kluco is still in it, and can pilot us home."

"Linda and I passed an airstrip once when we were being taken to another building to clean," Rachel says. "The *Galaxis* might be there, but I don't know about Mr. Kluco."

"He's still there," says Sherman, "he wouldn't have left."

"How do you know, Sherman?" asks Harry.

"Because it's the most logical thing to do," Sherman replies. "Kluco can be counted on to take the most pragmatic approach that would lead to all of us escaping, and still completing the mission."

Chapter 45

Harry has been sparring with other prisoners during his training. Most of them are humanoid but none of them seem to be a real match for him, if he really tried. They don't get the science of it as well as Harry does, or maybe don't have as good a trainer, or maybe both? Although there are other contestants that are larger than Harry, his size and strength are usually superior, and he holds back from hurting anyone. The same cannot be said of many of the other fighters.

"Yer first match iz in two dayz," Torka informs Harry.

"Yeah...great."

"Yerz dunt seem excited."

"I don't like being forced to fight."

"Well getz used ta it. Yerz gonna beez my champion, like itz or not."

Harry snorts.

"Who am I fighting?"

"Lingus, da weed."

Harry knows Lingus. A tall, skinny humanoid-type of creature. One of the few who is bigger (taller) than Harry, but Lingus is not a real threat. He is uncoordinated, awkward, and not one of the top fighters by any means.

"I'm not going to kill Lingus."

"First of all, yerz gonna do what yerz told. We make th' rules and yerz will follow 'em, thatz how it gowz, get it? But lucky fer all of yerz, th' matches will end when eeder a trainer or Gritzel stop 'em. We dunt wanna thinz out our fighterz yet. We dunt have enuff good onez and need all of yerz. But any fighter who duzzin' give us everything heez gotz is going t'pay fer it so he never duz thatz again."

Harry has seen Torka and other trainers juice their prisoners for the slightest infraction. He can only imagine the torture they impose when they are truly angry. And what really gets him is that while the victim is being tortured, the Glarbs are standing around laughing and hollering with joy. The more screaming and pain they can inflict, the better the show.

Harry looks at Torka with eyes of hate. Torka sees this, and knows that look.

"Thaz th' spiritz!" Torka is taunting him.

Harry hates this big, ugly, sadistic monster that he's forced to take commands from. The dark side of Harry stirs.

Torka is sneering at him now, almost daring Harry to take any action that would warrant "the juice." Well, if he's only going to get one shot, then he might as well make it a good one. Harry takes all of that anger and with everything he's got...

WHAM!

From the depths of his frustration, Harry's fist finds Torka's face, sending the big Glarb reeling backwards.

Harry has clobbered Torka with one blow. Big as he is, Torka was walloped like he was never walloped before. Harry wasn't really sure if this was *the opportunity* that he waiting for, but he could hold back no more, and would just have to make it work. Now is his chance.

If he can just get to Torka's belt before Torka recovers, and can grab the remote or the paralysis spray, or both, he can make a play for it.

His wallop has hurled Torka backwards a good ten feet. He has only seconds.

He rushes the fallen Glarb.

Torka is down and on his back, stunned. His vision is blurry. He kind of knows what just happened, but his mind cannot put it all together just yet—it is so...astonishing.

His vision clears a little, and he sees his enraged slave coming for him. He reaches for his belt to press the button, just as Harry dives at him.

Harry is in mid-air when Torka finds the precious button. ZZZZZzzzzzzzttt!

Surges of electricity pour through Harry's body as he falls onto his opponent. Torka immediately turns the juice off, but not before he is also shocked from Harry's body.

Though his tortured body is still twitching uncontrollably, Harry puts all of his focus on Torka's grip on the remote, which has loosened considerably and could probably be snatched. He has to forget about the juice and grab that remote. But he can't quite control his movements.

Torka manages to roll Harry's body off, but in the process, he drops the remote. It clatters to the ground between them. This is it—*the moment has arrived*— and putting all pain aside, Harry quickly reaches out and grabs it. He's got the device in his hand.

But Torka is much less affected than Harry, and he reaches out and snatches the remote right from Harry's hand. He points it at him, and pushes the button.

Immediately, the implants send waves of volts through Harry's writhing body, and he howls in agony. Torka stands above him now, and takes his finger off the button. He sneers down at his victim.

"So, ya think yer so tuff, eh, Earthling? Yer have the gall to betray me after everything I've taut yerz? Well, good fer you. Yer like yer frend the juze?"

Torka presses the remote again and Harry goes into spasms. Then he releases it.

Harry gurgles, "If you didn't have that control I'd..."

"Yer would what? Yer think yerz could beatz yer teacher, yer master?"

Torka turns and walks away from Harry about twenty feet. Then he turns around and faces Harry, who can hardly believe what he is seeing.

Astonishingly, Torka removes his belt and places it on the ground.

"There ya go Earthlin'. Yer freedom from yer chips iz right here. All ya hafta to do iz get past me t'get it."

Torka walks back half way to Harry and makes his stand.

"Come on, Earthlin', try it! All ya need to do iz get by me."

Harry can still feel the electricity tingling in his body. He's been weakened, but when will he get another chance like this? This may be his only one.

Putting all the pain aside he springs up and rushes at Torka. He makes like he's going to swing at him and then surprisingly, dives for Torka's legs.

Torka is impressed, and almost fooled, but manages to jump out of the way just in time, and Harry's clutching fingers grasp only air. A sickening thud is heard, as Torka's boot rams into Harry's side. And then Torka is on top of him.

Harry tries to roll him off, but Torka adjusts, and pulls back a fist ready to break Harry's nose.

Harry thrusts his knee up and into Torka's back, and Torka almost falls forward but reaches out and braces himself on Harry's face. Harry grabs Torka's hands and thrusts them to the side and arches up, and he manages to roll Torka off.

He takes a giant swing at Torka, but Torka catches his arm, and rolls and twists, now sitting on Harry's back.

Torka had been teaching Harry something about the back. What was it?

Too late. Harry feels Torka's arms around his neck and knows all too well the deadly chokehold which will follow. He's got to do something.

But try as he might, Harry cannot break free of the deadly choke hold before the lights go out. Torka has all the leverage. Harry's strength is for naught. He is at Torka's mercy as all oxygen is denied him, and the blackness settles over him.

A minute later, Harry wakes up. He sees Torka ten feet away, putting his belt back on.

He has failed. His one chance.

A wave of disappointment washes over him as Torka walks back his way, his finger poised over the button. "Getz up, slave!"

Harry plays groggy.

"Getz up now, slave, or I prez diz fer thirdy seconds."

Harry stumbles to his feet.

Torka shouts right into Harry's face, "Letz get one thing clear, slave. I AM YER TEACHER, YER MASTER, YER SUPERIOR IN EVERY WAY!"

Harry is hating this.

"Yer MY fighter, groomed t'beat udder slaves. I OWN YA! YER NEVER AGAIN t'raiz a han' againz me or I will sit on thiz button and never let go! DO YER UNDERSTAND?!"

Harry nods.

"SAY IT!"

"I get it," Harry mutters.

"I hope yer do, fer yer sake. If it ever happens again it will be yer las' time!"

Torka taps the button one more time for good measure, and Harry gets one more jolt of electricity to remember the lesson.

Chapter 46

Sammy, Sherman and the other enslaved construction prisoners, have put the finishing touches on the project that they had been working on—building another slave compound. It seems the Glarbs have high hopes of increasing their lot.

One might think that after working on a project like that for months, they would get the benefit of the rest of the day off when done? But no, there's more than half the day ahead, and they are being lined up and chained, ready for a trek to their new destination.

The soldiers are weaving the chains around each prisoner's feet, so they cannot possibly run, and then linking another two chains through the entire line, so they are all fastened to each other. Plus, they all have their implants, of course. There is little hope of escape, actually—none at all. The prisoners are completely secured, and controlled one hundred percent.

Finally, the last link is threaded and the enormous (and heavy) locks are latched closed. The humiliated queue of captive souls is led down the streets—a parade of slavery and ownership for all to see.

As they march, the Glarb guards are talking and laughing loudly. Their translators must be turned off because their banter cannot be understood, except to be derisive and cruel.

Just then, Sherman hears something...a whispering, coming from behind him.

"Sir...Mr...Pssst!"

Sherman cannot believe his ears.

Sammy is marching in front of him, and yet, he could swear the prisoner behind him is whispering to him in English.

He half turns, and sees a particularly ugly and bulbous lump of a boy, looking up at him, trying to get his attention without anyone noticing. Sherman quickly turns back to face forward, bends his head down, and whispers behind him, "Are you speaking English to me?"

"Yes. I've been waiting for an opportunity for a long time to speak with you."

"But how..."

"I have a mini-translator."

"You stole one?" Sherman is incredulous.

"No, it's mine, but that isn't important. What's important is your theory about the implants."

Sherman is stunned. How could anyone outside of their group possibly know? It makes him more than a little nervous.

"I don't know what you're talking about."

"Yes, you do," the lump-boy behind him answers. "You said something about how they might be able to be short-circuited?"

"How can you possibly know that?" Sherman gives up the ruse.

"I've been wandering near you and your group ever since you arrived."

"Eavesdropping," Sherman exclaims.

"That one isn't translating. Probably because this one is an older model," lump-boy answers. "I don't know what you mean. But you must know that there are many of us who would be willing to try anything at any price to get out."

"Really?"

"Yes. Look at what they've done to me. I was once a normal boy, but my father was overheard criticizing Gritzel. They turned my entire family into slaves because of that."

The impact of this statement has a profound effect upon Sherman. Realization dawns on him now, understanding just how cruel this planet is. Something that didn't add up before suddenly seems clear. He half-turns again and looks behind him, just a glance, but lets it linger for a moment or so, to confirm what he now knows to be true.

It didn't make sense to keep building more compounds. How often can you count on an errant space vessel flying through your territory of space, available to be captured and enslaved? It probably doesn't happen that often, Sherman reasoned.

But now that he saw the truth, it did make sense. For his quick glance was sufficient to see that lump-boy was indeed, or had been, a Glarb at one point. But someone in his family got on the wrong side of Gritzel, and so the entire family was punished. Each one of them had been reshaped, and possibly genetically altered, to be a slave.

"How did you get a translator?" Sherman asks.

"When you're enslaved you're supposed to be *processed*. For aliens like you, it means assimilating your knowledge of your home planet. For Glarbs who already live here, it means taking all of our possessions. Fortunately for us, Ditzin is usually in charge of processing, and he frequently forgets or overlooks things. I was given this mini-translator as a gift a few years ago, and Ditzin just missed it when he took my possessions. It's an older model, but it gets most of the words right."

As the chain gang marches on, Sherman considers what he has just learned.

The Glarbs turn a percentage of their own population into slaves and force them to join with the other captured beings to live a life of toil and servitude. They rule with absolute fear, for the slightest infraction can endanger the entire family. Even an accusation may be enough to doom you. There is no such thing as fair under Gritzel's rule. Speaking out against him, or any government wrong-doing, is simply unheard of—one could be tortured to death for such an offense, and the entire family enslaved for the rest of their lives.

Sherman is horrified at the cruelty which takes place on this planet. He looks at Dremmil and, for maybe the first time in his life, is overcome with sympathy. He introduces himself.

"I am Dr. Sherman Hollingsworth, what's your name?"

"They call me Dremmil, Mr. Hollingsworth."

"Dr. Hollingsworth."

"Oh, okay, Dr. Hollingsworth."

"What happened to you?"

"As I said, my entire family has been punished and forced through the mutation of becoming slaves."

"The mutation..." Sherman starts, then shuts up.

One of the guards thought he heard talking and comes near to investigate. Sherman looks down and shuts up immediately (which is not so easy for him to do).

#

The chain gang is led to their new location to start work on building yet another compound. Sherman has managed to tell Sammy about their new alliance with Dremmil. The three of them are anxious to speak to one another, but only dare to whisper at opportune times. The penalty for being caught talking would result in extreme punishment. Not only would they suffer "the joys of the implants", but if the translator were to be found, it would certainly be confiscated immediately, and followed by more punishment.

They arrive at the new work site and everybody is given instructions and gets to work. An hour later, finally a window has opened up where Sherman, Sammy, and Dremmil can work next to each other and talk without being overheard.

"There are many of us that have gone through the *transformation*," Dremmil explains. "Earlier on, when there were less slaves, sometimes even if you did nothing wrong, they might come and enslave you and your family. They need a portion of us to be unpaid labor just to fill out their workforce. And they feed us less than we would normally eat, unless you happen to be a top combatant and your trainer gets you decent portions. They also take all of our money and possessions."

Both Sherman and Sammy, even in the dire circumstances they find themselves in, cannot help but be moved to compassion for Dremmil, and the many like him. The *transformation* was explained in the most blatant terms with no embellishment whatsoever.

"They lock the victim down in their *hospitals* and proceed to give them painful injections three times a day. After each injection they either leave you strapped to the table or, if you're lucky, lock you in a small bathroom so you don't make so much of a mess.

The injections are meant to make you docile and apathetic about what's happening to you, and possibly your family. The side effects of the injections are these mutations you see on my body. Sores, rashes, scars, bumps, discoloration, and plenty of pain. After two weeks, you're finally finished and they dump you in a camp to start your life of slavery."

That was the most that Dremmil could explain throughout the day. It gave both Sherman and Sammy a lot to think about, and evoked much sympathy from them. They had found compassion, and a friend, amongst the horrific Glarbs.

Chapter 47

At their gathering later that evening, everyone is excited, and somewhat horrified at the same time, hearing Sherman and Sammy relate the tale of Dremmil.

"Which one is he?" Linda asks.

"Try not to look at him too much," Sammy warns.

"How can I not look at him if I don't know which one he is?" Linda says.

Sherman interjects, "He's not around right now. I'll point him out when he's nearby, but like Sammy said, we don't want them to know we have any ties or even a friendship with Dremmil. It would only arouse suspicion."

"They used to be Glarbs?" Rachel is amazed.

"They still are," replies Sherman, "Just genetically mutated."

"That's so horrible," Linda says.

"They do that to their own people?" Harry is astonished.

"Actually, it's a rather elegant solution to many of society's problems," Sherman reasons. "By deeming a portion of the population to be slaves, they solve many problems that occur in a normal society."

"Like what?" asks Sammy.

"Well, it may serve as a form of population and food control. Also, it could greatly aid industrial development. Slaves don't have to be paid. Nor do they qualify for any perks—no workers comp, no Medicare or insurance of any kind. Totally free labor. They don't even have to be fed more than necessary. They are forced to do the lowest level jobs that others don't want to do. If they're sick or injured, they could even be killed off if they are of no more use."

The group is silent thinking about this. This planet is truly reprehensible. A prime example of what absolute power, greed, and the lack of moral values could lead to.

Sherman speaks up again, "We also had our period of slavery in the 1800's. And as a matter of fact, it isn't really too much different from the caste system in India right now. The slaves here are maybe still a bit above the untouchables in India."

Chapter 48

The next day, on the construction site, provides an opportunity for Sherman and Sammy to work alongside Dremmil. They're even able to talk once in a while. Dremmil sidles up to Sherman, and in a low whisper, says, "There are many of us who would gladly fight for our lives given the chance. If only there was some hope of ever being able to fight without these damn implants. We probably wouldn't win, but we would go out trying. It would be good enough."

"It would be suicide," says Sherman.

"But at least it would be over," says Dremmil. "We can't even attack because there's too many of them, and even if we get one they'll just torture us long and hard by turning on the juice. And they wouldn't kill us. They would just shock us for fun over and over and laugh. And all we can do is scream in agony. Given the chance, we would all rather die than continue like this—but we can't even get the chance."

Sherman knows what's coming. Dremmil continues.

"I have not told the others yet, but if you really do have a way to deactivate these implants, you must share it with all of us. We would stand much more of a chance if we all join together."

"I am still working on a theory," Sherman starts to explain.

"*Tell me!*"

"Shhhh, don't draw attention. I'm not sure of anything just yet."

"*Please*! I heard you talking about rubbing them together before. Will that work? They get short-circuited?"

"Dremmil—quiet! You'll ruin everything. I don't know yet. First, I have to know what these implants are composed of, and better understand how they work."

"What do you mean, how they work? They shock you and damn near electrocute you."

"I mean, is there a metal alloy underneath the outer coating?"

Dremmil has never thought about that.

"I'm not sure."

"Can we find out?"

"It would be risky," Dremmil considers. "If they see us tampering with the implants, that's a great way to make them turn it on."

#

Rachel and Linda are inside a domesticile scrubbing the floors. Their supervisor is a large, overweight, and not too intelligent female Glarb. She looks at her two underlings, makes a decision, and points at Linda.

"You—come wid me."

Linda follows her outside. They continue walking a short distance and come to a large field. They stop at the edge of it. It's astonishingly beautiful.

Linda has never seen such exotic plants before in her life. There are tall, purple, twisting stalks interspersed with green, red, and yellow chutes and flowers. On the undergrowth, there are berries and seeds blossoming out in bunches.

Linda's boss stoops down on her knees to demonstrate the job.

"I wan' you pick 'em like dis. Look fer dis color," and she picks some red berries and puts them in a pail. Linda looks at her, but doesn't say anything or move.

"Git down here!" the Glarb yells.

Linda quickly gets down beside her and begins picking berries.

"No, dis color!" her boss yells at her, and again shows her the bright red berries are the ones to be picked.

Linda picks the right ones and puts them in the pail. Despite being yelled at, Linda feels good kneeling on the soil and getting her hands dirty. The soil feels unusually soft, even therapeutic. Picking berries isn't such a bad job after all.

Her boss finally leaves, but not before instructing Linda that there are five more pails she must fill before she can take a break. Linda begins picking berries and putting them in the first pail.

As she reaches in deep to pick the best fruit, she can't help but notice again how soft the Glarb dirt is. Something about it is alluring. It seems like it's been freshly tilled. It seems like it would feel good to stick her hands down into it. She does so, and feels...something.

Linda isn't sure what she's feeling, but senses a vibration in the soil. Not unpleasant, no, not unpleasant at all. She pulls her hand out and places it, palm down, on the soft dirt. Something is strange. It feels like some sort of vibration is going on in the soil.

Linda is on her hands and knees, looking down at the ground, when all of the sudden she notices a spot that starts to cave in, like a small sinkhole. And then, all the dirt caves in, and she sees a small, furry creature burrowing its way to the top. She jumps back in surprise.

The animal cautiously peers around outside the hole it just dug, not anxious yet to leave the safety of it. It has white/gray fur. It looks soft and surprisingly clean, and has a curious/friendly face, kind of like a hamster. It twitches its whiskers, looks at Linda, then scurries back down into the hole.

Linda is intrigued. What just happened? That creature was adorable. What was it? A rodent of some sort? But it was cute, and seemed to be friendly. Linda has good intuition with animals. She has a feeling that this one was unique in some way—very intelligent, almost as if it knew something.

Linda wants it to come back out. It made her feel good. She makes little calling noises to it.

"Here, little bunny thing...come on up...there's some nice berries you can eat."

Linda drops a berry down the hole. It wiggles around, and then falls through and hits something below.

It fell on the creature's head. Linda thinks she hears munching noises.

Somebody is really enjoying that berry. Then she sees two bright, large eyes. She drops down another berry. The little creature is right there. She hears it. But it is too cautious to come out.

Linda moves back a little bit to give it more space, and continues picking berries. After a couple of minutes, it pops its head out and looks around. It spots Linda and tilts its furry little head sideways, as if it is analyzing something.

Linda smiles. The creature makes a purring noise.

It comes all the way out now, sniffing the ground, keeping its eyes on Linda. It's furry, about the size of a ferret, maybe a little bigger, and has big eyes. It hops a little here and there, and then, ever so cautiously, approaches Linda's outstretched hand with the berry in it.

It darts out its little paws and quickly snatches the berry from her hand. Then it moves back a little, sits on its hind legs, and eats its prize. Upon finishing its snack, it plops back down and returns to all fours, looking at Linda. Maybe it's wondering if there is another snack coming? It turns its head sideways again, looking directly into Linda's eyes—almost as if it wants to tell her something.

Linda smiles. She wants to hold it.

She picks a big, plump, juicy berry and holds it up for her new friend to see. Then she sits back cross-legged, and places the berry on her lap.

The furry, little animal really wants that berry, but is not about to jump up on Linda's lap. It whines a little. "Give it to me" it seems to say.

"Come on, little cutie—you can do it. Look, here's another one." Now Linda has two berries on her lap.

This is too much to resist. It hops back and forth, back and forth, and then right up on her lap to get its treat. As the creature eats, it purrs.

Linda strokes its back, and then its head. It's funny, but she is feeling almost happy. Petting this animal, and having it purr on her lap, is a very good feeling. Somehow, the creature gives off comfort, and empathy, and warm feelings.

Linda has made a friend here, on the alien world of Glarb. Surely if a creature like this can exist on this planet, maybe the planet isn't all bad?

It tilts its furry little head up, and continues to look right at Linda, who can't help but smile. She gives it another berry, and it happily munches on it.

"Well, cutie-pie, I think if we're going to be friends, I'll have to give you a name. Hmmmm...what would be a good name for you?"

Linda ponders this, then comes up with it. She holds its head and smiles, "I think I shall call you...Jibly. Yes, I think that will do quite nicely."

Jibly looks up and seems to agree.

Chapter 49

It is the day of Harry's first fight. His opponent, Lingus the "Weed", is a very tall, green creature. Lingus is stringy, almost gaunt, and stands with a constant hunch. He looks a little like a weed, but scary—somewhat sinister. His appearance is, unfortunately, his greatest asset. Although his looks may influence the betting, it hasn't fazed Harry. He has seen Lingus train, and knows his skills are weak.

The fights all take place in a large, outdoor arena that is currently filled with several thousand screaming, blood-thirsty Glarbs, shrieking for their favorite. The Glarbs are absolutely over-the-top with excitement. This is what they live for. The tournament is sure to give them many gory scenes, much screaming, many deaths.

The betting has been a frenzy of ever-changing odds, always favoring the "Weed." Lingus is impressive to look at, being so tall. However, Torka, like Harry, knows better.

Torka knows that his fighter is highly skilled compared to Lingus—it shouldn't even be close. He has bet the maximum that he was allowed to on Harry. The betting structure for the fights permits the trainers to wager only so much, so that nobody gets cleaned out before reaching the next few rounds of the tournament. Gritzel learned by past tournaments that this measure is necessary in order to have plenty of money going around by the time of the finals.

All contestants, including Harry, have had their implants removed and replaced with a metal collar around their necks. The collar serves the same purpose as the implants, but delivers less voltage. This way, if they need to turn on the juice for whatever reason, the fighter can still recover after a moment and the fight can continue. Also, it's amusing to the Glarbs to see the combatants grab the collar of their opponents and hurl them down to the ground, or swing them around by their necks. That really invokes shrieks of delight from the sadistic audience.

Torka has scouted the "Weed" and given Harry a variety of holds and escapes to use against such a tall opponent. Harry is quite confident of his own abilities, and of winning this first match. His goal is not just to win, but to get through it uninjured and, if possible, without killing his opponent.

Harry and the "Weed" square off against each other, ready for battle. The "Weed" tries to intimidate Harry, grimacing down at him from his lofty height. It doesn't work. Harry's face is completely neutral, he doesn't look either excited or concerned.

Now *that* scares Lingus. You don't want a nonchalant opponent. Lingus was hoping to see fear in Harry's eyes. He moves in on Harry and raises two thin arms up menacingly, as if he's going to crush anything standing before him.

The "Weed" does his best to look like a giant, mean, crushing machine. But Harry doesn't see it that way. He sees the science of it.

Lingus has exposed himself for a clean shot to the mid-section. But Harry doesn't take it. Instead he deftly ducks under Lingus' long arms, and steps around to his side. He snakes both of his arms around Lingus' body, extends his foot, and trips him backwards.

From there, Harry has Lingus securely dominated in side-control. In an instant he has eliminated his opponent's primary advantage, the reach. The "Weed" squirms and flails wildly, not knowing how to get out, and quickly growing tired.

The Glarbs are loving it.

"Get him! Pound him! Kill him!" they shout, rooting for their favorite.

Torka is quiet. He sees his fighter do everything he was taught. Harry is not even breathing hard, while Lingus is going crazy, kicking at the air, waving his arms trying to punch—all for naught. Torka wants to tell Harry not to end it too early, but there are no rounds, no breaks, just one continuous fight.

Harry has a soft spot for Lingus and almost feels sorry for him. He saw him being tortured by his trainer one time, and then later, saw him shivering (crying?) by himself when Lingus didn't realize Harry was nearby.

Harry knows they are all in the same boat—being forced to fight. Even if Lingus survives their match, he may still get punished if he doesn't put on a good show.

Harry lets up for a moment and the "Weed" escapes from side mount. The crowd cheers wildly. Maybe the "Weed" can make a comeback?

Lingus jumps to his feet, mostly out of breath by now, but proud that he got out. Now he's going to show this human who's boss.

Harry lets Lingus throw a few blows, blocks all of them, and then rushes in and takes his opponent down to the ground again. This time he goes for one of Lingus' feet and secures it under his armpit, placing his right arm below the leg, and grasping his right wrist in his left hand from above the leg. Harry knew this move even before Torka taught it to him. On Earth it's known as a Kimura lock. Harry then arches back, putting tremendous leverage and pressure on Lingus' foot.

The "Weed" howls in pain.

They were taught not to stop fighting until somebody either dies or Gritzel stops the fight. Neither takes place, so Harry keeps at it.

Harry continues to stretch all the tendons and tissues in the "Weed's" foot and winces at the screaming. But he knows, although it hurts like hell, nothing is breaking or damaged too much. This lock is one of the milder and less devastating holds, plenty of immediate pain, but no real injuries.

"Come on Weed, get out!" his supporters yell.

But the "Weed" is completely captured and secured. Harry has the hold locked in perfectly.

After a minute of no more action other than Lingus' screams, his trainer throws a skull in the ring, the symbol of submission. Gritzel then steps in and stops the fight. The shouting from the crowd is a mixture of cheers and boos as the money begins to exchange hands.

"Yer dun great!" Torka beams.

Harry doesn't care too much to be congratulated by his trainer. He'd rather rip his throat out. But such is the situation he's in. He tries to remain looking neutral.

Torka looks down at him, "Youse all gonna eat gud tonight," Torka says.

Chapter 50

Harry and friends congregate later that day, sharing their stories over an excellent dinner. Torka was exceedingly pleased with Harry's performance, and they all benefit from that. A special cart was once again brought to them. It contained some kind of animal meat, like beef, and Glarb vegetables, and was very good. There was even a tasty potato type of vegetable. Good meals have a wonderful effect upon our captive friends and their spirits are lifted.

Harry has been relating the details of his first match.

"Oh, Harry, I'm so happy you were able to win, and without really hurting him," Rachel says.

"Oh, I hurt him plenty, but not anything lasting. He'll be okay."

"I almost feel guilty about eating this wonderful meal, knowing that someone had to suffer for it," Linda says.

"I don't," says Sammy.

"Me either," says Sherman, "Would you rather Harry lost and someone else gets to eat like this?"

Just then, an odd noise is heard coming from Linda. They all look at her. She is fidgeting and squirming. And then, suddenly, out pops Jibly from Linda's top.

Linda had hidden him the entire day and smuggled him back into their compound underneath her clothes. She had meant to tell the others, but Harry's story was so engaging she had almost forgotten that Jibly was there.

"Prrrrrrr, prrrrrrr..."

Jibly emits that delightful call of his, and coos softly from Linda's cleavage.

Everyone is shocked, but at the same time, immediately captivated. Who is this new creature?

"Oh, my!" says Rachel, "Well, who's this?"

A rare smile comes to Linda's face as she reaches in and brings Jibly out. There he sits in her hands, his friendly face peering out, regarding all of them with much interest. His whiskers are twitching, and his large eyes seem to shine with some kind of hidden wisdom.

Even Sherman is affected by Jibly's charm. Nevertheless, the dangers of smuggling an animal into their compound could have serious consequences. Sherman scolds Linda.

"Linda, are you crazy? You can't smuggle in an animal. If they catch us with some type of pet they'll more than likely kill it, and at the least, make us pay for it!"

Sherman is right, of course, and they all know it. Still, even after having met Jibly for only a moment, it's long enough to know that they don't want to part with him. Somehow, Jibly seems to be on their side. He gives off a feeling of comfort, and hope. As long he is alive, they still have a chance.

But of course losing him to the Glarbs would be devastating, even at this early point. They need to keep him, but absolutely keep it a secret, even from the other prisoners. Is this really possible?

Sherman continues to argue the point.

"It's not worth risking this creature's life, and all of our lives. We don't have any evidence he's going to help us, anyway."

"Oh, come on, Sherman!" Rachel exclaims. "Can't you feel it? He belongs in our group. He's one of us, in a way."

"You mean a kidnapped being from another galaxy, snatched from his ship while passing through?"

"I'm telling you, Sherman, and all of you, I know animals, and Jibly is on our side. He wants to help us, and I think eventually he will," Linda says confidently.

"How can you possibly know that?" Sherman demands.

"You know, I've gotta admit—I do feel something," Harry says. "Something good about this fellow. It's nice to have him around."

"I know what you're talking about," Sammy agrees.

"So do I," says Rachel.

Jibly coos again.

A ripple of calm washes over all of them. They are fine for the moment. But in an instant that changes. Jibly's presence is wonderful, but he also seems to bring with him a splash of what may come.

First, there's the soothing nature of his call, but it also leaves an aftertaste of a glimpse of a future that might be. Linda feels it the most.

She senses a feeling of impending danger. Something bad is going to happen—something really, really bad. And it could be life-ending for all or most of them, unless everything plays out just perfectly.

A wave of perception envelopes the group, as each one of them receives flashes, images in their mind, of events that could unfold in the near future.

Rachel sees Harry walking, when suddenly, a black and endless abyss opens up in the ground before him. He turns and tries to run the other way. But a giant, black hand reaches right out of the chasm and grabs him. She hears him scream as it takes him away—down, down far away to Nothing Land.

Linda sees troops and troops of fierce, loathsome, Glarbs hunting down and killing everything in their path. Ripping apart their own world, if need be, in order to ensure the Glarb way of life stays as it is.

Harry sees...nothing. He is somewhere else. It is black. He is totally confined, and, dying. He can't hear or see anything at all, and the air is quickly running out. It is a terrifying thought.

Sammy senses a long, downward plunge that never ends. He is falling into an endless pit.

Sherman sees his Hyperspace equations come alive, jump off of the whiteboard, and wrap themselves around his legs, then his body, then his neck. He is being asphyxiated by his own physics.

The phenomenon passes as quickly as it had formed, and leaves the gang disillusioned and confused. But the experience does not lessen their appreciation, nor their fondness, for this new creature.

The gang decides to keep Jibly on a trial basis. At the first sign of anything amiss, they will let him fend for himself outside the compound. Although they have a feeling, even if that were so, Jibly would still remain near. And, they have also decided to tell Dremmil about Jibly.

Dremmil is their ally. He had pleaded with Sherman to reveal his latest theories about the implants, but when Sherman flatly refused, had stopped asking immediately without a fuss. Dremmil also has a universal translator. It would be much easier to let the other prisoners know about Jibly and keep it under wraps, than to try and hide his existence completely. Dremmil could spread the word that Jibly was to be kept secret, and relay the plans to the other prisoners when they were ready to band together and make their move.

Oppression has always been a great catalyst in bringing people together.

Chapter 51

Gritzel, the Esteemed Leader, is in his office looking over some paperwork.

"Kirzul—tell Ditzin to come in here."

A few minutes later there's a knock at his door.

"Enter."

Ditzin steps into his office.

"Sit down, Ditzin."

He takes a seat.

"Which of the earthlings have been processed so far?"

Uh, oh, trouble.

"Um, none of them, sir, as far as I know."

"None of them, Ditzin? Did I hear you right?"

Damn it, he forgot.

"Uh—yeah—well, I was going to start tomorrow."

"Tomorrow? Oh were you Ditzin? You were just about to start tomorrow? And it's just coincidence that I brought you in today to talk about it?"

This could go really bad. He better confess.

"Um, well, I guess I just forgot."

"You forgot. I see, you forgot."

Gritzel is now pacing up and down with his head down. "Well, everybody forgets now and then, I suppose."

Ditzin feels something coming, and he doesn't know how to stop it. He remains quiet.

"As a matter of fact, I feel a bout of forgetfulness coming on myself. Yes, I think I do. I may even forget to feed you Ditzin—*for about a week!*"

This is no idle threat. It is the kind of thing the Glarbs would enforce, and Ditzin knows it. Ditzin is looking down at the floor. He needs to defend himself.

"I'mmmm...........mmmm...mmmmm" he can't even get the words out. He is scared of the consequences of saying the wrong thing, and of not saying anything. Gritzel gets up and walks over to him. Ditzin is visibly shaking now. Gritzel gets right in his face.

"NO MORE SLIP-UPS, UNDERSTAND?"

"Yes, sir," Ditzin says weakly.

"If this happens again, Ditzin, you're going to find yourself wearing the implants and joining them," Gritzel threatens. "*Now get out, and do your job!*"

Ditzin makes a hasty retreat. He can only hope he gets to eat something in the next few days.

Chapter 52

The next day starts out the same as all the previous days. Harry goes off to train, Linda and Rachel to clean, and Sherman and Sammy go to toil under the hot Glarb sun. The novelty of their situation is starting to wear off on Sherman. The reality of what their life has become is sinking in. Sherman has begun longing for home just as much as the others by now.

Sammy, Sherman, and the other construction prisoners are marched along the street, chained together by the waist, to start another day of labor. The Glarb soldiers are split, half of them walking at the front of the line, while the rest bring up the rear. They keep a close eye on their prisoners, looking for an infraction so that they can press their coveted remotes.

It's practically impossible to get away with any conversation, but Sherman can tell that Dremmil wants to talk. Sherman keeps hearing "Psssst, Mr. Hollingsworth," behind him. He wisely chooses not to turn around. After all, his name is Doctor Hollingsworth, not Mister. After a while, Dremmil gives up, just as one of the soldiers is coming up behind him. The soldier thought he heard something and marches alongside the center of the line, listening, but hears nothing now. Finally, the group reaches their destination.

After everyone is assigned their task and begins work, Dremmil manages to sidle up next to Sherman.

"Mr. Hollingsworth?"

Sherman gives him a look.

"I mean Dr. Hollingsworth—look what I've got," he exclaims.

Dremmil shows him a scrap of metal with a pointy edge. Sherman knows what it's for.

"Put that away—are you crazy?" Sherman scolds him.

"Yes. To get out—yes—anything."

"Dremmil, I know what you're thinking of trying, but it's only a theory at this point. It may just as well not work, or need some tweaking before it does."

"No matter. It is a hope, a chance, maybe our only one? We don't mind dying—only that we've tried."

The sincerity of Dremmil's spirit is not lost on Sherman. Nevertheless, he doesn't want his friend testing the theory prematurely. He must finish his analysis and be confident that his idea will work. He had promised the crew that he would adhere to tighter principles before releasing his latest physics masterpiece on them again. For God's sake, his last one skipped them over to the next galaxy.

"Please, wait until I'm finished with my analysis."

"How long?" Dremmil asks.

"I'll let you know."

"But we..."

Just then a guard turns their way and they quickly shut up. But did he hear something? He starts walking towards them.

Dremmil and Sherman had stopped talking just in time, and the soldier hears nothing. But he continues to linger around their area, looking for rule-breakers. He takes out his remote and holds it in his hand, looking around, ready to press it at the slightest provocation.

Sherman and Dremmil don't dare make eye contact. They both look down and seem to be very focused on their job. But inside Sherman's head, his thoughts are going a mile a minute. He *must* figure out the secret to unlocking these implants, and fast. He feels that time is short before Dremmil, or one of the others, starts to make desperate attempts at escaping, and ruins their long-term chances.

Chapter 53

The slimy Morling slashes its tail at Harry's feet, hoping to trip him. Harry had been warned about that tail and jumps over it.

The Morling growls, and comes straight at him. Its claws are open, ready to scratch.

Harry grabs it at the wrist and twists the limb the opposite way. The beast howls in pain and goes right to the ground, twisting and turning, desperately trying to relieve the pressure.

Harry steps over the wrist lock, putting even more pressure on, and the Morling tries to roll away. The second its back is turned to Harry, he releases the wrist and snaps on a deadly choke hold. The audience has seen this before and knows it's the end.

The Glarbs howl and cheer, as the lights go out for the Morling. His trainer throws the skull into the ring, hoping to stop the fight before his gladiator dies. Harry is so far, undefeated.

Harry has been winning and Torka has been getting rich. As Harry gets out of the ring, Torka approaches him, grinning that sick grin of his.

"Yerz been doin' great!"

Harry nods.

"Yer gonna getz to the finalz fer shure. I 'havenz told yer yet but I'm tellin' ya now...th' winner getz ta go home."

Harry looks at Torka, not sure of what he just heard.

"Yer heard me right, slave. Th' fighting iz never so gud az when we letz th' winner and hiz group go home fer the prize. All of yer frenz will be releazed wid ya—but only if yerz winz."

Wow! This is it. Here's the escape he was waiting for. Harry is overjoyed, but somewhat skeptical. Can it be true?

"Really? You'll release us and let us get back to our ship?"

"Only if yerz winz, slave. Yerz better keep it up."

Harry can't wait to tell the news to his pals.

#

Later that evening, Harry is relating the good news to his friends.

"My God, that's absolutely wonderful!" Linda exclaims.

"Yes, but can it really be true?" asks Rachel.

"There's no way of really knowing," says Sherman.

"Torka said the fights are always better when the prize is freedom," Harry says. "He seemed sincere, but he could also be lying. It's hard to tell."

Jibly is in Linda's arms. His eyes shine brightly with intelligence. He chirps a happy note.

"Jibly seems to think so," Linda says.

They all share a short laugh at that. One of the rare times laughter or happiness is ever heard from a compound.

Sammy asks Sherman, "What's going on with your idea about shorting out the implants, Sherman?"

"We don't have to worry about that anymore, do we?" asks Linda.

"Of course we do. First of all, Harry has to win to free us," says Sherman.

"And even if I do, we don't really know if Torka can be trusted to keep his word," Harry finishes.

"And it would be nice to let the other prisoners know if there is a way to escape," offers Rachel.

Rachel's thoughtfulness is not lost on Harry. He was thinking the exact same thing, and just about to say it.

He is very happy that if he is kidnapped on an alien planet, he has his woman with him. Well, kind of. He's not happy that she joined him in being a slave on another planet, of course. But very happy to have her near, still healthy, still beautiful, still thoughtful and considerate of others. And still tough as nails when need be, like now. He absolutely has to win their freedom from this planet.

Sherman continues, "Anyway, I'm pretty sure if we were to hold a metal scrap to the exposed metal plate while the implant is activated, it would short out. But you would have to insulate your hand somehow. You would need a thick cloth, or resistant material to clutch the metal piece with. I know Dremmil is anxious to try it, but I need to devise a way we can test it without giving up our plan."

Chapter 54

The next day, while Sammy and Sherman are working, they spot Dremmil carrying a very large load of materials. Not only is this unsafe for a variety of reasons, it bears no fruit whatsoever. There is no reason to do your job faster, or better. You are not rewarded in any way.

On the contrary, you are punished whenever something goes wrong, like dropping things, or doing the job wrong. You may be whipped, or breaks taken away, or food withheld, but 90% of the time it's turning on the juice. It's just so easy for the Glarbs to point that remote at you and push the button. And it seems to give them so much joy.

As Sherman considers this, he gets a dreadful premonition of what's to come. Oh, no! Dremmil must have overheard their conversation last night. He's going to get shocked on purpose just to test Sherman's idea.

At the same that Sherman comes to this conclusion, he hears a loud crash. There Dremmil stands—looking guilty. Everything he was carrying is all spilled around him. Two Glarbs are rushing over.

Through the translator, Sherman and Sammy hear, "You careless fool! You idiot! What are you doing carrying all this at one time?"

"He must think he's really strong," the other guard says.

"I think he's really stupid," says the first guard.

"No," pleads Dremmil, "not the juice, please!"

Instead, the guard smacks Dremmil on the back of his legs with a billy club type of stick, "Pick it up now! And carry it in two loads."

The disappointment on Dremmil's face is clear to see. And there's something else, that is not so easy to see.

"He's hiding something in his left hand," Sherman says to Sammy.

Dremmil picks up half the load, starts walking, then purposely trips and falls, making a real mess.

"That's it!" cries the guard as he points the remote at Dremmil.

"No, please, AAAUUUGGGGHHH!"

Dremmil is down on the ground, in agony, but manages to keep his back turned to his tormentors. Sherman and Sammy watch spellbound, as they see him rubbing the metal implant on his thigh over and over while flailing away, trying to keep his back to the Glarbs. He is testing Sherman's theory.

Finally, the Glarb eases off the button, scolds him again, and leaves Dremmil to pick up his mess. Dremmil is hurting, no doubt. But he managed to conceal what he was doing—testing Sherman's theory. Did it work?

The guards allow Sammy and Sherman to rush over to Dremmil. They pick him up and get him back on his feet. Dremmil is frustrated, angry, and still hurting from the after-effects of *the juice*. He scowls at Sherman and says, "It didn't work!"

Sherman's idea is busted.

"I'm sorry," Sherman says.

But while helping Dremmil up, Sherman takes a good, long look at Dremmil's implant. Dremmil was successful in sawing off the thin outer coating, displaying the shiny metal beneath. It was what Sherman hoped to see.

And even better, Sherman notices how thin the coating is on top of the metal. Seeing this, he is now working on his second theory, when just then, a guard marches right over to Sammy and demands, "Sammy McPearson—come with me. Ditzin wants to see you."

#

Sammy is led to a motorized vehicle with 3 wheels. It is the standard transportation other than walking. He is chained with his hands behind his back, and put into the backseat. The soldier drives to a large facility and stops in front of a well-kept and tall building. He lets Sammy out, and says, "Follow me."

As they walk inside the building, the guard instructs Sammy to take the stairs to the top (3rd) floor. Sammy does so, with the guard following him. Once he reaches the top, the guard commands, "Step aside."

He then leads Sammy down a corridor, finally stopping at an office, and he opens the door.

"Go!" and he gives Sammy a little push. Sammy stumbles, but manages not to fall.

There stands Ditzin, waiting for him.

"You are Sammy McPearson?"

"Yeah."

"You must be processed."

"What does that mean?"

"It means you sit down over there, put on the helmet, and we read your brain and take the data."

"What data?" Sammy asks.

"About your planet, your culture, things like that," Ditzin answers. He is one of the few Glarbs, maybe the only one, who will put up with questions and treats the prisoners with a morsel of kindness.

"How about if I just tell you?"

"This way is faster. Sit over there. It is painless."

This placates Sammy a little bit. But he still doesn't like getting his brain scanned. Sammy is placed on a chair, strapped in, and puts on the helmet. Ditzin then attaches electrodes to the helmet, and connects the wires to the brain scanning machine.

Sammy grimaces as it is turned on, but he only feels a slight tingling sensation. It is not painful, although it is very invasive. For over an hour the Glarb brain scanner reads Sammy's memories and stores them into the device. Finally, it is over. Sammy is sleepy. He is unstrapped and led back to work.

#

Later that evening Sammy is relating his experience to the rest of the group.

"I din't feel anything happening 'cept for a tingling sensation inside my head. But I hated it. I don't know exactly what they got but I felt... exposed."

Sherman is fascinated.

"I wonder why they started with you? No offense, but my brain probably has a lot more to offer."

The group looks at him. Sherman has done it again. He just says whatever he thinks. He is blatantly honest, but completely lacks normal social graces.

"Believe me, Sherman, I would gladly have switched places with you."

"Maybe your turn will be next?" says Harry.

"I certainly hope so," Sherman replies, not understanding the arrogance he has displayed.

"Oh, wait, no I don't hope so. But...I can't decide. I kind of like my brain analyzed—I'm not sure."

"It's out of your hands, Sherman," Rachel remarks. "Personally, I hope they never get to me."

"Me too," says Linda and Harry.

"I don't want them to know how much I'd like to get my hands around Torka's throat," Harry says, gesturing with his hands how he'd squeeze the life out of him.

"Oh, I think he probably knows that already."

"Yeah, I guess so. But if I win my next fight I'm in the finals. And if I win that, maybe it's home for all of us?"

"Oh, that would be so fantastic!" Linda joins in.

"If we can take Torka at his word," says Sherman. "I'm afraid I have some bad news about my implant theory."

Sammy almost forgot.

"What happened to Dremmil?"

Sherman tells the group about Dremmil's attempt to short-circuit his implants. They are all wide-eyed and then, extremely disappointed. They surreptitiously look around the camp to spot him.

"I don't think he's here tonight," Sherman says. "I haven't seen him since the incident."

"Maybe he needed medical treatment?" Rachel asks.

"Maybe. Or maybe he's being punished further?"

"Just for dropping something?"

"Well, they might have seen him sawing away at his implants with that metal scrap. I'm not sure."

The group is quiet for a moment.

"Sherman, does this mean that there's no escape from these implants?" asks Linda.

"No. Just that rubbing a piece of metal to the exposed metal plate didn't work."

"So then, we all hafta hope that Harry keeps winning and Torka keeps his word?" asks Sammy.

"Well, no, I still have another theory."

"Which is what?" Rachel asks.

"If two metal plates were touching each other at the same time they were activated; that is to say, if the exposed metal in two implants were rubbing against each other, I'm pretty sure both implants would short out."

The group is quiet—another Sherman theory. Sounds great, but who knows?

"We can't bend like that," Rachel says, as she bends over trying to get her shoulder implant to touch her upper thigh implant.

"We would have to pair off," Linda says. "We couldn't do it just by ourselves."

"Right," Sherman agrees.

"What if you're wrong?" asks Harry. "What if it possibly increases the shock and gets us killed?"

"It's highly unlikely that it would increase the shock," says Sherman. "You might see some sparks, but the voltage should be the same. Actually, I'm pretty sure it would really work this time. But testing it would be very difficult."

"Very," agrees Rachel.

They all think about this.

"Don't worry," says Harry. "I'll win my next two fights and then maybe Torka will keep his word?"

They can only hope for the best.

#

When they turn in for the night, Linda cuddles up with Jibly. He has been a wonderful addition to their group—a constant force of good feelings. Nevertheless, Linda's sleep is troubled.

She dreams of being home on Earth and riding her horse, Gopher. He's such a silly horse, always sticking his nose in the ground. Linda has quite a few pets, and misses all of them dearly.

Then she dreams of Harry fighting for his life. And, there is Jibly, tunneling through the ground, looking for something.

Something bad has happened.

Something horrible that has affected all of them.

Chapter 55

The next day, at the construction site, Sherman and Sammy see Dremmil back at work. He looks okay. But when Sherman makes eye contact with him, Dremmil grimaces and mouths the words, *it didn't work.*

Later on, the guards leave the prisoners to work unwatched for a short time. Dremmil comes over to Sherman. Sherman can tell that he's upset. Dremmil forgoes the usual "Dr. Hollingsworth" and calls Sherman by his first name.

"Sherman, you saw what happened, it didn't work at all. I practically got electrocuted! Nothing short-circuited like you said it would!"

"I'm sorry, Dremmil. I never told you to try it. I told you to wait."

"For how long? We've got to make our move already."

"These theories can't be rushed. We have to be sure."

"Well the only thing we can be sure of is that you don't know what you're talking about!"

"There is a way to deactivate the implants, I'm sure of it. I think if two implants were touching each other on the exposed metal, and they were both activated at the same time, they would both short out," Sherman says confidently.

"How can we ever test..." Sammy starts, but they all shut up quickly. The guards have returned and one of them is looking right in their direction. The guard approaches them with his hand poised over the button and the remote device pointed right at them.

"Shut up and work faster!"

The three of them immediately get to work. They are shaken up. They just barely escaped the juice.

Sherman's awe and wonder for this journey have totally worn off by now. He can't stand this planet any longer. They've got to get out.

#

Harry is in a battle, fighting for his life.

His opponent outweighs him, and is on top of him. He is being crushed. It is getting tougher and tougher. But he must win to get to the finals, and then, hopefully, freedom.

His opponent looks like a gremlin, or goblin of some sort. He is large and fierce, and has rotting teeth (fortunately) which makes his bite less effective, but his limbs are strong and agile. He is known as "Bone Crusher", or Crusher for short.

Harry is on his belly while his opponent sits on his back, but he manages to turn on his side, and then finally, roll over. Now his back is on the ground and his opponent is sitting on Harry's belly. Torka had taught him to avoid, at all costs, showing his back to his opponent, even if you're on the ground. You must always be facing your adversary.

He places both his hands on his opponent's large thigh, turns a little on his side, and tries to scoot out. This protrudes him maybe six inches, so that instead of Bone Crusher sitting on top of his belly, he now sits on Harry's waist.

Just before Crusher swings at him, Harry can now sit up a little and blocks the punch. Harry lays back down on the ground, turns and can scoot out just a bit more. Then Crusher tries for a bite, giving Harry the escape he was looking for. Harry arches up and Crusher falls forward. Harry snakes out through Crusher's straddled legs, then quickly side mounts his opponent.

The crowd shrieks their delight. This is a great fight!

Crusher tries to roll out, and mistakenly exposes his long, crooked, limb which Harry snatches to his chest. He then props up his left leg over Crusher's neck, his right leg over his body, and extends Crusher's arm straight while lowering himself to the ground and raising his hips.

The pain mounts for Crusher, as his arm is forced to bend the wrong way. This is a painful and deadly submission hold. Torka looks on, pleased as punch. Crusher is in tremendous pain, and looks to his trainer to throw in the skull.

But there is no rescue from his trainer, only shouts of "Get out of that! You are Bone Crusher, nobody can beat you! I've got a lot riding on yer!"

Harry extends Crusher's arm further and inches his hips higher. Crusher's arm can take no more. The sound of his joints is now evident as his arm prepares to break and Crusher's screams become panicky.

Just then, a skull is finally thrown into the ring, signaling a forfeit, and Harry releases the hold. He has damaged and hurt Crusher, but his arm was saved from being broken.

It was a brutal, devastating fight, and Harry has won again.

"Yer going to the finals, champ!" Torka beams.

Later that day, back at the camp, Harry tells everyone about his victory. He only has one more fight to win, and then they will all be set free, if Torka can be believed.

"Oh, Harry, that's wonderful. I knew you could do it!" exclaims Rachel.

"You're truly wonderful, Harry," Linda agrees.

"Congratulations," says Sherman.

"Way to go, Harry," Sammy says.

"It looks like we're really going to get out of here, thanks to you," and Rachel hugs him.

Harry basks in their praise. The whole group is elated. This is the best they have ever felt since they arrived, and he is truly their hero. He just hopes he can win his next match and that Torka will keep his word.

"Oh, Harry, do you think there's any way they might let us go to root you on?"

"Probably not, Rach."

"Why don't you tell Torka that it gives you added strength and encouragement? After all, it's in his own best interest that you win."

Harry considers that.

"You're right. I guess it wouldn't hurt to ask?"

If he had his friends at his side, that *would* help. Of course, he would be fighting his hardest anyway. The stakes are so incredibly high. But, who knows, maybe having your friends cheer you on in the audience could add something?

"When are the finals, Harry?" Linda asks.

"I don't know yet, but they'll tell me tomorrow."

Tomorrow can't come soon enough.

Chapter 56

Kluco, the fantastic robot pilot, wonders how he could have avoided this terrible situation. He has a lot of time to ponder this, and anything else. He has gone over the entire scenario which led to them being captured. He doesn't see any mistakes on his part. It is really Sherman's fault, and those at NASA, who decided to allow Sherman so much freedom to modify his hyperspace equations. But he really can't blame them.

There's no denying that Sherman is brilliant. Kluco has read all about the prodigy that is Dr. Hollingsworth. It's just that, sometimes he's wrong. Then again, trying to figure out hyperspace is no easy task. And, Sammy's mass was an unknown variable. It is an extremely unfortunate happenstance that they landed in this area of space, and were plucked out of the sky by the horrible Glarbs.

Kluco has also been thinking about himself. He ponders who he is, how he came into existence, and the purpose for which he was created. He desperately wants to succeed in that purpose, this mission (and others to follow if he ever gets out of this), but does not have any better ideas than to sit tight for now.

He ponders reality. How does one know if their very existence is *real*, and not just another being's dream? And does it even matter? What if everything he and his crew perceive is just an illusion? Perhaps they are all just characters in some fantastically intelligent, and handsome creature's imagination? Maybe this is all just a story and it will resolve itself when it reaches the end?

Kluco has examined all possible outcomes of the risks in leaving his ship, and trying to rescue his friends. It's just not feasible to think that he can remain uncaptured once any Glarb sees him. But how long should he wait? He can wait a year, ten years, 50 years, a human lifetime. There must be some limit before it becomes illogical to remain. What is that limit?

Kluco has been observing all on-going activities in this airstrip field, where he remains with his vessel. Most, or all, of the ships have been searched and looted. Not much activity anymore. His counterfeit tag worked perfectly in keeping himself and his ship safe from being boarded.

Perhaps he should now conduct some surveillance of his own? Could he enter the other ships at night and snoop around without getting caught? What possible good could it do?

Kluco considers this. Well, it would enable him to further advance his knowledge of his environment and perhaps alter circumstances. Maybe something new could come out of it that would shed some new light on escaping? Yes, like...weapons.

However, it's unlikely that anything of value, like a good weapon, would still be left. But maybe there's one hidden somewhere that they didn't find? It's possible.

This train of logic has led Kluco to make a decision that there may be some value in exploring the other ships. But extreme caution must be exercised to mitigate the risks of being caught. He will only go in the middle of the night, and as quick as possible, to the adjacent ship, with minimum time being exposed. His first jaunt will be tonight.

Later that night, the time has arrived. He cautiously opens the exit ramp of the *Galaxis* and disembarks. Although his primary mode of transportation is usually rolling on his wheels, he possesses a technique to handle stairs as well. His rollers can retract and allow two legs to come out which can bend at the knee and climb. The legs are not used too often, but they are available if he needs them to climb stairs or to navigate terrain that his rollers cannot.

The ship across the strip to the right is his target. He has watched the soldiers board it, and thinks he knows how to get in. He approaches it quickly in the dark. His night vision is excellent. Kluco locates the panel, finds the right button, and presses it.

A platform materializes on the ground before him. Kluco gets on it and it proceeds to rise up. The bottom of the ship opens, and then closes beneath him as the platform disappears. Very efficient. He now stands on the bridge of the alien ship.

The bridge of this ship is quite different, although he imagines many of the controls share the same functions; such as navigation, sensors, viewport, analysis, all the things any ship would need for deep space travel.

Part of the console is damaged in one area, like something big fell on it, or in some way it got smashed. Maybe this species was able to fight them off a little before succumbing? Kluco remembers the spray they used from their belts. His crew was instantly paralyzed—couldn't walk or move. They all just stood there while the Glarbs embedded those chips into their bodies. The takeover was extremely well-orchestrated, and, obviously, the result of a process that has been executed many times.

As he makes his way through the ship, he thought he heard something coming from the back. Kluco stops and listens—nothing. Maybe there are small animals or even insects roaming about? Kluco's hearing is excellent, and he listens intently for any stray noise, but there is none. It is as quiet as a morgue.

He looks all around, doing a complete 360. Nothing.

He turns up his auditory channel to the maximum. Kluco is in complete control of modifying all his parameters to best fit the situation. Hearing a pin drop at this level would sound like a bowling bowl. He remains perfectly still, listening.

And then...he does hear something. It's so faint, it's barely detectable. Could it be a heartbeat?

It's coming from...sounds like towards the back...behind that large console. Kluco is not sure what to do. He must reason this out.

If an alien is hiding from him, then it is not a Glarb. A Glarb would have attacked him by now. So whoever it is, must be afraid of the Glarbs, and probably thinks that's who he is—unless they saw him, which is hard to do in the darkness. Kluco makes a decision, and calls out.

"Hello, is anybody there? I'm not one of them. I'm also trapped on my ship worried about my crew."

He hears a shuffling. There *is* someone here. And then, a new voice, calls out in English, "Who are you?"

"I am Captain Kluco, from Earth. Please come out. I mean no harm."

"How can I trust you?"

"I don't know. Can you see me?"

"No."

"Well, do I sound like them?"

There is a long pause, then finally, "No."

Then there are clinking sounds.

Kluco's superb eyesight then detects something. A robot, in the female form, is standing up behind the console.

She is somewhat humanoid-looking, containing two arms and legs. But her body is android-like, while her head is more human-like than Kluco's, even though she has most likely never met a human before.

"I am Tica."

"Hello, Tica, I am Captain Kluco, from planet Earth. Where are you from?"

"I am from the nearby star system Ledro, planet Juran, about twenty-five light years from here."

"How is it that you speak English?"

"I don't. We are communicating through one of the Glarb's translators that was lost in the fight," she holds it up for Kluco to see.

"What fight?"

"My shipmates resisted the best they could when we were first captured. But once they got the implants in, the fight was over. I didn't see it, but I viewed it later through the ship's recorders."

"How come they didn't take you?"

"I hid in the elevator shaft."

Smart, thinks Kluco. She must have been hiding there all through the looting of their ship as well.

Tica realizes that Kluco is going to be her ally.

"Is your crew still alive?" she asks. "How many are there, or were there? There are eight of us."

"I can only hope my crew is still alive. I have no way of knowing for sure. Including me, there are six of us."

"We've got to find a way to save our crew," says Tica.

"I've been processing and trying to come up with a plan, but still don't have one that has a reasonable chance of succeeding," admits Kluco. "Maybe the two of us can think of something?"

Tica comes out and faces Kluco. It is dark, but both of them can see pretty good.

"Are you biological or robotic?" Kluco asks.

"Both. I was originally a normal Juruvian, but lost my life in an accident. I am a biochemical engineer and was working in my lab when there was an explosion. On my planet we're sometimes attacked by rebel terrorist groups, and occasionally, even the science labs are targeted. Or sometimes, the labs were hit by accident. I was actually killed, and my body was blown to bits. They were, however, able to save my brain, and successfully transferred it to this body I wear now."

"So you still have all of your memories from before the explosion?"

"Yes, completely. I only lost my body, my physical shell."

"But I was able to hear your heartbeat. How come the Glarbs couldn't detect you when they scanned for life?"

"If they scanned for sound they could have, if they were able to separate it from the other sounds, the other heartbeats, on the ship. But I have a feeling they were scanning for heat. My body gives off none."

"But why do you have a heart?"

"Our society is very advanced in what you would call cybergenics. We can mechanically mimic the Juruvian body very closely, including the heart."

Kluco is impressed. She does look much less robotic than he does. And she possesses a non-mechanical brain. Like Tica, Kluco reasons that the two of them will be allies, joining forces and increasing their chances of survival and escape.

"Were you in the elevator shaft when they returned to loot your ship?"

"Yes. I had to remain hidden while they stole everything they wanted to."

"Did they leave anything we could use as weapons?"

"No, they pretty much took everything valuable."

"How long have you been here?"

"It's been over 150 cycles. I don't know what else to do but wait and hope that at least some of my crew returns."

Kluco's excursion has yielded excellent results. Maybe if they combine their knowledge and ship's artifacts they can manufacture some kind of weapon?

"Can you show me around the rest of your ship?"

Chapter 57

Sherman and Sammy have told Dremmil about Harry's forthcoming fight, and the promise of freedom if he wins.

"They're going to let all of you go if he wins?" Dremmil asks incredulously.

"That's what Harry's trainer, Torka, told him," Sammy says.

"Don't believe it. They'll say anything to make the fights more interesting."

"We can only hope it's true," says Sherman.

But Dremmil isn't buying it. And doesn't really want it to be true.

"And what happens to the rest of us?" he asks.

Sherman doesn't want to say that nothing will have changed. But that's what he thinks. How will the fact that his crew leaves really change anything? They will just be thrilled to get away. But the cruel games and the lifestyle of the prisoners will just continue.

So instead he opts for a more diplomatic answer, which is usually not his forte.

"I don't know what will happen to the rest of you, I'm sorry," Sherman admits.

Dremmil is beginning to feel resentful and jealous. He doesn't want his new friends to leave without him. Nothing will have changed.

"Your theory didn't work at all," Dremmil reminds Sherman.

"I know," says Sherman. "But I may have something else for you."

"Another useless theory?"

"Perhaps, but then again, perhaps not. It would be very difficult to test without giving it away completely."

"What is it?" Dremmil wants to know.

"I will tell you in two days. After Harry's final fight."

"But what if I don't get to see you before you go?"

"We're bound to see each other. We aren't going to be staying anywhere else but the compound."

"Well, why can't you tell me now?"

"Because you don't listen and you'll just try it right away and possibly ruin it for all of us! You were in such a hurry to try it last time, you almost gave everything away. If they see the flaw that I found they'll just make corrections until it will be impossible to ever escape," Sherman scolds him.

Chapter 58

Kluco and Tica have been having their secret rendezvous every night for the last few days. They have been extremely cautious, and up until now, it was only Kluco who would visit Tica on her ship. Tica still possesses her original brain, after losing her body in an explosion a long time ago, and still manifests emotions, like fear.

On this night, she has finally overcome her apprehensions about leaving the safety of her ship and has boarded the *Galaxis*. Kluco is showing his new guest around the impressive vessel.

"This is Dr. Hollingsworth's room. He's the chief scientist of this expedition, as I've mentioned before. He's responsible for everything that has to do with hyperspace. It was his equations and understanding of nanophysics that made this expedition possible."

"Nanophysics?" asks Tica. "That one isn't translating."

"That's because it's a brand new line of physics that Dr. Hollingsworth recently invented."

"Oh, that sounds exciting! Do you think you can teach it to me?"

Kluco thinks about this. Would he be breaking some kind of protocol if he were to share Sherman's work with an alien?

"I'm not sure," he replies honestly. "I may be able to share the main premise, but not specific details behind it."

"Even that would be great!" Tica says.

"Okay. Well, let me finish. Anyway, this is Sammy's room. He's the stowaway I told you about. That one is Linda's room, over there is Rachel's room, and Harry's room is across, over there."

"You don't have a room for yourself?"

"I have one allocated to me, but don't really use it. I'm on the bridge most of the time," Kluco replies.

"You never sleep?"

"No."

"Do you deactivate?" Tica asks.

"Not regularly, but I can. I can set myself up for hibernation if I don't want to be aware of the passing of time and have to wait for a long time. But I don't mind being awake all the time."

"Not me," says Tica. "Since my brain is still organic, it needs rest, although a lot less now that I have this body."

"Interesting," says Kluco. "That could prove to be very useful."

"How so?"

"Because if you have limited downtime then we can both work most of the day and night, if necessary, in order to be more productive."

"But what is there to work on? I haven't come up with any reasonable idea yet to rescue my crew, and neither have you," Tica says.

"Not yet. But as time goes on the situation changes, and new paths open up. Just like I found you—now there are two of us and our chances have increased."

"Now all we have to do is find a few more thousand allies hidden in these ships," Tica says.

"Not very likely," Kluco answers, missing her sarcasm. "We have to find weapons, or the ability to manufacture them. Or something else that we haven't considered yet."

Tica sees that her new friend is always very logical. Not one for joking around. But she's very happy to have found him, and she is very impressed with the *Galaxis*.

"Can you show me your science station?" Tica asks.

Kluco leads her to the science station where Sherman works, and explains how they came to land in this area of space. Tica is fascinated.

"You jumped galaxies? My God that's fantastic!"

"Except for the fact that it deposited us here."

"Yes, but the physics behind it is extraordinary."

"It is," agrees Kluco, "thanks to Dr. Hollingsworth. But without refining our landing point, what good does it do? We can be skipping all over the universe for the rest of our lives trying to get home, and that's considering that I somehow get my crew back and escape from this planet."

Tica hears him, but is totally absorbed in studying Sherman's work on hyperspace.

"Do you mind sharing this information? Can I copy Dr. Hollingsworth's files and take them back to my ship?"

Kluco considers this. It's Tica's second request that may breach security protocol. He realizes more may be coming, and he will have to make a decision on what technologies he can share with her.

Of course, Dr. Hollingsworth's work is top secret. But they are in another galaxy. And he did agree to share information with Tica, who has held back nothing in sharing her information with him. It's possible that working together they might both improve upon Sherman's work so that if they do ever escape, they can skip back to their own galaxy, and find their way back home. Kluco still has hopes of succeeding in this mission, the mission for which he was built.

Despite the fact that he would be breaching NASA protocol, which he was meant to enforce, Kluco considers that working with Tica and sharing their science would improve their chances of escape. This is his number one priority, the safety and return of his ship and crew. It's logical to increase the chances of succeeding in any way possible.

"Yes, you may, "Kluco tells her.

#

Kluco leads her to the *Galaxis'* science laboratory, and begins to show her around. Tica is extremely interested in all of the new technologies it holds.

"What are these for?" she asks, referring to a glass cabinet storing what appears to be a stack of metal bars.

"This is part of an experiment that tests cold fusion. We can bond these metal bars together in temperatures approaching absolute zero."

"Fascinating."

Now something else has caught Tica's eye.

"Excuse me, Captain Kluco, but what is this for?" she points to a cabinet containing multiple jars with chemical symbols on them. Kluco opens the cabinet.

"That one," Tica says, pointing to a jar labeled X2Y4.

Kluco takes it out, and reads the details of the label.

"It contains a man-made chemical, xeryxium, used for spraying a protective seal on metal alloys."

"That word is not translating. What are the chemical properties?"

Kluco tells her.

"May I see it?" Tica asks, and Kluco hands her the jar. She studies it, reading the details of the label.

"Fascinating!" Tica exclaims.

"Why?"

"It uses just the right amount of stable and non-stable isotopes," Tica mutters, lost in thought.

"Just the right amount of isotopes for what?" Kluco asks.

Tica holds up her hand, she doesn't want questions now, she is thinking. A possible solution to one of their problems is forming.

Chapter 59

It is the day of the finals of the tournament. Harry is to fight his toughest opponent yet, the undefeated Horaxian, "Kraline".

The tension is so thick you could cut it with a knife. Thousands of screaming Glarbs are packed in the stadium. The odds on this fight are even.

Kraline looks like a small monster, and is closer to a female than a male. Her species is divided into three different sexes, and it takes three to mate.

She is the middle sex, maybe 60% female. Her reproductive task is to receive fertilization from the male, and then pass the egg on to the pure female for birth.

The Glarbs were not able to capture a pure male Horaxian, which is good news for Harry. But still, it is a daunting task to beat one, even 60% female.

They are small, fast, and extremely vicious. They look like gremlins. Their teeth are sharp and pointed. The females can be even more vicious than the males, although not quite as strong.

There she stands, across the ring, waiting, sneering, drooling.

She has gone through her opponents just like Harry, only much more viciously. She has killed two of them, and seriously injured most of the others.

Her trainer gave up trying to teach her the science of fighting, it just wasn't necessary. He was barely able to teach her to stop when the skull was thrown in. She zones out once the fight starts, and only knows to kill. The Glarbs kind of like that.

Harry's friends are not in attendance, although he has many supporters within the arena. They have seen him go through his opponents using superior fighting techniques, along with that great, primal strength. It is a battle between a good fighter and an absolute raving, psychotic, vicious monster.

The stakes are incredibly high. Harry fights for freedom from a life of slavery for him and his friends, and to leave this planet and return to Earth. It is the most important fight of his life.

The fight begins.

Harry takes one step towards the center of the ring, and in a split second, Kraline has crossed the ring and is right on him, slashing and biting like a bat out of hell.

He tries to block and she sinks her teeth into his arm.

It hurts like hell, and Harry's instincts take over and he jabs both his fingers into her eyes. She releases her bite and stumbles backward, shrieking like a Banshee.

The crowd roars its approval.

Harry has temporarily blinded his opponent and moves in to make the most of it. Kraline is rubbing her eyes and backing up.

Harry takes two steps towards her and tries to grab her by the neck, but she ducks out and dashes about to the other side of the ring. My God, she is quick.

Harry tries to rush her, but she races around while her eyes recover, and unbelievably, he feels another bite on his thigh. She was so quick that she got behind him and bit him before he knew what happened. Now Harry is bleeding from his arm and thigh.

The blood seems to excite her even more. Harry backs into a corner where she cannot get behind him. No matter, Kraline screeches and darts straight for him, claws ready to slash.

Just in time, Harry raises his foot and kicks the blitzing Horaxian square in the chest, sending her reeling back towards the other side of the ring.

She rights herself, and attacks again. God, she's fast! Now here comes a full frontal attack, as she launches herself, claws first, at his head.

Just in time, Harry ducks, and the screaming Horaxian goes flying out of the ring. The Glarbs throw her right back in, and this time Harry is ready.

He catches her, raises her up over his head, and smashes her to the ground. For once, this slows Kraline down. She tries to scramble and right herself, but is unsuccessful. She is hurt.

Harry tries to stomp on her neck, but it is partially blocked with her claws, and now his foot is bleeding as well. Harry resorts to a knee drop, square on her belly, knocking the wind out of her. He is on top of her now, wailing away at her face. He's going to win, he can feel it.

And then something weird happens. Her body starts to fade. She's become invisible. The Glarbs are screaming at this turn of events. This is turning out to be a fantastic show. Where did this invisible stuff come from? Kraline was always visible before. Torka glares across at Kraline's trainer, who has a big grin on his face.

That dirty cheater, Torka thinks. Kraline is fighting without a collar just so they could pull off this trick. Torka is furious—he should have noticed that, and now it's too late. Once the fight starts, it goes to completion.

Horaxians don't wear clothes, they are somewhat hairy, even the half-females, and her trainer dared to remove her collar so she couldn't be seen at all when going invisible. Her trainer was not required to release any information about this unusual talent. There's really not too many rules in the tournament. You send out two contestants and the winner is basically the one who lives.

However, all contestants are supposed to be wearing metal collars so that they can be forced to fight, or punished for not giving it their all. Kraline is a vicious and savage competitor, who took out a number of her opponents just in training. She would never be accused of not fighting hard enough.

Torka must do something to even the score. He has spent a good deal of time and wagered quite a lot of money on his slave. He watches the fight, seething with rage, absolutely hating what is happening now.

After going invisible, Kraline has managed to get another bite in, this time on Harry's arm, and then snaked out from beneath him. Then Harry is walloped in the back. He turns and tries to grab her, but gets only air. He stands up, grasping this way and that.

Suddenly he is tripped, and then kicked. He reaches out, desperately trying to get a hold of her. His only chance is to turn this fight into a grappling match, otherwise he is going to end up being a punching bag, and eventually disemboweled. But Kraline is lightning-quick and he continues to come up empty. Where is she? He stumbles around the ring throwing punches at the empty air.

Suddenly, there is a cut to his neck. He quickly grabs in that direction—nothing. He feels a sting on his leg, and a trickle of blood forms from a new scratch. Harry kicks at his invisible opponent, and again comes up empty.

The crowd is going crazy. Harry is going to lose. He can't fight what he can't see.

Kraline stomps him in the midsection and he doubles over. Then his head snaps back as she kicks him in the face.

Torka is looking at all of this with disgust, and boiling over with anger and frustration. The dirty cheat. She shouldn't be allowed to fight without a collar. And he should have noticed that before they started. Somebody should have disclosed this invisibility thing, too, it's not right.

Torka hates this with a passion because it's usually him who comes up with a cheating way to win, when necessary. He loathes being outsmarted. And he hates losing money, or bets of any kind. But Torka is not to be outdone. His evil brain comes up with a plan.

Torka's first instinct was to confront Kraline's trainer, aggressively and threateningly, and demand they put the collar on Kraline. But he knows there is no chance that will pay off. Gritzel will not stop a fight once it's started. His second idea is much more proactive. Torka makes his move.

He reaches down, grabs two handfuls of dirt in those giant mitts of his, and tosses it in the ring. He does this a few times. Some of the dirt clings to Kraline. Harry can see a faint outline of her now. That's all he needed.

Kraline is right beside him, ready to start slashing and biting, and then dart away. But this time Harry can see her. He grabs at her body, picks her up, and once more smashes her down. Then he picks her up again, this time by the feet, and smashes her head into the ground, still holding her feet.

Kraline is trying to block her head from being smashed by putting her arms up, but the third time is the charm, and Harry's smash goes completely unblocked. Her head cracks open and she is bleeding now, greenish slime is oozing out. Harry lets go.

But astonishingly, Kraline rights herself and stumbles towards him, still on the attack. She is wobbly, not so fast anymore, and her tactics no longer are working. She gets a big fist right in the face and goes down. And now Harry is on top of her, pummeling her into oblivion.

Her trainer throws the skull into the ring and rushes out. Harry and Kraline are separated. The fight is over, and it may be too late for the injured Horaxian.

Harry doesn't really care about that. He is totally exhausted, hurting, and bleeding, but ecstatic nonetheless. He has won his freedom and saved his friends. They are going home. They are going to leave this God-forsaken planet, and their lives of enslavement are now over.

Freedom—it's wonderful! Harry can't wait to celebrate with his friends.

Torka escorts him from the ring.

"Yer dun great! Nobody haz ever dun that t' her before."

"Why didn't you tell me she could go invisible?"

"Louzy cheat! They kept zat frum all uv us."

"They?"

"Her trainer knew—louzy cheat!"

"So do we get to go home now?"

"Shur, az soon az ya win th' finulz."

"I JUST DID!"

"The finulz are two dayz."

"WHAT DO YOU MEAN? THERE'S NO ONE ELSE TO FIGHT!"

"Therz me," laughs Torka.

Chapter 60

Later that evening, back at camp, Harry is telling everyone about his victory over the vicious, cheating, Horaxian. Initially, they are absolutely elated. However, he quickly gets to the part where Torka has informed him the finals aren't over, and his next match is with Torka.

"Those lousy, stinking, cheats!" Linda exclaims.

"Damn those lying, dirtbags!" says Sammy.

"The Glarbs are nothing but low-life, cheating, hoodlums!" Rachel agrees.

Everybody is mad as hell. They all feel that they should be on their way home after Harry's latest victory.

"Well, we all knew we couldn't believe them," says Sammy.

Rachel nods her head, "You're right,"

"It seemed too good to be true," Linda adds.

"I don't suppose if I beat Torka it will make a difference?" Harry wonders.

"It might," says Sherman.

"How so?"

"From what Dremmil tells me, even the Glarbs have some rules they have to obey. First of all, they don't expect anyone to beat Torka. But if somebody did, they would be held in very high esteem. The Glarbs honor brutality, viciousness, and above all, winning. Torka didn't really break his word to you."

"He did so," Rachel insists. "He never told Harry the finals were two days long with two fights!"

"And Harry doesn't really have time to recover," says Sammy, "He's been fighting non-stop while Torka is fresh."

"Oh, I'm not saying that it's fair. And it's certainly sneaky and deceptive. But Harry never asked what the finals consist of, nor how long they are."

"The *finals* mean two contestants battle it out to be the winner," Rachel says. "It's only logical."

"In our minds, yes," says Sherman. "But we just assumed their tournaments were like ours. The Glarbs all knew that the finals were two days, and it was never explained to Harry, nor did he ask."

"Whose side are you on, anyway?" asks Linda.

"Ours, of course," says Sherman, "I'm just saying that Torka still has not broken his word, and if Harry can beat him tomorrow, there's a good chance we will be going home."

"It's not tomorrow," Harry interrupts. "The finals are two days long as far as the fights go. I get two days to recover before fighting Torka."

"Then they are being somewhat fair," says Sherman. "If they really wanted to stack the deck against you they would have had you fight tomorrow."

The group is silent thinking about this. Maybe Sherman has a point?

"I think Sherman's right," Sammy says. "I think if you beat him, we're going home."

Linda is nodding her head in agreement. "I think so too."

"Me too," Rachel adds.

"Maybe you're right?" Harry says.

"Can you beat him, Harry?" asks Linda.

Harry muses to himself. Can he? After all, Torka is big and strong and knows every dirty trick in the book. But Harry's confidence has been soaring through the clouds since he started training. He feels like he really gets it.

He now sees fighting like a chess match. It's not so much your strength, even though that helps a lot. It's your ability to counter your opponent's moves, and think a couple of moves ahead. It's knowing how one move can open up an opportunity for the next one, eventually leading to a submission hold. He feels he can do that extremely well, even if his opponent is bigger and stronger.

Finally, he answers, "Yes, I can beat him."

"But will you be okay in two days?" asks Rachel.

"I don't have much of a choice about that. I'm really sore, but my cuts will heal and if they keep giving us good food, I should be fine."

"We'll do everything we can to get you there," says Rachel smiling at him.

"Thanks. Oh, Torka did tell me that all of you can come and watch."

"Really?"

"That's great!"

"Yeah. Don't ask me to explain it, I can't. But he said I can bring as many friends as I want."

"Well, maybe if we're all allowed to go, it's an indication that we might be let go as well if you win?" says Sherman.

"Maybe you're right," says Harry.

"Oh, Harry, you simply have to win!" Linda exclaims. "I think we'll all be going home after all."

The desire and fervent hope are so strong, that the group quickly latches on to the possibility that it will happen.

The gang is fed exceedingly well, as Torka had promised. This further cements the idea that they are only one victorious match away from going home.

Linda and Rachel nurse Harry's wounds all evening. Rachel does her best to give Harry the best massage/rubdown in the world.

Finally, they all turn in.

Hoping, hoping, hoping...

#

Harry goes to bed with the weight of the world on his shoulders.

Everything is riding on him. All their hopes and dreams of freedom and home are at stake. He must beat Torka. Can he really do it, he wonders?

Even at 100% he honestly doesn't know if he could take Torka. They had fought once before, at the beginning, before Harry knew anything about the science of fighting. Torka had taught Harry a lesson that time. True, he was still recovering from the shocks of the implants, but Harry has a lot of respect for Torka's abilities.

Could the student really beat the master?

Well, he would just have to, that's all there was to it.

And, of course, this time his friends would be watching. There was no way he was going to let them watch him fail. He had come far, far along since his first spat with Torka. He wasn't the same person or the same fighter anymore. He was now highly skilled, and experienced to a degree.

Of course, Harry knows that Torka is bigger and probably even stronger. But not faster. Not even with his sores that are still healing from Kraline's bites. Torka is somewhat slow.

And Harry is more determined than he has ever been in his life to win this next fight. Not so for Torka, who is really just a bully and a show-off. If he really thought he could best Harry fair and square, then he would allow more than just two days of rest and recuperation. Harry thought about this and realized he had one more advantage on Torka.

He now understands that Torka is afraid of him.

Torka has seen Harry grow as a fighter and knows better than anyone else how far he's come, and what he's capable of. Yes, Torka must be afraid, or at least...leery. A smile forms on Harry's face.

He likes the idea that Torka is afraid of him. His confidence grows.

Yes, he can and will beat him. Torka will probably try some dirty trick to distract him, but Harry won't fall for any of that. He will be focused, vicious, and victorious. He is ready.

Chapter 61

It is the day of the fight. The biggest fight of Harry's life. The biggest event in all of their lives.

If only he can find a way to defeat Torka, they should all be on their way home soon.

Every one of Harry's group has been allowed to come and watch. This seems to all of them as a reasonably good sign that the Glarbs will keep their word, if only Harry can win.

He must. He will have to find a way.

Torka has kept his word regarding allowing Harry to bring his supporters. Harry's friends are escorted to a special section meant for the slaves. Even Dremmil is there. They take their seats.

Harry had talked himself into feeling pretty confident the night before. But now, he cannot help but feel nervous. The stakes are so incredibly high.

He forces himself to remember what he's gone over in his mind. Torka is afraid of him. And Harry is quicker, and has been fighting consistently, improving his skills and gaining experience with each match. His sores and stiffness from his last fight, with Kraline, have largely healed. He is strong and in good shape.

Gritzel leads Harry to the center of the ring, and leaves him there. There are no announcements. Each fight starts as soon as both contestants enter the ring. And here comes Torka, confidently making his way to the ring.

"Well, if it aintz my slave. Ready to getz pulverized?" he calls out at Harry.

Harry notices that Torka is trying to hide something in his hand, but doesn't say anything.

"I'm ready for you, Torka," Harry answers.

"Notz gonna make anyz difrenz, slave. Yer still gonna getz pulverized," Torka threatens.

"If I win, we all get to go home?"

Torka climbs into the ring and stands at one end, Harry at the other.

"Absolutzly," says Torka. "Yer juzt have to beatz little olz me, and yerz all goze free. If yerz could juzt manage notz to die!" and Torka gives a loud laugh.

Torka takes a step towards Harry. The crowd is roaring in anticipation of what's to come.

Harry plays his best card.

"You're scared of me."

For just a moment, Torka's eyes reveal the truth. Then he snorts, and says,

"Me, scaird of yer?" he laughs derisively. "I thinkz we both knowz watz gonna happen t' yer, slave. We've dun thiz befur. I can beatz yer with one hand," and he holds his free hand out. He's hiding something in the other one, and Harry knows it.

"That was before," says Harry. "I'm much better now."

"Yer thinkz so, slave? I've taught yer not even halvz of what I know."

Harry is silent. He is watching that hand.

"Letz get the rulez strait firzt," and Torka approaches him like he's going to explain the rules.

But quick as a flash, he thrusts the other hand towards Harry's face and throws salt at his eyes.

Harry was ready for Torka's dirty tricks and closed his eyes while turning his head, just in time. Torka, who was confident that this ruse would work, is rushing him, thinking he was going to get the drop on Harry.

WHAM!

Torka runs straight into Harry's foot. A direct kick in the chest, and Torka goes reeling backwards falling on his lumpy posterior. Torka is pissed off as hell. Blinding Harry at the outset was his big game plan, and would have held a huge advantage. Instead, he's down and Harry is coming at him.

Screams, cheers, and jeers fill the arena. The crowd is going crazy. They are ready for the fight of the century and these two are going to give it to them. As long as there is plenty of violence and injury, and some good screaming, they're going to love the show.

Harry sprints over to attack his opponent while he is still down, and kicks him in the side, twice. But the second kick is caught, and Torka hangs on to Harry's foot and twists and rolls. Harry comes down on top of Torka, kicks his foot out, and goes for a punch in Torka's big ugly face. But Torka feints back, catches Harry by the wrist, and twists it the wrong way. Any other opponent would be down on the ground, but quick as a whip, Harry follows his wrist with his head, somersaulting out of the hold and springs to his feet. Again, the screams from the crowd are deafening.

"Ahm juz toyin' with yer, slave," Torka taunts. "Gotz to give 'em a good show."

"I'll make sure of that," says Harry. "You'll be screaming real good."

"@#$!" Torka curses Harry in Glarb. "Ahm threw bein' niz to yer!" Torka threatens.

Harry gives him a gesture with his hand, the "come hither" sign. This infuriates Torka. They are both on their feet now, circling each other with clenched fists.

Torka rushes at Harry with a barrage of jabs, uppercuts, and kicks, but all are blocked. Harry spins and nails Torka with a big roundhouse kick to the chest. Torka, stumbles but does not go down. He is furious and looks at Harry with intense hatred radiating from his eyes. Harry gives him a smirk in return. Torka's blood is boiling with rage. He swipes at Harry's eyes, but Harry leans back and once again Torka comes up empty.

Torka lets loose with a yell from hell, "Now, yerz going to diez, slave!"

One more time Torka rushes in. But he cannot penetrate Harry's defenses so easily.

Torka's maniacal attacks do not intimidate Harry, and have so far not resulted in any gain, as Harry blocks, feints, and counter-punches perfectly, just as he was taught. The two combatants exchange blow after blow with nobody really scoring a clean shot.

Torka comes at Harry with arms raised, which surprises Harry because it leaves him exposed for a kick to the stomach. Harry shoots his right leg out towards Torka's gut, but Torka quickly catches it, and is about to take him down, but Harry leaps off his left foot while Torka is still holding his other one, and kicks him in the side of the head. Torka stumbles and lets go of Harry's foot, but doesn't go down. None of his tricks are working.

Up to this point, it has been a very even match with neither fighter being able to claim the upper hand. The crowd is loving it. Harry's friends are cheering him on with everything they've got.

Torka has never been so frustrated. This fight should have been over by now. He throws a wild left hook but Harry blocks it with his right arm, steps forward and smashes him in the face with a big fist.

Again, Torka reels backwards, but does not fall. Harry hit a clean shot with everything he had.

"What will it take to knock him out, or at least off his feet?" Harry wonders.

Originally, he thought that the longer it goes, the more the advantage would go his way. Torka, he figured, wasn't training and was too big to last very long. He should run out of gas.

Yet, it doesn't seem to be happening. Torka is as tough as they come, and Harry has hit him with sledgehammer blows, but it's not enough to even knock him down. Harry is beginning to think his best bet is to grapple him and try for a submission hold. If Torka won't submit, Harry will gladly break his bones. But grappling with such a large and skilled opponent, although it hasn't happened yet, could lead to getting locked up in one of Torka's many holds. Harry, stays on his feet, crouched, and focused. He will continue to wait for an opening.

Torka is absolutely furious. He wants to kill Harry and make him suffer. They've been going back and forth for a while without anyone getting an advantage, and it's embarrassing. Torka has never come face to face with such a focused, superb, and powerful fighter like Harry Stone. And he made him this way. There must be a weakness to exploit, but his cheating ways have gone for naught. He tries another dirty trick. He's got plenty of them.

Torka starts to wobble. Harry sees this and comes at him. Maybe this is his chance?

Harry stops two feet away, just out of Torka's reach. Torka fakes stumbling. Harry's not buying it. He thinks it may be a trap, when just then, Torka goes down low and spins, trying to take Harry out with a leg sweep. Harry jumps over it just in time.

Damn, damn, damn—Torka is beside himself with rage. He blasts Harry with a sidekick, but it's blocked, and at the same time Harry's left jab connects cleanly with Torka's face.

That does it, I'm killing this slave right now," Torka thinks, and he unloads a right hook that would knock out Muhammad Ali, but Harry ducks under it and answers with two blows to Torka's midsection.

The crowd is screaming. They are all standing, pumping their fists in the air, and shouting at the top of their lungs.

Torka doubles over from the one-two punch he just received. He wants Harry to get close enough so that he can grab him and take this fight to the ground. Harry knows that combination must have hurt, and comes forward while Torka is still bent over.

Torka dives at Harry's legs in a desperate attempt for a takedown, and succeeds in grabbing them. As Harry is falling he manages to roll onto Torka, and they both tumble to the ground.

Torka catches Harry's arm and twists, going for an arm-breaking Kimura. Harry rolls out of it and catches Torka's neck with his legs and starts to squeeze. Torka twists around to almost a headstand and rolls, forcing the release, and goes for a body choke by wrapping his legs around Harry's torso, but doesn't quite get there. Harry counters by grabbing Torka's foot and going for an ankle lock—but just before he can snap it on, Torka kicks away and unbelievingly turns his back on Harry in order to stand up.

And there it is, clear as day, the opening Harry has been waiting for.

In his haste to right himself, Torka has made a cardinal mistake in fighting, and has shown his back to his opponent. Harry doesn't even have to think. Not a moment is wasted, as his instincts take over. He jumps on Torka's back, slides his right elbow under Torka's chin while placing his left hand in back of Torka's neck, and starts the squeeze.

He has Torka locked in an inescapable choke hold. Harry has all the leverage, though Torka is fighting for all he's worth, trying to bite, kick, scratch, anything to get out of this. It is the exact opposite of their first encounter, and now Harry is in control.

The hold is locked in perfectly, and Torka feels the blackness coming over him. Harry is about to win the greatest battle of his life, and freedom for himself and all of his friends.

The crowd is in a screaming frenzy. They have never seen such a battle before, and also have never seen Torka lose.

Harry's friends are cheering ecstatically. Their hero has done it again. It looks like their life of slavery is over and they are on their way home.

As Torka is about to go unconscious, he makes an unusual gesture with his hands—a signal of some sort. And just as quickly, oxygen comes flooding back into his lungs, as Harry lets go of the hold, and falls to the ground howling in pain. His collar has been activated.

While Harry is writhing around on the ground in agony from the electricity shooting through his neck, Torka recovers enough to give him a few good kicks.

"Thaughtz yer cud beatz yer mazter, huh slave? Not todayz, not everz!' and yet another kick.

From the stands, Rachel and the rest are screaming their protests.

"Stinking, dirty cheaters!"

"He had you beat fair and square!"

"Turn it off, you're killing him!"

But they can hardly be heard above the shrieking Glarbs' laughter and cheers, as they howl with joy at Harry's predicament. Gritzel has his hand on the remote, grinning broadly.

Torka is still kicking him, and Harry is clutching at his collar, his neck.

It's getting really bad.

"Pleeaaase, turn it off, you're killllliiiing hiiim!" wails Rachel.

But Gritzel doesn't turn it off. Not until after a good, long time, when Harry's eyes finally shut closed, and his body goes limp.

And still, Torka gives him a few more blows for good luck until, finally...it's over.

Rachel, Linda, and the rest cannot believe their eyes. There lies Harry's limp (lifeless?) body in the center of the ring. And there is Torka, standing over him, sneering and laughing.

Harry had him beat fair and square—they were all going to go home. But the lousy, cheating, stinking Glarbs couldn't bear to lose, so they simply turned on his collar while Torka kicked him.

"You cheats! He would have won! You couldn't stand to give him a fair match!" screams Rachel.

"You liars! You're all filthy, lying, snakes! I hate you!" cries Linda.

All of Harry's friends continue to shout and curse at the injustice they have just witnessed. They were so close. They were supposed to be going home. Instead, they are doomed to continue on as slaves for probably the rest of their lives, and most likely without Harry. They can't tell if he's alive or not, but it doesn't look good. He's not moving.

One of the Glarb guards looks at them, grinning and loving it. What a great show it's been. The audience is ablaze with shouts of praise and celebration. Torka has a big smile on his ugly face. He walks out to address the cheering crowd.

"Thank yerz. Thankz all uv yerz. I toldz yerz I wud beat 'im. Look atz him nowz, ha, ha!" Torka breaks out into unrestrained laughter as he points at Harry's motionless body.

Gritzel motions Torka to come over and then announces, "And we have here your winner—the great and undefeated, Torka!"

Deafening screams and roars fill the arena. It was the best fighting ever seen. The audience continues to erupt in cheers and jubilation.

Cheating is a good thing to the Glarbs. It shows that you outsmarted your opponent, regardless of whether or not it was fair. It doesn't matter how you win, just as long as you get there in the end.

The fact that Harry never had a chance, and would have beat him if it wasn't for the collar, doesn't register with the Glarbs. They just want a good show peppered with brutality, plenty of pain and injury, and some good cheating just adds to the fun. They got a smash hit tonight. And, sadly, it isn't over yet.

Gritzel turns to Ditzin, "Bring the crate over here."

A rectangular wooden crate is brought to Gritzel. Two guards are carrying Harry's limp body over as well.

"Put him in and nail it shut."

When Rachel and friends see what they're doing, she screams hysterically, "Nooooo! You can't! Pleeeease...Noooo!"

But her screams of protest cannot be heard above the roaring crowd, as Harry is placed in the crate and the lid is closed. Two guards have already started to dig the grave. Harry's friends are screaming at the top of their lungs, to no avail.

"Noooo!" wails Rachel, "You can't!"

She tries to leave the area and rush up to the front, but the guard pushes her back. Rachel backs up, and then, with all of her might, rushes at the guard, who already has his remote out and is pointing it at her.

Rachel never hesitates, yet before she can reach him, he's already pressed the button and down she goes. There is nothing any of them can do, but watch their friend be buried.

"Wait," Gritzel says as he opens the crate, "Take his collar off first, Ditzin. We can use it again."

Ditzin positions the collar-removing tool and starts to take it off. The collar is still warm and is not coming off smoothly. He's having trouble and wrenches it and the collar bends a little but doesn't come off. Torka is getting impatient.

"Letz him diez with hiz collarz on," says Torka. "I wantz him t' be a slavz in his death."

"Fine," says Gritzel, "It's already ruined anyway."

Ditzin, as Ditzin is wont to do, carelessly leaves the collar-removing tool in the coffin.

Torka gets the last word in, "Sweet dreemz, fer eternity, slave!" and then the lid is closed.

"Nail it shut," commands Gritzel.

Two guards immediately take up hammer and nail, and nail the lid shut, while the other guards finish digging the ten-foot grave. That's how it's done on Glarb.

The coffin is then lowered into the ground to the roar of the crowd, and the screams of protest from the few there who love Harry.

The deathbed containing our hero finally comes to rest gently at the bottom of the grave. They begin covering the coffin and filling the hole with dirt.

"Nooo, nooo, nooo, you can't!" cries Rachel.

But they can and they do. The Glarbs have just started filling in the grave when amazingly, Gritzel seems to have a change of heart.

"Clear the dirt off and bring him up!"

To Rachel's utter joy and relief, she sees them bringing up Harry and opening the lid.

"Oh, thank God! Thank God!"

Gritzel says something to Ditzin who then disappears for a moment, and quickly returns wheeling a rectangular metal box with an airtight lid.

The guards lift Harry, still motionless, out of the crate. When this is done, the collar-removing tool that Ditzin left in there is clearly evident. Gritzel reaches in and takes it out.

"Whose side are you on?" he asks Ditzin, while holding up the tool.

Ditzin sees this and becomes frozen with fear.

"I-I-I didn't..." he can't think of any excuse.

"Maybe you'd like to take his place?" Gritzel asks him.

"Oh, no, please sir," Ditzin pleads.

"Why don't you get in there and lie down?" Gritzel threatens.

"Please, anything but that, sir," Ditzin has never been so frightened.

Gritzel looks at him. Ditzin has started to tremble. Then Gritzel makes a decision.

"Get in the crate, Ditzin," Gritzel commands.

Ditzin's eyes grow wide. His shaking increases.

"Please, not that, sir. I'll never make another mistake again, I promise."

"I'm only going to say this one more time, and then you will be tied up if necessary—get in," and Gritzel points to the empty crate which only a moment ago contained Harry.

Ditzin is terrified. If he disobeys he's going to be tied up and thrown in. If not, he may be taking his last few steps in life, en route to a horrifying death. He is freaking out.

Now his teeth are chattering, his body still shaking, and he slowly takes a step in, then another one. He looks up at Gritzel, "Please, sir, please, no more mistakes. I promise."

Ditzin is standing in the empty crate, terrified, his fate possibly decided in Gritzel's next statement.

"Lie down!"

"Oh, no, sir, please, please, please," Ditzin gets to his knees and begs some more.

"All the way," and Gritzel pushes Ditzin down. Ditzin is now crying, begging, and shaking uncontrollably as he lies on his back, waiting to be buried.

Gritzel leaves him there, terrified, and turns his attention to Harry.

"Put the slave in here instead," orders Gritzel, pointing to the metal casket with the airtight lid. "And make sure it's locked and sealed."

With Ditzin's fate still unknown, the guards do an extremely thorough job of locking Harry in the new casket, making sure there's nothing else inside, and sealing it shut.

Rachel's horror is now dialed up just as high as it can possibly be. First, she thought her beloved Harry was getting a second chance (if he's still alive). But now, she watches as his body is placed in an airtight, metal coffin, without any hope of escape. If he's not dead now, he surely will be in a few hours.

Once again, Harry is lowered to the bottom of his ten-foot grave. As his friends scream their objections while watching their hero buried alive for the second time, Rachel can take no more and faints in utter grief and despair.

Linda is crying and screaming too. Although it makes no sense to do so, she leaves all common sense behind and rushes towards the front, trying to get around the guard. With just a flick of a finger, the guard renders her helpless and she falls to the ground, writhing in agony, the implants doing their job.

The guards are now piling the dirt on top of Harry's coffin. The audience is going crazy, screaming and cheering—it's deafening. Gritzel looks at all of this, and decides to add one more element to the frenzy he's created.

"Get out Ditzin!"

"Oh thank you sir, thank you so much. You're the greatest. I'll never screw up again. You can belie..."

"Shut up! You better not screw up again because you just got a taste of what will happen if you do."

"Yes sir, yes, oh, thank you. No more screw-ups, I promise."

Gritzel then leans over and says something to him, and Ditzin proceeds to run off just as fast as he can. A few minutes later he returns with a soil compactor. One of the guards takes it from him and goes to work, packing the covered grave just as tight as possible.

Gritzel knows this is not really necessary seeing as how the coffin is locked and cannot possibly be opened or cut through, but he enjoys stretching this moment out—it's good for the show.

Rachel comes to, amidst the chaos that is going on. She cannot help herself from crying and screaming once again. She prays with all her might that all this is just a scare tactic and that they will once again, begin removing the dirt from the grave and bringing Harry up.

Unfortunately, this time there will be no order from Gritzel to do that. Torka walks over to Harry's grave, stamps his big foot on it, and raises his arms in victory. Gritzel joins him. The crowd erupts again, in a new burst of cheers.

Even if he wakes up, there is no way he can force the lid open. Not only is it locked, but there is ten feet of compacted soil on top of it. And there are no tools in it to assist him in escaping.

It looks like this is the end.

Chapter 62

Jibly had followed the gang to the arena and had been scurrying around at their feet during Harry's fight with Torka. Of course, he doesn't understand everything that's been going on, but he does understand that his friends are extremely upset, and he wants to help.

Jibly is what is known as a Snurdle on planet Glarb. They are a mysterious species, very secretive, and not too much is known about them. If one is fortunate enough to spot them, they are usually near the company of children, not adults. There is much folklore about Snurdles. They are said to be empathic, telepathic, and quite intelligent, but these things have never been proven because they are impossible to catch.

Linda is standing up now, trying to recover from *the juice*. She is weeping, and beside herself with grief. She feels Jibly going in and around her legs, and picks him up and holds him close. Jibly purrs, trying to make her feel better.

All of the sudden, Jibly goes perfectly still in Linda's arms. And then, surprisingly, hops out and dashes off.

"Jibly," Linda exclaims. "Come back!"

But it's too late. Jibly is off and running, and Linda cannot follow him.

"Where are you going?" she shouts after him. "I need you!"

Jibly has scampered quite a distance away, but stops for a moment, once again going perfectly still. He closes his eyes, then, after a few seconds, continues on.

Linda cannot see him, but she suddenly feels something. She senses that her beloved friend is not abandoning her, no, not at all. He'll be back eventually. He wants to help in some way, she knows that, but can't imagine what it is.

Jibly continues to scurry through the crowd, reaches a point outside the arena, and begins burrowing. He emits a sound for help, and two of his friends, not too far away, hear it and begin burrowing towards him.

This is a wonderful start, but they will not be able to pierce the metallic coffin. Their teeth and claws would break first.

#

Ten feet below, buried alive, Harry stirs. He is not dead yet, but he is close. His body fights to recover, to live—and from the blackness, consciousness returns.

Harry's eyes flutter open. But he is not sure if his eyes are open or closed. He's not even sure if he's awake. He blinks, and groans, but there is no light. All he sees is black. He wonders if he is dead.

Somewhere in Harry's mind, a tiny little seed of horror is born, but not yet acknowledged.

He rethinks the last moments that he can remember.

He was fighting Torka—and winning. Yes, he was just about to win. And then, what happened? He doesn't remember.

He struggles to recreate the events in his mind. He had Torka in a choke hold, it was locked in, and Torka couldn't escape, And then... what happened? He can't remember anything except, oh, yeah, there was agonizing pain.

Electric pain. They had turned his collar on. Oh, my God, they had turned his collar on to keep him from winning.

That's right, he remembers now. He was on the verge of winning his friends' freedom—they were all going to go home. Torka was going unconscious, courtesy of Harry's choke hold, when Torka made some kind of gesture and they activated his collar. Those lousy stinking, cowardly, cheaters.

The little seed of horror grows larger.

And what had happened next?

Harry vaguely remembers Torka kicking him while he was writhing around being electrocuted. That's all he can recall. He must have blacked out.

And Harry just now realizes how much pain he's still in. It hurts everywhere.

The little horror seed grows larger still, and starts making its way toward the front of Harry's mind.

Harry reaches this way and that, feeling the sides of the coffin. And now, realization quickly dawns on him what must have happened.

He is...confined...in a box...trapped.

The air is stale, stuffy. There is no light. My God, it can't be...it just can't be. It is too terrifying to imagine. This just can't be real!

And then, the horror steps up and clearly introduces itself. Yes, the Glarbs and the sadistic Torka have really done it. Harry comes to the full realization that he is buried alive, in a coffin, with no way out. He will most likely remain here until he goes mad, and dies.

Harry has no tools of any kind. The metal coffin is very strong. Not even Jibly or his friends can pierce it. And it is airtight, so there's not much time left.

Rachel, Sherman, and the rest can't possibly get to him. They are totally controlled by their implants, and the Glarbs are guarding them closely.

#

There are all sorts of people in the world. Some have great intelligence in one area, while lacking the most common sense in another. Others are strong and athletic, but are severely lacking in academics. There are artists and musicians who excel at creating the most glorious creations, but cannot make ends meet nor manage their lives.

No matter what qualities one possesses, there are some characteristics that are difficult, or impossible, for many to learn. But there is one attribute that separates the true men from the boys. It is something that you can't buy or have taught to you. You have to develop it yourself, and once you do, you are forever a different person than you were before. It is an attribute that the greatest heroes throughout history have all possessed, for without it, a hero you could never be. And that is: courage.

And Harry has it in spades.

But realizing you are buried alive in a coffin can shake up even the bravest of men. Harry is about to be tested like never before.

Full blown panic is knocking at the door to his mind. He must not succumb, or all will be lost.

The claustrophobia can be overwhelming. It's enough to drive anyone insane. He can't let that happen.

Nevertheless, for just a moment, Harry loses it. He kicks and punches from inside his black deathbed, all to no avail.

He abruptly stops, realizing that he is using up too much air, and he will not be able to punch or kick his way out.

He fights to control his breathing and his panic. He needs to calm down and think.

He calls upon his courage, closes his eyes, takes a few deep breaths, and does what he can to settle down.

His breathing slows. His pounding heart stops racing and returns closer to normal.

And as he calms down, he seems to hear something. Not audible, nothing from beyond his metal cage, but from inside his head.

Help you.

Friend.

Find you.

Harry has no idea where this is coming from, or maybe it's just his imagination, but either way it still helps somewhat. Maybe help is on the way in some form? But how?

He opens his eyes and it's the same as when he closes them, completely black. He reaches up and feels the top of the coffin just a few inches above his face. His heart starts pounding. *I can't stand this another instant,* he thinks. Panic and totally freaking out are ready to completely consume him.

No, he thinks. *I can't let it. I'm going to get out somehow. There was something there, inside my mind, to help me.*

Once again, he calls upon his courage to ward off the insanity that wants to overwhelm him.

Harry takes a deep breath, and tries to relax as best he can, despite the extreme predicament he finds himself in. He needs to go inside his mind, and listen. He's got to calm down, and steady his heart rate, and relax...and listen.

Slow down heart, we're going to be okay. This is just temporary. We're going to get out. Something is there.

He continues taking deep breaths, and clearing his thoughts and panic. *There was something there. I just need to listen,* he tells himself. Harry feels his pounding heart slow down a little. He can do this.

Come in, whatever was there before, I'm listening.

And then, a single word, not his own, but from some external place, forms and expresses itself:

Tunnel.

Yes, he heard that, or rather felt it. Something that was not him said *tunnel*, or implanted that thought into his mind. Could his friends be tunneling to him? He didn't think so. The Glarbs would never permit anyone to rescue him. He stops thinking and listens.

And there, inside his mind, forms a picture of Jibly's face with his little whiskers twitching.

Oh, God—could it really be? Is Jibly going to dig him out? He didn't think the little guy could possibly claw through the metal, but hey, let's give it a shot.

Thinking about Jibly tunneling towards him floods Harry's spirit with hope. He's got to keep it together, and wait for the little guy to find him. He begins knocking on the ceiling of his casket, hoping the vibrations can somehow be felt by the furry little creature looking for him.

He calls out, "Jibly, Jibly...I'm over here!"

The sound of his own voice, helps a little. But, as time passes, and he neither hears nor detects anything else, he begins to think he must have imagined it in the first place.

Nobody's going to find me. There's nobody on the way. I'm going to die here.

His heart starts racing again. His breathing quickens, using up the air much faster.

Again, he calls upon his courage, and says to himself,

No, you're not going to die! Get control of yourself and calm down. Help is on the way.

Harry clears his mind, takes deep breaths again, and thinks about his heart slowing down. It works—he's able to feel the pounding stop. He tells himself to keep breathing slow and to work on consuming as little air as possible. This is not the end, he's not going to go out like this.

Yes, he is beat up, bruised, and in pain, with little air left.

But he is still breathing, and he is still alive. He will get out of this.

He thinks of Rachel, and all that they've been through. He must see her again. He must see all of them again. This can't be it, it just can't.

If only he could look at Rachel one more time. And hold her beautiful face in his hands, and tell her he loves her.

Harry's emotions are running rampant—anger, terror, despair, longing, love, hate, vengeance.

He tries to keep it together, but it's already getting hard to breathe, and he can feel the panic closing in on him.

One more time, he pounds at the ceiling of his casket, and hurts his hand. He can't stand it any longer. Maybe succumbing to madness isn't such a bad idea after all?

Damn it—he just cannot get out! He will never open it.

My God, how he wants to escape and kill Torka!

How he wants just to hold Rachel one more time.

But he cannot get out, is finding it harder to breathe, and harder still to keep the crushing claustrophobia and insane panic at bay.

#

The arena has emptied out and our mortified friends have been returned to the compound. Rachel is beside herself with grief and is inconsolable, as are most of the others.

They just saw their leader, friend, and hero, Harry Stone, on the verge of winning their freedom, only to instead be electrocuted and buried alive. At least they hope that he's still alive, they're not sure. But if he was when he was put underground, he's not going to last long in that sealed metal coffin. And he might lose his mind before he runs out of air. It's absolutely terrifying—if only there was something, anything, they could do.

The tears flow like rain. Their hatred for these monsters consumes them. And the fact that they've all been duped only adds to their anger and frustration.

The injustice of it all. How could they ever be lulled into thinking that they were going to be set free? Rachel weeps to Linda, "We must do something! He's dying out there!"

Sammy is pacing around and around.

"How can we help him? What can we do?" he shouts at nobody in particular.

Linda has been unusually quiet. Yes, the tears have flowed, but stopped a while ago. Linda has been very still, and has had her eyes closed, for a couple of minutes now. Then she says something shocking.

"Poor, dear, Harry. Listen to me, everyone. I don't think all is lost. We'll get him out somehow—Jibly's on the way."

This statement stuns all of them into silence, as they look around and notice that Jibly is gone. But what can Linda mean that *he's on the way?*

"He is?" sobs Rachel. "What...how can you, what do you mean?" and she looks at Linda in amazement.

Linda knows what she's about to tell them may sound crazy, but she believes it to be the truth.

"Jibly can find him, and he's got his animal friends. They're going to find him and dig him out. They've got to!"

This information brings a wave of relief and sustenance to the group. It's a hope. Something believable, however far-fetched. Because the truth of the matter is that neither his claws nor teeth can pierce Harry's casket.

"When did Jibly go?" asks Sherman.

"He jumped out of my lap after Harry was...buried (she can hardly get the words out). And then ran out of the crowd to find a place to dig."

"How do you know that's what he's doing?"

"I can't explain it, but I just know. I felt it. Somehow he placed a picture in my mind."

Linda's words are like medicine. Jibly has captivated all of them, and they just know that this animal is indeed very special, and on their side. There has always been something mysterious about Jibly, like he knows things, and has some hidden wisdom.

Rachel's spirits are on the rise, as are everyone's. Somehow, they're going to get out of this—all of them, including Harry. They're going to fight their way out and kill these damn stinking Glarbs if it's the last thing they ever do.

Chapter 63

Ten feet below, sealed in his airtight coffin, Harry is doing what he can to survive and not panic. If only he had some light, or a little more room, so that he could turn over. It's so dark and terrifying. He can feel himself losing the fight to keep his sanity.

Maybe he can turn over, he thinks, just to change his position. He turns to his right, but his left shoulder hits the top before he can completely turn on his side. It's just so damn tight—damn it!

He tries turning to his left, and of course, his right shoulder hits the top. He needs to move, to turn, anything. He's so confined, he can't stand it another moment, and bangs his fists against the top while violently kicking his feet. The panic is mounting.

Harry cries out a shrieking scream of utter distress, "DAMN IT, HELP ME SOMEONE! GET ME OUT OF HERE, PLEASE! I CAN'T STAND IT ANYMORE! GOD HELP ME—PLEASE, I'M DOWN HERE! LET ME OUT, LET ME OUT, SOMEONE, please, let me out..." It ends in a whimper.

He realizes he's losing it. He wants to sob, give up, give in, why fight it? This is hopeless. But then he thinks of Rachel and the others—on top, where there's air, and light, and open space. He desperately wants to have that again. Harry calls on his courage once more.

Damn it to hell, I'm not going out like this, he thinks to himself. *At least I'm going to turn,* he decides, and with an overwhelming effort, banging his left shoulder on the top of the coffin, he wrenches his body over and completes the turn.

"There, I did it," he says out loud.

Now he's on his belly, in the pitch, black darkness, and he places his hands in a pushup position. He knows he's using up air, but can't help it. It's going to be used up eventually anyway. He's got to try something.

He tries to get to his knees a little, pressing against the top of the lid with his back. But he's too big, and it's too tight. However, he could do a pushup. Harry pushes up as hard as he can with his legs straight, on his toes, and his back is pressing against the ceiling. He lets loose a big grunt, "AAARRGGHH!" determined to shove the lid open. It stays put. Just as closed as it was before.

Harry begins to lose it. Nothing is working. The claustrophobia is full-blown, and overwhelming.

"God, please don't let me die like this," he begs. "At least let me go out on top, fighting for something. Not like this. What did I do to deserve this?"

But then, he thinks he knows what he did, or rather didn't do. He didn't listen.

For how many years did he receive that *DON'T GO* message? So many.

Yes, it's true he got it wrong, thanks to Sherman, thinking it said NOT GOD. But he still had a chance to act on it when they first lifted off. He could have insisted that they abort the mission for any number of reasons. It would have been terribly upsetting to everyone, but AT LEAST IT WOULDN'T END UP LIKE THIS! He would gladly trade embarrassment, his career, his reputation, everything he had, not to be where he now finds himself.

His breathing takes on a frantic pace, and he closes his eyes and feels his heart racing again. *Can't let it, going to get out,* he tells himself. He fights desperately to keep his mind in control.

In this face-down position, he now rests his head on his folded arms, and tries to calm down. He pictures himself outside, above ground, free—looking for Torka. Oh, how he hates those stinking Glarbs, especially Torka!

That lying, cheating, drooling, ugly, arrogant, smelly...oh, he just hates him so much. Somehow, he is going to claw his way out of this and kill Torka, and make him suffer. He had him beat. He legitimately beat him, was choking him out.

Harry's terror has now turned into rage. Once again his heart speeds up, and the adrenaline storms through his blood, this time fueled by hate and frustration.

He pictures himself fighting Torka, getting him into painful holds, and never letting go. He sees himself breaking Torka's bones, while that big, ugly face screams for mercy, and Harry gives him none. Oh, he would just love that.

Damn it—he's got to get out of this!

He wrenches another turn over, and is now lying on his back. He tries to bring up his knees once again, but they hit the top of the lid. He's just got to get out! What can he do? Someone needs to help him.

And then, he remembers that Jibly is trying to find him. Oh, yeah, Jibly. Once again, Harry starts deep breathing, and prepares to go inside his mind, listening for his little friend.

Just thinking of the little guy seems to help a little. He feels the pounding subside, and goes deeper and deeper into his mind. Listening, clearing out the panic—*come in Jibly, where are you? I need you. Help me.*

#

While Harry is meditating on this, Jibly and his two friends are burrowing just as fast as they can. Jibly had to start his tunnel quite a distance from the grave the Glarbs had dug. He couldn't be out in the open and let everyone see what he was doing.

Jibly has been tunneling down and horizontal, towards the general area of Harry's underground torture. Jibly is extremely sensitive to Harry's mind calls, but is too busy digging just as fast as he can to acknowledge, and then send a mental picture back. He doesn't want to let up for an instant, and is already engaged telepathically with his two helpers, who are also burrowing towards him.

#

Harry, still with his eyes closed and his mind in listening mode, knocks on the side of his coffin, just in case Jibly is really out there looking for him. This helps immensely.

Jibly can feel the vibrations, and digs even faster towards their source. Suddenly, the soil takes on a different constitution. It becomes much denser, and harder to tunnel through. Jibly stops tunneling horizontally and begins digging straight downward. He hears the tapping louder now, directly below him.

Harry stops tapping, just for a moment. What was that? He thought he might have heard something, and not from inside his mind, from outside his metal cage. He lies perfectly still, and...there it is! There *is* a scratching or something, very faint, but it seems like it's getting louder.

My God—maybe a rescue is coming? Harry's spirits soar. Is it really possible that he will escape this? He resumes tapping on the side of his coffin. Maybe it's Jibly? If it is, what can he do? Jibly would need some kind of tool. Maybe Jibly has other tricks that they don't know about yet? Maybe he can emit lasers from his eyes and burn through metal?

The digging sound gets progressively louder quickly. It must be Jibly. It's constant, not a shovel or a machine, it's an animal. He calls out, "Jibly, is that you? I'm in here! Oh, God—can you save me?"

And then he hears a chirp, and clinking on the outside of his coffin.

"Jibly, it is you! Thank God! Can you cut through this? Please get me out!"

Jibly starts attacking the coffin with his teeth and claws. In a short time, his two friends join him. Inside, Harry hears the sounds have increased and seem to come from all over the coffin at once.

"Jibly, you've got some help? That's great! Thank you guys, thank you so much! C'mon, you can do it, I know you can!"

He is excited and hopeful, but the air is getting stuffy.

Try as they might, the Snurdles cannot pierce the metal casket. They are damaging their claws and teeth, and getting nowhere.

After a while, Harry sadly realizes the animals cannot pierce the metal. It just can't be! He's so close to escaping that he can just feel it. How can he get this close, only to fail? It's not fair, it's not right, it's not just. He's got to get out!

If only to see Rachel one more time, and tell her that he loves her. Just to see the sky again. Just to see anything—anything beyond this black box. He hears Jibly chirp. Then the others chirp. Then he feels something, this time on the inside of his mind.

"What? What is it, guys? What are you trying to tell me?"

But Harry thinks he knows. He doesn't want to know, but, yes, he knows. The crushing truth is what they're trying to tell him. They can't break through.

They can probably assist digging upward and helping him to tunnel out, but they can't break the metal. He has to do that himself. And he knows already, that is impossible. Oh, God, to get this close. He'll never get out. He's really going to die here. And there's not much time left.

Harry's breathing is becoming labored—the air is running out.

Even in his jubilation upon hearing Jibly and his friends digging, he had his doubts. Their claws and teeth cannot cut through metal. They would need some kind of tool, which, of course, they don't have. The only way out is up to him, and Harry has nothing but his fingernails.

He feels around in his coffin for anything that may help. He finds nothing.

He tries to scrape the top of his coffin with his nails. It's totally useless.

He doesn't have much time left. He can tell the air is stale. If only he hadn't used up so much oxygen with his screaming and pounding. But what difference does that really make? He would just die later, rather than sooner.

"Jibly, help me! I can't cut through it!"

Jibly chirps, and seems to say, "You must! We can't either."

Utter despair and frustration overwhelm Harry as he sadly realizes that this is it. His mind, starts to turn towards, even welcomes, insanity, as he now feels the cold embrace of death is imminent.

He cannot get out and will never see his friends and beloved Rachel again. He desperately does not want to die in this blackness, with help so close on the other side of his coffin. But there is nothing that he can do about it, and so he begins to reluctantly accept his fate.

Chapter 64

Millions of light years from earth, on the alien planet Glarb, ten feet below the ground, Harry Stone is lying on his back inside a pitch black, metal coffin, waiting for death.

He has given up on escaping and is trying to die while thinking about his life, and his loved ones. But it's not easy. His thoughts are spinning out of control.

The walls are pressing in and the claustrophobia is off the charts. It's enough to drive anyone mad. He has tried to fight off the rising panic and overwhelming terror and despair, but they're going to win eventually, what's the use? The door to insanity has already cracked open and his mind is peeking through it.

If only there was a way just to poke a hole in this tin can, he might have a chance. At least it would provide a breath of fresh air, because it's really getting stuffy. But there are no tools of any kind, and so, this it. It's so horrible, to go out like this.

He figures that he could quicken his fate by yelling, screaming, and pounding, just going nuts and use up the air as fast as possible, and be done with it. That might very well happen, any minute now.

He thinks about his fight with Torka. That cowardly, cheating Torka. Stinking, lousy, smelly, ugly, @#$!% Glarbs—he wants to kill all of them!

If it wasn't for the hideous implants and collars, he would have taken all of them on early in the game, and things would be totally different.

Torka, always resorting to the collar when he can't beat Harry fair and square. What a cheating coward! Damn collar, how he hates it!

He reaches to his neck to feel his. He wants to smash it to death, even if he has to die, he'd rather die with it off. Hey, it's bent, and... damaged?

Harry reaches up with both hands, feeling his collar. It feels different, like it was almost removed. He puts both hands together and grips it at the bend, and rips and tears and pulls for all he's worth.

The collar separates in two and comes off in his hands!

Harry is momentarily elated. How did that happen?

He can't see it, but examines it in his hands. He feels all around it, and it has broken in half, with a sharp edge jutting out. Harry cautiously feels the metal point where it's jutting out. And then, it happens. Realization dawns on Harry, and a wonderful feeling of hope envelopes him.

Is it possible that the thing he hates the most, the most crippling, debilitating, humiliating object that he despises so greatly, is ironically his salvation? He gently feels the jutting edge again with his finger, and positions the collar with the edge pointing up. He places it against the ceiling of his coffin, and starts scraping and poking. Little bits of metal start tumbling down onto his chest. This could work!

But the air is growing thicker still, and he realizes that he is running out of time.

Harry shuts his eyes to avoid the sparks and debris as he pokes and scrapes the broken collar point against the ceiling of his metal coffin.

Fortunately, the jagged and pointed break in the collar proves to be stronger than the metal. Harry can't see it, but he is making a dent in the ceiling and the broken collar point remains sharp and unbroken. He works the point around and around while pushing up.

Harry's mind, just recently welcoming the dawning of insanity, has completely turned around, and now is firmly grasping hopes of survival. If only he can push that collar point through before the air becomes too poisoned to breathe in any more. He realizes it's going to be close.

He must exert great force to cut through, which uses up the air even faster. It is now so stuffy and thick, and he understands that he's just breathing his own recycled air—coffin air.

His mind and thoughts are getting cloudy. He's going to lose consciousness soon, and he knows it.

The Snurdles have stopped attacking the casket with their teeth and claws. They have, instead, concentrated on digging just above it, to provide space for the lid to open, and for Harry to crawl out, should he ever get that far.

One of them has even begun digging straight upward to provide light and fresh air from above. The compacted soil has made their tunnels much more secure, and less risky of caving in.

Harry keeps his mind focused on his task, although he fears he may not have many breaths left. Thoughts of seeing Rachel and his friends again dance around in his mind. How great that would be! He must make that happen, he's so close.

Along with these pleasant thoughts, another one, from the opposite direction, invades his mind. The thought of meeting Torka one more time.

Because if he ever gets that chance...oh boy...does he ever look forward to that. He will stop at nothing to torture and kill him with his bare hands! Oh, does he ever hate Torka. What a pleasure that would be, to come face to face with that big, ugly lout again. And this next time there would be no crippling collar.

By God Almighty, he desperately wants that to happen. This hope drives Harry to push and poke harder and harder. Revenge can sometimes be a stronger impetus than love.

As Harry exerts more and more effort, he gets to the point where he feels a tiredness starting to form in his brain, and fears this may mean the air contains too much carbon dioxide. He realizes how serious this is. One breath of too much bad air can be disastrous. He could go unconscious and his fate will be sealed. All of his hopes to see his loved ones, and kill his enemies, will be forever gone. His corpse would rot away in this horrible casket, ten feet underground on this disgusting planet, and nobody would ever see him again. And so, Harry takes one more breath and holds it, hoping it's got enough good air to give him the time he needs to poke one blasted hole through.

He stabs and pushes and twists that broken collar point—he feels like it is close to poking through, but it's got to be soon or he's going to pass out.

With only seconds to spare, he puts everything he's got into shoving that collar point through the top of the coffin...and...it...breaks through—revealing just a sliver of light, and beautiful, precious air! He puts his mouth up to the hole, exhales, and then sucks in. Fresh air fills his lungs and it is a wonderful feeling. His head begins to clear immediately.

Harry places his mouth over the hole, and continues to take some deep breaths. He is elated. He's got air and even a little bit of light. And he's got that wonderful broken collar. What started out as a tool to keep him enslaved, ended as a tool to freedom.

Harry takes another deep, long, wonderful breath, and then lies back down with a huge grin on his face. His entire body calms down, the impending madness recedes, and his spirit soars.

As Harry steadily works on enlarging the hole, he sees friendly, bright, intelligent eyes on the other side.

"Jibly," he cries out. "Thank God for you! You're a wonderful friend!"

Jibly purrs in reply, and once again that wave of comfort seems to be emitted with his purring. It washes over Harry and makes him feel good. With Jibly on his side, he's bound to win. Harry sits up and takes another deep breath through the air hole. Jibly and his friends scurry around the outside of the casket, and Harry gets a glimpse of the two accomplices.

Even just seeing this activity, and being close to the Snurdles, brings Harry some peace and helps him to believe that things will be okay. Finally, he lies back down, pokes his collar through the hole, and gets to work enlarging it.

When Gritzel gave the order to have the soil compacted after burying Harry, it was done mostly for show. He wanted to prolong the moment and give the audience something else to cheer about. He also figured it might make an impression upon Harry's friends who came to watch. As if burying their hero alive wasn't enough, he thought compacting the soil could intensify their anguish, if possible. Both Gritzel and Torka excel at sadism.

However, he failed to consider any type of rescue attempt by, say, a kind-hearted and furry little Snurdle who had befriended Harry's group. The compacted soil made the tunnels much more secure. Most likely the dirt would have caved in and fallen on top of the casket if it was loose. Now the tunnels are the gateway to clean oxygen, which Harry inhales with gusto. Fortunately, all the spectators have cleared out and there is nobody around to see the small tunnel hole, and the mound of dirt, on top of Harry's grave.

Jibly and his friends continue tunneling around the casket in order to make space for Harry to peel back a flap and miraculously climb out of his deathbed, and start his ascent towards freedom and revenge. God help those who have hurt him and his friends. When Harry finally digs his way out, and emerges unfettered by a slave collar or implants, he is going to be the most hell-bent, devastating, ruthless nightmare Gritzel and Torka have ever seen.

With each poke and cut, the small hole in the top of his coffin grows larger, and more air and light spill in. Harry's mind is no longer filled with dying thoughts and reminiscing about his life. He is revitalized and dead-set on living a long time. He is going to break out of this thing and wreak havoc on all who have wronged him.

Of course, there are many factors still against him. There are too many of them to simply beat up, and he is not quite certain how he will free his friends. And, at the moment, he is still on his back in a mostly-sealed coffin, bruised and battered. But Harry's spirit is indomitable, and his courage and confidence continue to soar.

There is enough light now to allow Harry to see what he's doing, and see the tunnels above him. The claustrophobia, previously driving him to insanity, has completely left. He outlines the flap he is cutting and relentlessly pokes, cuts, and scrapes.

Harry has a long way to go cutting that coffin open with his broken collar, and somehow getting out and clawing his way to freedom. In the meantime, we haven't visited Kluco and Tica in a while.

Chapter 65

We are in Tica's ship. Kluco is with her. They are looking at a computer screen. Tica has constructed a simulation involving wormholes and space vortexes. On the monitor, it shows what looks like tunnels piping throughout the Andromeda galaxy.

"We have mapped out many, of what you would call wormholes, throughout this sector," Tica explains. "We have had limited success in predicting where the end point will be for any of these wormholes."

"Yes, it's a very unpredictable science," Kluco agrees. "But Dr. Hollingsworth wasn't using just wormholes to skip through hyperspace. He was aggravating them with something he invented called *hyper-dimensional subspace solenoid.*

"Yes, I see that," agrees Tica, "and his work is very innovative."

"Yes, but we never landed even close to his estimates."

"But you had a stowaway that you didn't know about. It wasn't really Dr. Hollingsworth's fault. He must be an extremely brilliant man, Kluco. You all must feel honored to serve with him?"

If Kluco had emotions that would have done it. Fortunately, he does not.

"Perhaps, if the circumstances were different," Kluco agrees, "but I do not think, although I don't know for certain, that my crew is busy honoring him too often."

"But his contribution to science and physics, to what your species calls *mankind*, cannot be overlooked," Tica adds.

"I'm aware of that," Kluco replies, "and in that regard you are right. But the reality of the situation is that, here we are trapped on an alien planet, and I don't even know if my crew is still alive."

"I think they are. My crew is probably alive, too," Tica reassures him.

"How can you be so sure?"

"Logic. What little we know of the Glarbs is that they are fond of slavery. That is why I wait. Because I have no way to fight them and rescue my crew. Same as you. But most likely they have been enslaved and are working, doing menial work."

"If they are alive, then we still have a chance. What do you think we should do?"

"Well, if it's okay with you, I would like to continue to share and study each other's science. Tica says, "Especially Dr. Hollingsworth's work."

"Yes, it's fine," says Kluco, "I would also like to study your science station, if that's okay."

Kluco watches Tica bend over and study Sherman's work. The tiniest of sensory feelings creep through his system.

Or it could just be his self-lubricating, autonomous diagnostic center going to work.

Chapter 66

The Snurdles are digging for all they're worth, making tunnels around the casket so that Harry has room to peel back the metal flap that he is cutting, and squirm out. Some of the dirt is removed, brought all the way to the top of the hole, and dumped out. Much of the dirt is repositioned and put on the sides of the casket.

Snurdles are pretty adept at tunneling and clearing space where it's needed. One of them has also been bringing berries into the tunnel. As soon as the hole is large enough, they will drop the berries through it.

Harry has so far been able to cut the beginning of a rectangular flap out of the top of his coffin. He is now pushing up on it, trying to bend it back. He turns his head as some dirt falls onto his face. But only a small amount of dirt falls in. Jibly and his friends have done an excellent job clearing space around the top of the casket.

It takes a lot more than being buried alive, electrocuted, and forced to fight the toughest beings from planet Glarb to fell Harry Stone. The dark side of him, which previously landed him into so much trouble, has helped him to overcome the tremendous odds stacked against him in his current predicament.

Harry is extremely resilient, and holds a deep loyalty towards his crew—not just as a friend, but also as a leader and rescuer, if need be. He is totally focused on crawling out of this grave, killing Torka and as many Glarbs as possible, rescuing his friends from slavery, and leaving this God-forsaken planet for good.

With tremendous effort, fueled by fresh oxygen in his lungs, he places both hands along the top of the jagged flap he has cut, and pushes up. The metal starts to bend back.

A wave of fresh new air greets him, along with a good amount of new light coming down from the tunnels above. This further elates Harry—he is absolutely getting out of this thing. But by God, is he ever hungry and thirsty.

No sooner does this thought enter his mind, when just then, one of the Snurdles deposits their collection of berries through the new opening. The berries fall into the coffin, and some land right into Harry's mouth. Oh, my God—is that good! It's like medicine. As the berries squirt and slide down Harry's throat, the Snurdles rush to get more, and Harry eats everything that falls in.

Although he is still lying on his back in a coffin, he is feeling a thousand times better than before. After a short rest, Harry gets back to the task at hand, enlarging the rectangular flap. His collar, once the most despicable and hateful object he had ever known, is now the most beloved, as he continues to cut his way to freedom.

#

It is an hour later, and the Snurdles have brought more berries and even some vegetables. Harry takes short breaks from his cutting to consume everything that they bring him. It tastes so good. He feels his strength growing.

And now, for the first time since being buried, Harry pushes back the metal flap even more, and can sit up. His furry friends have done an excellent job of clearing an area above the coffin. He's got his arms and head out, and tries to maneuver his feet underneath into a kneeling position.

Using the broken collar, Harry digs and claws and pushes up. He struggles to get vertical and pushes hard, rising up from what was supposed to be his final resting place. He is now almost standing up, in a crouching position.

Harry's face shows grit determination. His confidence surges with the absolute certainty that he will dig his way to the top. Up he goes, inch by inch. His animal friends are doing what they can to help.

He wriggles, twists, wrenches, and tries to lift his knee up—it's so tight. He uses the broken collar to expand the width of the tunnel. All three Snurdles continue to burrow every which way. They are a tremendous help, not only just for widening the tunnel, but even their company lifts his spirits. He is not alone—he is with friends.

Harry can now step on top of the casket. He is fully out and vertical. As he digs up and the soil spills down, he manages to step on top of it. In this manner, he continues his progress upward. In his mind, he sees himself out, and joining his friends again. And he pictures the vengeance he will unleash upon his enemies.

Thoughts of what he will do to Torka consume and fuel him. Oh, just wait until he gets his hands once more around Torka's neck. My God, he will squeeze that thick, burly neck into a pencil thin strand, with Torka's big, ugly, bumpy head bobbing this way and that.

He sees himself getting Torka in various holds, breaking his arms and legs, while Torka is pleading for mercy. Ha, ha, ha, that will be so great. Just listening to Torka beg will bring Harry so much joy. Torka's pleas will certainly fall on deaf ears.

Why should he show Torka even a grain of mercy? Harry will just laugh with glee. He was electrocuted and buried alive just when he was about to win. He will pound Torka into the next galaxy, if he ever gets the chance.

And he's going to get that chance. He will stop at nothing. Never in his life has Harry hated someone as much as he hates Torka and these stinking, cheating, cowardly Glarbs.

Inch by precious inch, he ascends. The coffin is now two feet below him. And then, the strangest sensations come over Harry. Something weird is going on.

Is it his imagination, or is the ground around him vibrating? Is it an earthquake? What's going on? The vibrations are increasing.

Suddenly, something happens that he never expected in a million years.

Harry nearly jumps out of his skin as a stray hand reaches out from below, and grabs him by the ankle!

Harry's heart skips a beat. There is a hand gripping his ankle, pulling him back down to his grave! What the...?

He looks down. There is light coming up from below. It's hard to make out, but it seems to be connected to...well, it looks like a Glarb. There is a Glarb grabbing him by the ankle and trying to pull him down. And then he hears a voice coming through a translator, slightly muffled by all the dirt.

"Harry, please, don't go back up. They'll kill you!"

What the heck? Harry is bewildered.

"Who are you? Let go! Where did you come from?"

"Come back down and follow me, and we'll tell you everything."

"Back to the coffin? Are you crazy? Who are you?"

"I am Dravitz. We have tunnels. Please turn around and follow me."

It is then that Harry notices that below him, around the casket, there is a rather large and newly dug tunnel shooting out from the side. Dravitz is holding some type of drilling machine. Did he come up from somewhere below?

"You're one of them! How can I trust you?"

"I was on my way to rescue you. It took a while to find you, and you already, somehow, got out. Yes, I'm a Glarb but I'm not one of them. We're trying to overthrow Gritzel and we need your help."

Something seems to ring true for Harry. Dremmil spoke once of a rebel group, but they thought it was only a myth. Guess not.

"Come on. We will feed you and help you rescue your friends."

If this stranger wanted him dead he would have left Harry in his coffin instead of tunneling to him. And the promise of food is very enticing. Harry believes him.

"Okay, lead the way."

And strangely enough, Harry turns around and follows Dravitz back down, towards the very grave he had just escaped from.

The End.

Note: Volume 2 is already completely finished and follows Harry and the gang to the completion of this journey.